THE SKULL CHRONICLES
Book I

LOST LEGACY

D K Henderson

With best wishes
D.K. Henderson

Published by Lyra Publishing

Lyra Publishing
Wiltshire, England

Copyright © Dawn Henderson 2012

The right of Dawn Henderson to be identified as the author
of this work has been asserted by her in accordance with the
Copyright, Design and Patents Act 1988

Cover design by EbookLaunch
www.ebooklaunch.com

ISBN 978-0-9571952-3-3

www.dkhenderson.com

To Sue Coulson

A dear friend and fellow traveller on this crazy madcap journey into the unknown, without whom this book is unlikely to have ever been born

Other books in The Skull Chronicles series

THE SKULL CHRONICLES
Book I

LOST LEGACY

Prologue

250,000 years have passed since the thirteen crystal skulls were first brought to Earth from the distant star systems of our galaxy. 250,000 years in which, with their help, humankind has evolved and prospered. In which our consciousness and understanding has expanded to bring us to a point where we are ready to move into a new way of being. That point is now.

The crystal skulls, vital catalysts throughout this long journey of ours, are preparing to make themselves known to us once again as we reach a turning point in our history. We are about to make a huge leap forward in our evolution, a leap that will carry us into a whole new world. They will be there to guide us through this sometimes turbulent transition, if we are prepared to listen.

Long before the golden age of Atlantis, these skulls were held in the tender arms of our world, nurturing and guiding our growth and, when we were ready, sharing their knowledge and wisdom with those who were open enough to hear it. A knowledge and wisdom born of and carried on the vibration of love.

At several points in the far-off past these skulls were revealed to the people of the Earth, came to live openly amongst them, to teach and to guide them more closely than ever before. They came too soon. Humanity was not yet ready for them to stay and they were hidden once more.

At one time, long since disappeared, all could hear their voices. But as centuries and then millennia passed, and our connection to One-ness of all was forgotten, we stopped listening. Their messages and guidance were lost to all but a few. To those few who refused to assume the dark cloak of fear and separation that was spreading

6

throughout the world and instead held themselves proudly and strongly in the light. They became the wisdom keepers of those ancient times, handing down their secrets and mysteries – their sacred knowledge – from mouth to ear, from master to student, throughout the ages. Keeping the secrets hidden so that the many who sought to pervert or destroy their truths could not discover them.

No more. Now is the time when this wisdom and knowledge is coming once more into the light. When it is being made available to all who wish to learn. Now is the time of awakening for us all. And soon, when enough of us have learned to listen to their voices once more, have made the choice to step out from under the dark shadows of our fears, the skulls will once again live amongst us.

These are the stories of these skulls and of one of those whom they are now contacting...

Chapter 1

Whoa! Yet again I found myself sitting bolt upright in bed, my heart nearly jumping out of my chest. Breathing hard. Groping for reality.

Another dream. Again, so real. Again, so vivid. Too real and too vivid. Not like a dream at all really. For one thing, it made sense. You know what dreams are like. They tend to jump from one scene to another with scant regard for continuity, and be filled with weird and wonderfully surreal images and happenings – a series of bizarre events in impossible scenarios. One minute you can be driving a toy car through the desert, the next it turns into a pink submarine with wings. Or maybe you are being chased by giant three-legged cabbages only to find yourself the next moment in a crowded tube train, playing a ukulele and talking to a teddy bear. Well, you know. You've been there. All the rules of time and space vanish in dreamland, which more often than not resembles the exotic product of somebody's hallucinogenic fantasies. And however real they seem while we are in them, once we are awake – properly awake – we are never in any doubt that we have been dreaming.

This dream, like all the others I'd been having over the last few weeks, was different. It was coherent. It made sense. The story followed logically, like an excerpt from a film with a beginning, a middle and an end. Moreover, I wasn't really part of it, merely an observer to the events that were unfolding before my eyes. There simply to watch. Every detail was clear to me – the characters, their surroundings. Sound, smell, feel – all were as tangible as if I had actually been there, walking along with them.

That night was different though. That night, I did something different. As my eyes opened I glanced at the clock: 3.20am. I got up, pulled on my dressing gown and went downstairs. At 3.20am? Brrrrrrr. It was freezing. Absolutely flipping freezing. Had I finally gone completely crazy, rifling around for a pen and paper at that unearthly hour on a winter's morning? But the compulsion to put the story onto paper was overwhelming. I scrambled back into bed and wrote without really paying attention to the words that were flowing from the pen although even now, wide awake, every detail was crisp in my memory. Why tonight of all nights? I had no idea and I really didn't care. All I wanted to do was finish it and get back to bed. As soon as the last word had touched the paper, I dumped the pad on the bedside table, switched off the light and immediately fell back into a deep sleep. I had no idea that something important had begun that night. Something I didn't yet understand. I hadn't even taken the time to re-read what I had written.

Chapter 2: Inception

The huge discus-shaped craft hovered silently above the forest canopy, an incongruous visitor in a virgin landscape that was as yet unshaped by man. The elegant curves of its dark silvery hull, flashing blue and violet as it reflected the sun's rays, cast over the land below a glowering shadow that deepened further the already dense gloom of the forest floor.

The ship had travelled here from way beyond Earth's own solar system, its origins the distant star systems of the galaxy, bringing with it gifts of a value and importance that Earth had never received before and never would again. Earth's nascent human race was being given a helping hand; one that would open the door to the evolution of its consciousness and the achievement of its full potential. It would be nurtured, protected and guided. At first from a distance, a subtle energetic influence would lightly touch and, when the time was right, awaken the latent skills and abilities that would otherwise remain undiscovered and unused. This loving, benevolent and guiding hand would set humanity on its path to true understanding and lead it gently forwards.

Far below, a small party was battling its way through the fetid humidity and dense, clutching undergrowth of the jungle. Vines and creepers, some swollen as thick as a man's waist in the dripping warmth, hung in tangled, impenetrable curtains. The explorers were making slow, energy-sapping progress, besieged by biting insects while the moisture-laden air robbed every breath of oxygen. There was no trail for them to follow, and they had no choice but to hack out each hard-won step of the way through vegetation that even their toughened knives, honed to a razor edge that no Earth-found metal could ever hold, struggled to conquer. They had descended to the surface at the nearest possible point to their destination, which was hidden deep in the trees, and they did not have far to travel – a few miles at most – but in these difficult conditions it would be almost a day's punishing trek.

It was an incongruous and exotic looking group of men and women, drawn from each of the races involved in this ambitious operation. Tall slender Pleiadians, golden-haired Thetans and bronze-skinned Sirians trekked side by side with short, squat Metulians, small, delicate-boned Eleusians, and the strange childlike forms of the Arcturians. At the head of the group, two powerfully built males from the Alpha Centauri system opened up the path, wielding their huge machetes like machines. Yet others followed on behind. They carried with them a small square box of a dull grey metal, inscribed with strange symbols and geometric shapes. This box held the final element of that precious cargo. All the others had already been set in their chosen places, concealed securely within the protective embrace of the Earth.

Their objective was a small gully that sliced through the hillside, so well camouflaged by the vegetation that the Alpha-Centaureans did not see it until they were right on top of it, and only narrowly missed plunging headlong. It was not deep, barely thirty feet at most, and its floor was pleasantly cool after the heat of the trek. At the gully head, a small waterfall tumbled prettily over moss-covered rocks, its stream gushing through a narrow channel at the far end where the slope of the hill descended to meet it. One by one the party climbed down, appreciating the fresh, pure water that quenched their thirsts.

Behind the waterfall, a narrow crack pierced the wall of moisture-drenched grey rock, opening out into a deep recess a little further inside. This was where the treasure would remain until the time was right to bring it into direct contact with the human race.

One of the taller men now stepped forward. He was slender with blond, almost white hair that hung like silk to below his shoulders. His moustache and beard were of the same colour and from beneath his pale eyebrows, intelligent, vividly blue eyes looked out on the world. This was Artem, elected leader of the Galactic Council. In his hand lay a strange-looking key made of pure gold. It was about the length of a man's hand and shaped like an 'f' and a 'j', attached at 180° to each other from a small centre circle.

Artem indicated for the box to be brought to him. It had no visible catch or lock, but as he pressed the key into a matching indentation on its side the top slid open; reaching inside, he drew out the carved skull that it held. This was the priceless gift that the people of the stars had brought to the Earth and its infant race.

*   *   *   *   *   *   *

There were thirteen in all, thirteen skulls skilfully and lovingly carved by races of beings from far beyond our world. Beings who wished to see us thrive. These races had each created a skull and downloaded it with all the knowledge and wisdom they possessed: technology, physics, mathematics, understanding of the ways of the universe and the energy that guides it, and much more besides. Every skull held immense power, carrying the specific essence of the beings who had fashioned it, able to generate huge levels of energy. In addition, each held the consciousness of the unity within it – a deep understanding of the One-ness, of the supremacy of love and of its power to create. Thirteen skulls, each powerful in its own right, but which, when brought together, could create – or destroy – worlds.

The peoples who had brought forth these treasures were highly evolved, with an understanding of life,

12

consciousness and unseen energies that remains beyond the grasp of humankind even in the twenty first century. Each of the skulls was created from a powerful mineral that would enhance its individual essence – clear quartz, amethyst, blue and black obsidian, and rose quartz among others – and add its own vibration and characteristics to the whole. They would be placed at selected points on the Earth's surface, points carefully chosen to carry their influence throughout the entire planet. Thirteen skulls, precisely positioned around the world. They would be spread thinly, but it would be sufficient. Neither would they be evenly spaced geographically. It was not necessary. Every chosen location was an energy centre or major confluence of the planet's energy grid lines, from where these voices could spread rapidly outwards in all directions, carried freely through the web of this matrix.

* * * * * * *

The skull that emerged into the light that day in the gully glowed a deep rich purple, pulsing with a power that could be felt by all those who clustered around it. This was the final skull and perhaps the most important: the Master, created jointly by the twelve races who were part of this ambitious and world-changing project. When all the skulls were one day re-united, it would be the Master who would act as the nerve centre, gathering, focusing and amplifying their energy.

Artem raised the skull and touched it to his brow in a gesture of gratitude and respect, then handed it to the small figure of the Arcturian, the only one there small enough to squeeze through the narrow fissure. Entering the cave was like entering a magical fantasy world. Glittering crystals grew from the walls, the roof, the floor; some were miniscule, others as tall as he was. It stretched deep into the hillside, far back beyond where the light reached. To one side was a small pool, inky black and bottomless, and behind it, jutting out from the wall, a low shelf that glistened milky white. It had the smooth texture of a stalactite, and had been formed from the calcite deposits in the water that dripped constantly down the wall at this point and ran into the pool.

He laid the skull on the ledge and immediately it flamed with an inner fire as it connected to the energy lines that ran through this place. Fingers of gold flickered through its depths, crackling audibly in their intensity; an ethereal net of electric blue lines blazed through the cave. It had begun.

GEMMA

Chapter 3

It all started, I think, with the painting. I was rummaging around in an antiques shop – well, that's what the sign said, it was more like a tatty second hand junk shop with delusions of grandeur – when I shifted a broken chair and there was this painting, leaning drunkenly against the wall, half buried under an old puce candlewick bedspread. The frame caught my eye first. It was rather ornate and an improbably garish bright gold colour, so I dragged it out for a closer look. It was not my thing at all. A group of near naked Indians, complete with exotic feathers in their hair, knelt in what I imagined was homage in front of a stone altar on which rested, surrounded by a halo that would rival those of the saints in fifteenth century religious paintings, a skull.

It repelled me, yet at the same time something about it – and to this day, I still have no idea what – fascinated me in equal measure. But I had no intention of buying it and so I shoved it back where I had found it and carried on rooting around through the clutter.

To my intense frustration though, it wouldn't let me go. All through the week I just couldn't get it out of my head as its image kept popping into my mind at the most unlikely moments. So the following Saturday I found myself back at the shop handing over, for some unfathomable reason, my hard-earned money for a picture I didn't even like.

As she wrapped it and held it out the woman behind the cash desk peered at me over her spectacles. 'Are you sure you want this?' she asked.

'No.' I answered brusquely, to be honest already regretting my purchase, but something – pride maybe? – stopped me from telling her I'd changed my mind and asking for my money back. I stuck it under my arm and, with what I hoped was a haughty air (I probably just looked plain ridiculous), marched out of the shop.

*　　*　　*　　*　　*　　*　　*

Dan, my husband, was not impressed. 'It's not going in the living room. I can't look at that all the time. It's hideous.'

I agreed with him completely. So I put it in the study, out of the way, standing it on top of the bookshelf. Yet still it drew me. I found myself sitting gazing at it in the evenings, trying to find out what its fascination for me was. I couldn't. I told my friend Joe at work about it. Joe has had a life-time love affair with skulls.

'But you hate them,' he said in bewilderment. He was right, I did. I found them creepy and sinister, the stuff of horror movies and nightmares. 'So would you like to play with Spikey, then?' he asked mischievously. Spikey was Joe's own miniature skull, bought from a gift shop during a holiday in Cornwall. He was about an inch and a half tall and a deep purple colour, carved from some kind of rock or other.

'No, I wouldn't, Joe. It's revolting. And so is the picture.' I slumped down in my chair, shaking my head, totally at a loss. 'That's what I can't understand. Why, when I find it so creepy, am I so pulled to it?'

Joe looked at me closely, an odd look on his face. 'I think you are going to have to change your mind about them. I think they have work for you.'

'What? Who have?' He'd tossed out the bait and I'd bitten.

But Joe just shook his head mysteriously and refused point blank to say any more, despite my offered bribes of daily cakes from the local bakery and making his morning coffee for the next six months. Not even my threat to reveal his secret Abba LP collection to the rest of the

17

office worked. All he would add, with a knowing, enigmatic glint in his eye, was, 'You'll find out when you are ready and not before. I get the feeling you're going to be in for one hell of a ride.'

I had become so intrigued and desperate to find out what he was talking about that I could have killed him, but nothing I said or did could get him to change his mind.

Chapter 4

And then my whole life changed. Actually, fell apart would better describe it. Not exactly overnight, but pretty damn quickly. One moment, there I was drifting along in a stable, secure (if to be truthful soul-numbingly dull) current of existence, nothing inspiring, but then again nothing horrible, happening. The next, my safe if mediocre little boat hit an iceberg, and I found myself suddenly pitched headlong into a swirling, inescapable maelstrom of uncertainty and chaos.

So what happened? Well, firstly my marriage ended. Out of the blue. Dan simply walked in one evening looking like hell, sat me down and told me he was leaving. He had fallen in love with someone else and was moving in with her. That weekend. Just like that. No warning shots, no clues. One day he was there, the next he wasn't. As quickly and simply as a door closing. Oh, and by the way, would I look for somewhere else to live please because he wanted to put our house on the market straight away.

Work was the next foundation to crumble. My job had never been particularly fulfilling or stress-free but it had always been tolerable and pretty secure, and it paid a decent enough salary. All that was about to change. Not long after Dan and I separated, an unforeseen take-over of my employer's company threw everything into disarray. Overnight, the atmosphere switched from friendly and easy-going to one that at times you could cut with a knife as the threat of redundancy hung over us all and work demands rose to impossible levels. I started to dread going in to the office every day.

And to top it all I got ill. Nothing life-threatening, thank God, but definitely life-stealing. As recent events finally caught up with me, I became locked inside a thick bubble of exhaustion, depression, and an almost irresistible urge to find a cave and hibernate for the next ten years. My world was tumbling down around my ears, and most of me no longer cared.

I began to wonder whether the painting was cursed, then scolded myself for allowing my sometimes active imagination to launch into overdrive. Voodoo, black magic – it was all nonsense. The stuff of lurid Hollywood films and sensationalist paperbacks. I had never believed in that sort of mumbo-jumbo and wasn't about to start now. Life is what we see. Nothing more, nothing less. Well, I was soon to find out that, in so many ways, I was so very wrong. Life is infinitely more than we can see and touch, or even imagine, as I would gradually come to discover. But all that is for later. I'm getting too far ahead of myself.

Chapter 5

When I look back on all those events with the greater knowledge and understanding that I now possess, I can see how inevitable they were and how I was led (well, let's be honest, dragged kicking and screaming...) out of that stagnant conventionality and, eventually, into a life I love.

I hadn't been happy. I would have denied it with all guns blazing at the time but it was true. I vividly remember sitting in the study with my best friend Cathy, shortly after I had bought the painting. We had decamped there so as not to disturb Dan who was watching TV in the living room, and were slumped on the tiny sofa, a glass of something red in our hands, gazing at the picture and just chatting about nothing in particular, as women do. Then, out of the blue – and to this day I don't know what made me say it – 'God, Cathy. I wish something would happen to liven up my life a bit. You know, a bit of excitement, adventure. Some new experiences. This same old, same old is suffocating me.'

She looked at me sharply. 'I thought you were happy?'

'I am.' So untrue, but I was refusing to see it at the time. 'I am happy, just... Oh, I don't know. Bored? Dissatisfied? Looking for something more?'

'Well, be a bit careful. When we think about something enough we tend to bring it into our lives.' She was perfectly serious.

'Yeah, right!' I'd heard all this reality creation stuff before from Cathy and I wasn't buying into it. Life was life. Good or bad, it just happened and there wasn't much you could do about it.

'OK, but don't say I didn't warn you.' And with those words she changed the subject.

* * * * * * *

I tried to ignore it but now that I had voiced my dissatisfaction, or unsettledness, or whatever it was, it wouldn't go away. I still considered myself happy. I had a loving husband (or so I believed), a beautiful home, a well-paid job, and good friends. How could I not be happy? Still though this feeling sat like a rock in my stomach, growing heavier by the day, squeezing the breath out of me.

I spent more and more time just staring at the painting, often not even seeing it as my mind day-dreamed me off on all sorts of adventures. It drew me as a moth to a flame; I even caught myself talking to it in my mind. Sharing my thoughts, my hopes, and my grumbles. This was becoming seriously weird, but at the same time it felt safe and reassuring. And if I was going round the bend, at least I was doing it in private.

Until that evening…

Dan was out and once more I was feeling completely out of sorts. That heavy, suffocating brick was back, sitting firmly and immovably in my solar plexus, although once again I could not put my finger on any particular reason for it. I had been busying myself with trivial jobs since I'd arrived home in an attempt to take my attention away from it but tonight it was shouting too loudly to be ignored. Eventually I gave in. Drawn as usual to the study. Perching on the edge of the desk. Letting the frustration course through me. Shouting out loud in my exasperation. 'For heaven's sake, what is wrong with me? Why am I constantly feeling like this? Whatever it is, I am sick and tired of it. I have had enough! Do you hear me? I have had ENOUGH! I don't want it any longer.'

22

I stopped, suddenly feeling ridiculous at shouting to an empty room, and got up to go and clean up in the kitchen. I had just reached the door when I whirled round at an almighty crash behind me. The painting – that hideous, fascinating, disturbing, bewitching painting – had somehow toppled off the bookcase and was now lying face down on the floor, its canvas gaping where the corner of the metal waste paper basket had sliced through it as it fell.

That was it. I admit it. I freaked out. I grabbed the picture, pretty much flew outside and flung it in the dustbin. That was the end of it.

*   *   *   *   *   *   *

The next day, Dan left me…

And then the dreams started…

*   *   *   *   *   *   *

It was so quick that I could have almost convinced myself it hadn't happened – except that it had. I can still see it as clearly today as I did at the moment when it appeared right in front of my face and I woke up with a startled scream, my hands clutching at the duvet in fright. A black skull, shining like polished glass, gazing at me from its empty eye sockets, seeming somehow alive. Just hovering there. So real I felt I could have reached out and touched it.

That was the first time.

It was particularly unnerving for me because I haven't dreamed for years, not properly. OK, OK. I know. We all dream, all the time. What I mean is that although I dream – and I'll take the experts word for it – I hardly ever remember doing so. On the rare occasions I do remember, it is only ever of vague disjointed snippets hovering

23

elusively, probably images from the last few moments before I wake up. These dreams were different. I remembered them in their entirety, every last detail, and they remained etched unfaded on my mind even days later.

They continued, perhaps one or two a month, and I told no-one about them, did nothing about them, until that night when I grabbed a pen and started writing. From that time on I kept the pen and notepad by my bed and recorded every one. Not knowing why. Never reading them back. Just needing to get the words onto paper. Needing to record the stories those dreams were showing me.

GILEADA: The Black Skull

Part 1

THE ICE TOMB

Chapter 6

The small group moving through the barren, rock-strewn valley were making slow progress. It had been a long, hard trek – over half a moon's cycle since they had crept out of the village. All five men were on the edge of exhaustion. They were strong and tough, raised from birth in the harsh conditions of their land, each one hand-picked by the man who led them, but even they were now almost at the end of their endurance. They had to be close to their destination but they did not know for certain. All had been told of the task they had been charged with. Only one of them – Halsgørd, the big blond man who led the way – knew where that lay. They had followed him blindly, and would continue to do so no matter what came upon them for their loyalty was unquestioning and total. He was their chieftain, a great warrior, and a just, honest man for whom all those with him would willingly give their lives.

'Ho!' Halsgørd raised his hand and the men behind him stopped, gently lowering their load to the ground. 'There.' He pointed ahead where, through the gloom of the encroaching night, a low escarpment was just visible, a deep grey shadow against a scarcely paler sky.

'How far?' asked one of his companions.

'An hour, maybe a little more if we push on'. Halsgørd's voice was deep and powerful but the vicious blast of the wind stole his words so that only those nearest to him heard the reply. Although the men with him were warriors – strong, tough, and battle-hardened – this journey had sapped even their great resources. They had to keep going, to reach their destination before the long night and the packs of ravenous animals that hunted through those hours of darkness once more risked overwhelming them. They had to succeed.

No snow had settled yet on the ground here, but it wouldn't be long before the freezing death-grip of winter took its pitiless hold on this land. It was bitterly cold. The ice-raw wind seared their lungs with each painful breath and like a razor sliced through their thick furs to the flesh beneath.

Over the last few years winter had come earlier, stayed longer and been harsher than ever before in living memory. This year was no different. It was barely one moon past the equinox and yet the soil was already beginning to harden. Even the clan elders could not recall a time when such cruel conditions had endured for so long. The gods were angry.

This was a bleak, dead landscape with no sign of life. The few stunted trees that existed, tortured by the elements, barely clung to survival. Heads down, their shoulders hunched against the penetrating cold, the group pressed on. Behind Halsgørd, the remaining four men carried between them what looked like a rough litter: a framework of pine saplings covered in rough-hewn planks, lashed together with cured sealskin strips. On top rested a small box, no more than two hand spans square and beside it, a large, fur wrapped bundle. The men carried their load carefully and with a reverence that bordered on tenderness, protecting it as best they could from the jolting and jarring of the trek over the rough terrain.

*　　*　　*　　*　　*　　*　　*

The distance was deceptive and it was three bone-numbing hours later, hours which had felt like an eternity spent in a frozen hell, before the dark bulk of the cliff loomed up in front of them. A tangible sense of relief ran through the men. After two weeks of exhausting effort in energy-sapping conditions, and through barren, inhospitable landscapes, they had finally reached their destination. The return would be harder still, even without their burden, as winter tightened its hold and daylight all but disappeared, but they were not thinking of that now. The final step of their task was upon them, and the rough, bearded faces were grim as they contemplated it.

The bearers carefully laid the litter on the ground once more and looked closely at the almost sheer cliff face in front of them. A jagged wall of black basalt rose steeply far above them before it flattened out gradually to a rough plateau. They spread out to look for the opening that was their goal. It was a difficult task. The walls of the cliff were uneven, folding this way and that on themselves, and the moonless night reduced visibility to almost nothing. Promising crevices continually turned into false hopes and blind recesses. Even when they lit one of their few remaining torches, the guttering flame provided them little assistance, itself creating deceptive shadows with its unsteady light.

'Here! Over here!' Finally. Picking his way carefully over the uneven, rocky ground through the darkness, Halsgørd headed towards the sound of the voice, barely audible over the sound of the wind that still battered them brutally.

'Bring the torch,' he shouted over his shoulder. Frustration and the biting cold, but primarily a deep abhorrence for the task that was now upon him, had shortened his temper to a hair trigger and his men sensed it as they followed rapidly after him. The dark silhouette of Oldin, the eldest of his warriors, suddenly appeared out of the night, looming out of the background blackness of the cliff.

'Here,' the warrior said. 'If you touch the rock here you can feel the mark.'

Halsgørd pulled off his bearskin mitten and touched the rock face where Oldin had indicated. Sure enough he could feel an indentation, but his frost-numbed fingers would not tell him its shape. 'Where is that torch?' he bellowed.

The smoky yellow flame sputtered as he seized the torch that was held out to him, spattering him with hot seal fat, but he paid no attention. His eyes were fixed on the black wall in front of him. There it was. A simple symbol, carved deliberately into the hard, black rock. They had found it. He hesitated for a moment, feeling the weight of the golden key in his belt bag. No-one else knew about this key, which exactly matched the image in front of him. This symbol was the verification that they had indeed found the right place.

Halsgørd stepped back a little way and lifted the torch higher. Yes, there to the left of it was the cave entrance, just as the shaman had told him it would be. It was small, barely five feet high by three wide. Even the smallest of his men would find it a tight fit, especially bundled up as they were in their furs and sealskins. Well, he was their leader, he would be the first to enter. Warily he squeezed his tall, muscular frame through the small opening, holding the torch at arm's length. If a wolf, or worse a lion or bear, was sheltering in the cave, the fire would buy him a few moments at least.

To his silent relief the space beyond was empty, and opened up a little to allow him enough room to stand upright. The torch light flickered eerily on the roof and walls, glancing in rainbow prisms off the quartz crystals embedded in it. In one corner was a pile of freshly chewed bone, and a pungent odour rasped his throat indicating that, while it might be empty now, some animal was clearly using it as its lair and would at some point return.

'Lion!' Oldin had followed him in and recognised the creature's trace. Halsgørd nodded his agreement. A lion would not stay away from its den for long in this weather. Or its meal, he thought, spotting a half-eaten carcase lying amongst the bones.

The last of the torches were lit and jammed into cracks around the walls of the small cave. In the enclosed space, the acrid odour of seal fat and the thick smoke it produced was almost overpowering, but Halsgørd ignored it as he scanned the cave's interior.

It was exactly as the old shaman had described. There was the huge squared rock that had once been used as an altar – and more. As it would again. And there, behind it, carved into the wall of the cave at waist height, the small alcove. He closed his mind to the thoughts crowding in of what was to come. Of the task he had been charged with. He would not allow himself to weaken.

The men had carried their burden carefully into the cave and set both the box and the fur bundle on top of the ancient altar stone. The bundle was wriggling now. As the covering slipped a little, the face of a young woman was revealed. Wrapped in furs and sealskins to keep her warm throughout the long, arduous journey, the woman was bound hand and foot. Her eyes were wild, terrified, yet she did not utter a sound.

Halsgørd did not look at her. It took a huge effort as her pleading, desperate eyes seem to pull at him, compelling him to look into them. Through an immense act of willpower he did not, knowing that if he succumbed to that golden gaze his resolve would fail and he would be unable to go through with this. So he forced himself to harden his heart and turn his back on her.

She was beautiful. By all the gods she was beautiful. She always had been, first as a child, and growing more and more so as she developed into womanhood. He had hoped… No, he told himself angrily, there was no point in following those thoughts. That would never happen now. Furious at himself for allowing these feelings to seep through the mental and emotional walls that so recently he had deliberately and strongly erected, he turned his attention back to the task he had come here to fulfil.

Chapter 7

The cave was small and with everyone inside, it was
cramped. No matter, they would not be here long.
Halsgørd removed the golden key from his belt bag,
ignoring the glances and indrawn breaths of his men as it
came into view. He was not concerned about its theft.
These men were loyal to him, courageous, intelligent, and
unquestioning of his command to the death. It was a
loyalty that was going to be put to the test sooner than they
realised, he knew. Shaking the dark thought away, he
moved to the small box that lay beside the woman on the
altar. He turned it until he found what he was looking for,
a symbol identical to that on the rock face by the cave
entrance. A symbol that exactly matched the golden key he
now held in his hand. Again, he could feel the woman's
eyes on him, watching his every move. She seemed calmer
now. Had she resigned herself her fate, he wondered?

Taking the key, he fitted it into this matching
indented symbol on the box and with a soft click, the lid
slid aside. Carefully, reverently, he lifted out its contents.
He sensed rather than saw the fear flicker in the eyes of his
men as the skull appeared. Black as midnight, polished
like glass, even in daylight it looked eerie, supernatural. In
the dim flickering torchlight, it had an almost malevolent
air as the orange flames reflected through the empty eye
sockets and danced over those standing there. Only the
woman seemed soothed by its presence.

Halsgørd could sense its power, feel its energy
pulsing through his hands. Until this moment, no-one other
than the clan shaman and the skull's guardian had ever
touched it. Few had even seen it. Such a sacred and
powerful object could not be left open to the gaze of
everyone. The clan chief and his successor were the only

others allowed to view it, have access to its wisdom, which was channelled through the voice of its guardian. Its guardian – the lovely young woman curled on the cold stone beside him. From now on, their roles were to be reversed; it would become her guardian for eternity.

Lifting the skull above his head, its energy flowed through him, turning him giddy. Possessing this, he thought, he would be invincible. Maybe he could overpower those around him and flee with it. With its assistance, he would become the mightiest, most powerful clan leader in the land…

'Halsgørd! HALSGØRD!' Oldin's voice slowly penetrated his consciousness. He was disorientated, trembling. The force, the power of this object, staggered him. It had overwhelmed him, taken control of his mind. Now he understood why he had to do this. This was too much to be under the control of any mortal man. It risked corrupting even the strongest and purest of hearts.

'No.' A soft voice entered his head like the whisper of spring rain. 'It does not corrupt. It reveals to you your greatest fears so that you may face and defeat them.' She was in his mind, reading his thoughts, and speaking to him through her own. 'You have the strength and wisdom to understand this. Few others do. That is why this skull must be protected and hidden safely until humankind is mature enough to use its power wisely. That is why you were chosen for this responsibility. And it is why I was chosen. Do not fight this. It is how it must be.'

Halsgørd turned and looked at her properly for the first time since their journey had begun. There was nothing but reassurance and confirmation in her golden eyes. Feeling more at peace than he had since the night he had learned of this duty, he lifted the black skull above his head and uttered an invocation to the gods. Then he turned and placed it on the glittering cluster of quartz points that lined the base of the alcove.

He nodded to his men, who stepped forward and stripped the furs and skins from the young woman. From the depths of the bundle a lovely young woman emerged, small and delicately built in contrast to the tall, rugged men who surrounded her. Her hair was as dark as the men's was blond, raven dark of an almost blue-black hue. Large deep gold eyes flashed in the torchlight, her previous temporary calm once more overtaken by sheer natural terror at her fate. She stood, a slender, vulnerable figure wearing nothing but a thin linen shift, and immediately began to shiver violently in the damp, freezing air of the cave. She began to struggle, to try to free herself from her bonds, yet still no sound came from her. Men lifted her shoulders and feet and laid her gently back on the stone altar. None of them relished this task – the young woman was known to them all and well-loved in the clan – but all understood why they had to carry out their orders. As her bare skin came into contact with the frigid stone, she jolted in pain.

Halsgørd forced himself to look into her pleading eyes. 'It will be easier this way,' he told her gently. 'It will come more quickly. We will leave you the light. Soon the cold will simply embrace you and you will fall asleep.' He indicated his men to leave the chamber and followed them to the doorway, then turned and looked back at her. 'I'm sorry,' he whispered, the walls around his heart beginning to crumble. 'I'm sorry. Sleep now, my lovely lady.'

He could not say more. Could not bear to see the fear, the suffering, and the hopelessness in those wide eyes. Could not bear to feel the biting anguish rising within him. He pushed through the narrow cave entrance, welcoming the sharp pain as he scraped his forehead on a spur of jagged rock. This was not him, he raged silently. He was a warrior, not a murderer of innocent young women and, despite the explanations and reassurances of the clan shaman, what was happening here was murder. As clan chief's son, it was his duty. Well, he had done his duty, but however they tried to justify it to him it was still the cold-blooded killing of a defenceless victim. Moreover, the young woman's would not be the only murder – the shaman preferred the word sacrifice, but it all came down to the same thing – that he would commit to protect the whereabouts of this treasure. This was a darkness that he would never be able to shake from his soul.

Chapter 8

Outside the cave, Halsgørd's frost-numbed fingers fumbled once more for the key, although their trembling was not solely down to the frozen air. Deadening himself to the turmoil within him, he felt his way across the rough surface of the rock face until he finally found the indentation he was seeking, and pressed the key into it. Immediately a haze started to fill the cave entrance, rising up from the floor. As it thickened, it began to change into solid rock, sealing the entrance in minutes. Open-mouthed, Halsgørd's men watched in disbelief and fear at the sorcery unfolding before them. They were brave men, but this was beyond anything they had ever experienced. And though the old shaman had foretold of this miracle, it could not prepare any of them for the reality of what was unfolding.

What the five men were witnessing was not in reality any form of witchcraft or supernatural event, but the process of an ancient and highly evolved technology that had been embedded when the skulls were originally set in place. A seeding of self-replicating molecules had been pre-programmed to create a matrix that would seal the cave entrance completely, a process activated when the key Halsgørd held was inserted into the impression in the rock wall.

'Let's get out of here.' All the men were keen to leave, and yet within them all was a conflicting reluctance to do so. It would be a hard parting. Although all wished to escape this place, to walk away from the dark cliff behind which was entombed their innocent victim, none of them wanted to abandon her in this way. But they could do nothing for her now. She was beyond rescue; there was no way to get back in to the cave. The entrance had disappeared completely. Heavy thoughts and sorrow filled them all. The more distance they could put between themselves and the cliff face, the easier they hoped they would feel, although none really believed it. Halsgørd was the only one of them carrying the grim knowledge that the events started on that dark night only a short while before were far from at an end. As they set off into the icy wilderness once more, his mind was filled with punishing memories of the evening this had all begun…

*   *   *   *   *   *   *

Halsgørd stood before the clan chieftain, not knowing why he had been summoned. Recognising in the sombre face that it would not be a pleasant meeting.

'Sit down, son. We have much to discuss.' The voice was tired and strained, and this fatigue showed in the old man's whole demeanour. Despite his advanced years, he still stood strong and powerful, but this evening he seemed bowed and beaten, the weight of his duty resting heavily upon him. Halsgørd lowered his tall frame onto the thick furs that covered the stony ground, a cold darkness flowing over him. Whatever was coming was not good. He could sense it with every cell of his body.

The chieftain began to speak, telling Halsgørd of how the shaman, Tulka, had come to him, having foreseen death and destruction fall upon his people. Death and destruction committed by the hostile hands of those who wanted to seize the skull and its power for themselves. All would be slaughtered by the vastly superior numbers who fell upon them.

None of this was new to Halsgørd. Year after year, generation after generation, aided by the shaman's powerful magic, the clan had mercilessly and successfully protected both the skull and its guardian from attempts by rival clans to steal them. The clan were powerful warriors, who fought hard and fiercely, but they were also led by just, honest men with a deep sense of what was right. That is why they had been chosen from amongst all the others to hold the power of the skull. They alone possessed the inner strength and integrity that would not allow for the abuse or mis-use of its power. As time passed the mere presence of the skull reinforced these virtues in its keepers.

But the other clans were gradually growing stronger. Over the past few years, as life had become even harder for these tribes of the icy wastelands, one by one they had begun to forge alliances with formerly implacable enemies. With one aim – to wrest the skull from its custodians and harness its power for themselves. They had seen how healthy and well-fed the clan were, how they had learned to forge metal to a hardness that no-one else could emulate, to harness the sun's rays, study the cosmos, and anticipate the weather. They had resisted all attempts by the Skull clan to share some of this knowledge, too suspicious of their motives to recognise the goodwill in the gesture. They wanted it for themselves and themselves alone, and now they weren't prepared to let anything – or anyone – stand in their way.

The threat now was greater than it had ever been. Their enemies were ready. If not stopped, they would soon launch an attack that would wipe the clan off the face of the planet. Worse would follow.

'Worse?' thought Halsgørd. What could be worse than the total annihilation of his beloved people?

'The annihilation of all of humankind.' The tall, thin figure of Tulka materialised out of the shadows behind the old chieftain. It was as if he had read Halsgørd's thoughts. 'They cannot be allowed to acquire this treasure. They do not know of its power as we do. They have no experience of it. They will mis-use it, be unable to control it, and in doing so will destroy our future existence in this world.'

37

No thought of scepticism or doubt entered Halsgørd's mind. He knew the skills and abilities of this wise man, who had dedicated his long life to prophecy, guidance, the well-being of the clan, and the safekeeping of the its most precious artefact, the black skull. When he spoke everyone listened and believed, for they had long learnt of the accuracy of his predictions. If he had foreseen these events, they would take place.

'There is a way to avoid it.' Halsgørd looked at him questioningly. This was it, he thought. This was what was creating such trepidation within him. He waited, his heart pounding, for the shaman's next words. 'The skull must be returned to its place of origin. It must be returned and concealed so that it will not be found until humankind has evolved enough to use it safely. Until the time of the rising.'

'Where is this place? How do you know its location?'

'I have seen it. Night after night I have been taken there in my dreams. I can show you how to get there and what you must do when you arrive. It is a long way from here, across the wilderness lands. It will not be easy.'

Halsgørd was confused, trying to find order in his thoughts. This wasn't what he had been expecting. Yes, it would be a hard trip, but the task was by no means impossible. He was strong, resourceful, and easily able to deal with anything he might face on the journey. So why did the coldness of death still surround him, chilling him, and swamping him with an almost overwhelming compulsion to get out of this place. All at once, he understood. There was something more to come, something almost unthinkable.

Tulka spoke again, and as his words fell into the space between them the darkness around Halsgørd grew deeper, suffocating him, as if seeking to squeeze the life from his body. In his deepest, blackest imaginings, he could not have anticipated this. This... this horror he was being asked to carry out. He heard the words, registered them somewhere, even as his mind refused to acknowledge them. The girl, Linka, the guardian of the skull, was to be taken too.

'No!' At last the reality of what he was being asked to do penetrated Halsgørd's numbed mind. He leapt to his feet, rebellion and anger pulsing through his voice and his body. He could not. He would not. She was young. She was beautiful. And he loved her. Hoped to make her his wife one day soon. He would not be the instrument of her death.

The shaman continued, paying no attention to Halsgørd's outburst. It had been foretold clearly in his dreams that this had to be done. The sacrifice was essential. There was no choice. The future of humanity was at stake. At this point, however, his level voice cracked. Halsgørd raised his head from his own despair and saw tears falling down the old man's face. Linka was like a daughter to him. When her mother had died giving birth to her younger brother, he had taken her in and raised her, teaching her what he could. He loved her as his own child; the visions he had received, the guidance he had to relay, was breaking his heart.

'No.' More quietly this time. Halsgørd shook his head. 'I won't do it. I can't do it. There has to be another way.' For the first time in his life, he questioned the words of the shaman, and defied his father.

'You have no choice, Halsgørd. You are my son and heir. As future chieftain of this clan it is your duty and you are bound to fulfil it. You cannot refuse. You must not. Know that I find this as painful and abhorrent as you, my son, and it is with a heavy heart that I command it, but it must be.' The chieftain's voice shook a little, but stayed resolute.

Halsgørd looked at the two men standing before him. They were both good, wise men who held the wellbeing of their people uppermost in their hearts. But could the future of all of mankind truly be at stake here too? As he looked at Tulka, he knew that the old man believed without a shadow of a doubt that it was. The pain and suffering in the shaman's eyes as he stood there, having effectively signed his adopted daughter's death warrant, was proof of that. It was those eyes, more than anything else, that woke in Halsgørd the bitter understanding that this had to be. That try as he might to fight it, he could not. He would do what was demanded of him, if only to ensure that the girl would suffer as little as possible. But it was with an ice in his veins and a weight in his heart that he agreed to undertake this mission and all it entailed, knowing full well what it would cost him.

Even as he nodded his reluctant acceptance, he understood that more was waiting for him. Tulka's sorrow-filled eyes held further secrets, secrets of which even his father the chieftain was ignorant, and which Halsgørd knew he would soon learn. Secrets that he would rather not hear.

As he rose to leave, his father stopped him. 'You cannot speak of this to anyone, Halsgørd. You must leave the village unseen and in total secrecy. There are those amongst our people who also covet the power of the skull and are prepared to aid our enemies in taking it. They will not act themselves, but they will pass on information if they learn of it. You must cover your tracks and stay vigilant.'

'I will need men, father. I cannot do this alone. If it was just the skull, then yes but if we are taking...' Here Halsgørd's voice failed him.

'You know who you can trust with your life. Pick four of your best, most loyal men. Warn them to be ready to leave at any moment, but do not tell them why or give them notice of your departure until that moment arrives. When you have left the village you may tell them of your mission, but keep the destination as your secret. The less people who know the details, the less chance of careless words or deliberate betrayal.'

* * * * * * *

'Come!' commanded Tulka, turning away. 'There is much you need to know.' Halsgørd threw a searching look at his father.

'What we have discussed here today is all that I know,' came the answer to his unvoiced question. 'I will not seek to find out more. As you well know,' a faint smile of affection played briefly across his father's face, 'as you have learned the hard way my son, I do not like to remain in ignorance. But on this occasion, it is how it must be. Everything else remains only between you and Tulka. From this moment, the responsibility and knowledge is yours alone. What I do not know, I can never tell, no matter how severe the pressure for me to do so.'

At these last words, the ice seeped deeper into Halsgørd's veins. He understood their meaning only too clearly. Should their enemies take the clan, they would show no mercy in obtaining the information they sought. No man, not even one as strong and stubborn as his father, would be able to resist their savage interrogation for long.

'Come!' Tulka repeated impatiently. 'Time is not our friend in this.' With a final look that told his father more clearly than any words that he had understood, Halsgørd followed the shaman out into the darkness, climbing in silence to a cave in the hillside that overlooked the encampment. Here they could speak without being overheard. Throughout the remainder of that long, difficult night, he listened and absorbed. He was sickened to his stomach, yet he forced himself to pay close attention, knowing the importance of what he was hearing.

41

Distances. Directions. Instructions. He committed them all to memory.

They would be leaving within a couple of days, at the dark of the moon. He had to ready his men, make preparations, and do it all in total secrecy. All this he heard and accepted, started planning in his head, even as his heart fought against what was to come. He had to act normally until their departure. No-one must suspect that anything out of the ordinary was going on. Tulka had made that absolutely clear. They could not risk anyone discovering their plans.

*   *   *   *   *   *   *

Halsgørd still didn't know how he had made it through those two interminable days, but somehow he had succeeded without raising suspicion. In company he had forced himself to laugh and joke as usual, to lead and advise, as was his duty as the chieftain's heir. It had been as if he was watching someone else from a distance, someone completely separate to himself. When he found himself alone, though, the darkness constantly threatened to overwhelm him. Slowly, painstakingly, he began to build a wall around his heart, shutting away and deadening his guilt and his pain. He knew he had to; he could not carry this through otherwise. The detachment that this gradually brought to him, as he contemplated what was to come, unnerved him. He knew it wasn't who he was, but he could not allow himself to weaken.

He avoided Linka completely. He could not risk coming face to face with her. Being near her would bring all those carefully constructed barriers crashing down. The pain and guilt that would explode within him would be unbearable. Moreover, he was clearly aware that she could somehow read his thoughts, his emotions. He would not be able to help giving himself away and he could not allow that to happen.

He had chosen four of his most trusted men to accompany him, speaking to each individually so that none knew the identity of his companions, swearing them all to absolute secrecy. He did not inform them of what their mission entailed or when they were to leave, merely commanding that they be ready whenever he called, bringing with them provisions and equipment for a long and arduous journey.

Chapter 9

The thickening molecular mist continued to creep noiselessly across the entrance, sealing it completely. A sudden, terrifying and suffocating silence engulfed the cave where Linka lay helpless. The howl of the strengthening gale, which had held her final desperate link to the outside world, disappeared and with it her last faint hopes of escape.

Violent panic erupted in her, yet still she did not scream. She could not. Her only voice came from the skull that now rested just inches from where she lay. Otherwise, she was quite mute. Her race had never needed speech, communicating solely by telepathy. The clan were not yet open enough to hear her thoughts. Except the one – Halsgørd. He had heard her. She knew he had. Had sensed his shock and confusion as her words entered his mind.

Halsgørd. The man she loved above all else and who, although he had never shown any indication, loved her in the same way. Despite her desperate situation, a faint smile touched her eyes. She knew. She could read his mind as well as he could read the stars. Halsgørd. The man who had brought her here to her death. She could not hate him for what he was doing. Could not condemn him. She knew that he had had no choice, that this had to be. Felt, almost as agonisingly as he did, the pain, conflict and despair that he was suffering despite the barriers he had so carefully erected. Saw too that he would be enduring so much more before his journey ended.

Halsgørd. She was grateful that he had left the torches, although the light would not last long. To have been left here alone and in blackness would have been more than she could have borne. Grateful too for his actions is depriving her of her furs. The cold would take her quickly this way. It would be brief.

But she did not want to die. She had not yet lived. Had not yet known the heat of a man's passion or of his body. Not known the comfort of shared love. The despair, the loss, the hopelessness returned then. Hot tears of grief flowed down her ice-cold face. Painfully she twisted her frozen body until she faced the alcove. 'Help me,' she pleaded, gazing into the empty eye sockets. 'Please, help me.'

A faint golden haze began to shimmer around the skull, the aura growing in intensity until it filled the alcove and spilled out over the stone block.

'Rest little one,' whispered a voice in her mind. It was a voice she recognised: that of the skull that rested on the quartz cluster in front of her. 'All is well. You are safe.' A gentle sensation of warmth began to soften her chilled skin, comforting and reassuring her.

Was this it then? The end? This was how the cold would claim her when it came. But no. It was something else. A deep sense of peace and safety crept into every cell of her body, warming and soothing her to her deepest core.

*   *   *   *   *   *   *

The black skull was a masterpiece. Life-sized, intricately carved from a single block of inky obsidian, it was an object of infinite beauty and accuracy. It had been brought to the people so many generations ago, carried by a young woman who had simply walked out of the bleak plain and into their encampment one day. The stranger was stunningly beautiful, unlike anyone the clan had ever seen. They were a tall, strong and sturdily built people, well adapted to their harsh climate and life, blond haired and mostly blue-eyed. She was slender and delicate, with hair

45

the colour of midnight and eyes like liquid amber. She had been the first guardian of this treasure.

No-one had ever discovered who she was or where she had come from, for she never spoke a word unless deep in trance, serving as the voice of the skull. At first she had been cared for by a long ago shaman, but soon her kind ways and gentleness – and in no small measure her bewitching magnetism and loveliness – won her a husband whose children she bore. All but one of these children were clearly their father's offspring: strong, blond and tall. That one was the image of her mother, seemingly untouched by her father's genes, a pattern that was repeated in every generation. Always only one, and always a female, never varying from the distinctive build and colouring of her mother. Never varying from her gentleness and beauty.

Each of these girls became guardian in her turn, taught the knowledge and understanding she needed by her mother. As generations passed, some of this wisdom was lost or distorted, but the powerful connections to the skull were not. It was a bond that not even the guardian herself understood as its source became forgotten over the passage of time, but which nevertheless remained as strong as the day it was forged.

Linka had in time assumed the role in her turn, but she was different. She had not been able to learn at her mother's knee as all those before her had done. She could barely remember her mother, who had died in childbirth when Linka was only three years old. With her last laboured breaths her mother had conveyed to Tulka her request that he take in Linka and raise her as his own. Entrusted to him the golden key that until then none but the guardian and her heir had ever seen. Gasped out its purpose and its importance.

So Linka did not know of her origins. That she was not of this world that she lived in, and that neither was her beloved skull. That the other young woman, the one who had walked out of the wilderness and into the encampment so long ago, had come from beyond the stars, sent to bring this gift to these people. Sent to act as a channel for its knowledge and its wisdom, but also to watch over and protect her precious charge. To prevent the misuse of its power, which was beyond comprehension.

Linka's ancestor was Eleusian, a gentle, loving, and highly advanced race from far beyond the Alpha Centauri star system. Long ago, when man had first began to walk the surface of the planet, the Eleusians and eleven other star races had each brought a crystal skull to Earth and placed them in carefully chosen locations. Then they had watched and waited for humankind to reach a level where it could hear and understand the knowledge of these skulls. When that time arrived, a guardian was chosen from each of those twelve races to recover its own skull and, for the first time, bring it into direct contact with those infant earth societies who were evolved and aware enough to use its power wisely.

These carvings were objects of breath-takingly skilled craftsmanship, perfect replicas of the human skull in every detail. They had each been programmed with a vast amount of information that would help the benevolent advancement of the human race, and awaken it to ever higher levels of consciousness. In addition, each carried its own 'essence', a signature vibration linked to the material from which it was created. The ultimate location of the skull was determined by its resonance to this essence.

If Linka did not know anything of this, she had always known of her deep and powerful connection to the black skull. As she passed through childhood, it stood alongside Tulka as her teacher, comfort, guide, and friend. She learned to use her mind to communicate with it, and to act as its oracle when the tribal elders sought its advice.

She could not know that this small cave, that had become her tomb, was one of those former hiding places. But deep within her, in that part of herself that still held those ancient memories, something awoke. An understanding – that this skull had, in a sense, come home.

* * * * * * *

'Rest now,' the voice repeated. 'Rest little one.' She could feel the air pulsating around her, first a gentle tingle on her skin, now settling around her to enfold her in its protective embrace.
'Thank you.' The gratitude spilled from her as her eyelids closed and she fell into a deep sleep, a sleep from which she would never awaken.

Chapter 10

'Let's go.' Oldin's gruff voice broke the sombre silence. He was a veteran warrior, tough and battle-hardened, but his words were uneven and heavy with sorrow as he spoke. He turned and moved determinedly forward, beginning to retrace the route that had brought them here only a couple of hours earlier. A couple of hours that to every single one of them felt like days.

Halsgørd called him back. 'We go this way.' He pointed along the base of the cliff in a direction at right angles to that of their arrival, and saw the confusion sweeping across the faces of his men. 'We need to lay a false trail in case we are being followed.'

He could tell his own face would betray him so he busied himself stowing the key back in his belt bag. They knew he was hiding something from them, he could sense it, but their loyalty was such that they did not question his orders. Without hesitation they set off in the direction he had indicated. Each of them was forcing his mind away from their recent actions, away from the prospect of a long, hard, and uncomfortable journey home in the almost constant darkness of late autumn, filling it instead with thoughts of the good meal and warm woman that waited for him the encampment at the end of his ordeal.

The forceful words of this, Tulka's secret final directive, played over and over in Halsgørd's head as he trudged through the darkness ahead of his men. It was the ultimate betrayal of their loyalty and friendship. He had always been totally honest and open with those who risked their lives with him but now… Now he had lied to them, and would continue to lie as long as was necessary. He was finding this as hard as what had just taken place. Instead of the soft embrace of a woman, he was leading

49

them into the cold arms of death. And he had not told them. Soon, Halsgørd promised himself. He would tell them soon.

*　*　*　*　*　*　*

The night of their departure had been the darkest for many days. The moon was nowhere in the sky – the old moon had died, the new was not yet reborn – and the light from the stars was obscured by heavy clouds that threatened the first snowfall of the winter. It was the perfect night, Halsgørd thought, his heart heavy at thoughts of what was to come. Even if anyone had been out wandering around the camp, they would have found it difficult to see anything in the all-enveloping blackness.

Noiselessly, he raised his men from their beds and led them to Tulka's hut where he signalled for them to remain outside. They looked questioningly at each other but did not give voice those questions. He had impressed clearly on them the need for silence; their voices would carry a good distance in the still night air. They trusted him completely, trusted that he would tell them when they needed to know.

Inside the hut, Tulka was waiting for him. Beside him, asleep on a rug, was Linka. Tulka had drugged her, partly to prevent any disturbance that may wake the village as they took her away, but also so that she could be blissfully unaware of her impending fate for a little while longer. She was bound hand and foot, and wrapped in so many furs that she resembled a small bear lying on the floor. Halsgørd didn't need to wonder what these actions had cost the old shaman. The answer was clearly written in his anguished eyes and the tears that flowed freely down his lined cheeks. Against the wall beside her lay a litter that had often been used to move the sick and injured of the clan to this hut for healing.

Halsgørd felt the bile rise in his stomach as he gazed on the small defenceless figure, sleeping so peacefully and unsuspectingly. He swallowed hard and turned to summon his men. As he did so, Tulka laid a hand softly on his arm, holding him back.

'Don't let her suffer. Please.' The low voice was almost a sob. Halsgørd nodded, an understanding of their mutual love for this young woman implicit between the two of them – the old medicine man who had raised her as a daughter, and the young warrior who had intended to make her his wife.

As his men entered the hut they stopped short, unprepared for the scene that met them. Each of the men knew this young woman, whose gentleness and good nature had won the hearts of them all. But not one of them challenged Halsgørd's orders. Gently, tenderly, they moved the warm, still bundle onto the litter. As they stood, lifting it between them, Tulka pulled a small square grey chest from under a blanket and placed it carefully beside the drowsing Linka. The men carried the litter and its passenger carefully through the doorway and waited outside for their instructions.

As Halsgørd turned to follow them, the old man once more waylaid him.

'Take this.' He placed a small wrapped package in Halsgørd's hand. The package was heavy; the young chieftain unwrapped it to reveal a strange golden object. 'It is the key I spoke of. You remember what you must do with it?'

Halsgørd nodded, looking at the key closely. It was an unusual shape, a small circle with two equal length arms coming from it at 180° to each other. One of these arms was shaped like a 'j' and the other like an 'f'. The workmanship was exquisite. He had never seen anything like it, had never seen anything to equal it. But there was no time for delay. Every moment they stayed here

51

increased the risk that they would be seen. He rewrapped the key carefully and pushed it deep into his belt bag.

'There is something else.'

What now? Halsgørd was impatient to get moving, mindful of discovery but also wishing to dispel through physical exertion the agitation and emotions that were beginning to crowd into his body. Tulka sensed his irritation, but held his ground. 'There is something else,' he repeated, and the tone in his voice caught Halsgørd's attention. 'Something I couldn't tell you before. Something else your father does not know.' Tulka had lowered his voice even further, to barely a whisper. Halsgørd's already strong feeling of unease deepened further as he saw a new sorrow in Tulka's eyes.

'There must be no trace, Halsgørd. Do you understand? No trace. Our enemies must never be able to discover where you have been.' Halsgørd looked at him, unwilling to grasp the full implications of his words. 'No-one must ever be able to learn of its whereabouts,' Tulka repeated forcefully. 'There must be nothing left that could point to its location. There must be no-one left who can tell.'

A chill crept into the depths of Halsgørd's soul. The shaman had just asked him to sign not just his own death warrant, but also that of his men. Good, loyal men, his friends, who were following him faithfully and unhesitatingly, trusting in him completely.

The next words were like acid in the wound. 'You must not tell them. I have been shown this clearly in my visions. They must not know. You must swear that you will not tell them.'

Halsgørd stared at him disbelievingly. He knew that to a man they would willingly lay down their lives for him, as he would for them. Countless times in the past they had risked just that. They had to know, to have the choice. This would be the ultimate betrayal of his men's love and loyalty. A bitterness that he could not master rose up in him, and he turned on the old man.

'No-one?' he hissed. 'What about you?'

Tulka looked back at him steadily. 'No-one.'

Halsgørd felt his anger dissolve in an instant. No, Tulka would never ask others to do what he would not. Placing a hand softly on the old man's shoulder in apology for his outburst, wordlessly the young clan heir turned and walked out of the hut, leading his men and their charge out into the inky empty wilderness from which they would not return.

*   *   *   *   *   *   *

Late in the following day, the lifeless body of the old shaman was discovered in the cave high above the village, frozen contorted in the agonised death spasms of his final moments. Agonies that had been inflicted by the poison he had taken, a poison distilled by his own hand. He could have ended his life in a gentler way. Why suffer such an excruciating death when he had to hand the means by which he could have simply fallen asleep and not woken up again? Because he had wanted – needed – to punish himself cruelly for the tragic events he had set in motion. For sending his beloved daughter to her death. So alone he chose to endure those last hours, as wreaths of fiery torment relentlessly wracked his body and he screamed his suffering to the silence. Until, finally, it was over and he lay dead.

Chapter 11

They were heading north. Away from the cave tomb, away from their homes, into the frigid darkness of the deepening arctic winter. Halsgørd marched in silence, lost in his own disturbed thoughts, unwilling to speak. His men, sensing that something was wrong, that he was gravely troubled by something more than the horror that they had so recently been part of, did the same, growing ever more uneasy as the hours and distance passed.

Late on the second day, the snow that had been threatening since their departure from the village almost a full moon's cycle before finally began to fall. Not in soft, gentle flakes that lightly brushed the skin like a lover's caress, but in icy shards that sliced at their exposed flesh with a stinging ferocity, hurled at them with all the fury the wind could muster. In that bleak, exposed wilderness it almost knocked them off their feet at times. They had to find shelter, Halsgørd knew, or they would perish here, and they were still too close. They had to stay alive for as long as they could; to put as much distance as possible between themselves and the cave. At least the snowfall would hide their tracks.

'There, look.' One of the men pointed ahead. Halsgørd squinted through the storm, almost blinded by its icy onslaught. Yes, he saw it – a cave opening, nestling into the hillside. It would protect them from the blasting fury of the blizzard and give them a dry, sheltered place to rest.

As they neared the cave entrance they grew cautious, wary of a hibernating bear or sleeping lion within. It was empty. The chamber stretched back for some way, curving in a slight dog leg so that, at the rear, the howl of the storm fell to a muffled groan. The men sank to the floor exhausted, relieved to be out of the wind's barrage at least for a while.

Where was Oldin? He had been right there as they climbed the rise to the cave entrance. Had he not followed them in? Halsgørd frowned, a little anxious. Oldin was wise and experienced, but in these conditions…

A noise outside caused him to turn. Oldin was standing in the cave entrance, grinning. On the ground behind him lay the skeleton of a dead tree. Wood! Wood meant fire, and fire meant warmth. More than anything at this moment they all needed to warm their frozen flesh and dry their sodden furs. Trees were few and far between in this wind scoured landscape but Oldin had spotted this one as they made their way up the hill. Resourceful as always, he had wrenched it from its anchor in the rock and dragged it to their shelter.

* * * * * * *

Before many minutes had passed, a cheerful fire was burning in the cave and its flickering flames warmed the cold stone with their orange light. They had been careful to site it beyond the dog leg so that it could not be seen from outside, although it was almost impossible to believe that any other human would be wandering around in this bleak, frozen landscape. The men slept deeply, their exhaustion evident. They had eaten well, the spoils of a successful hunt the previous day, enjoying the luxury of hot, roasted meat rather than the tough, dry flesh that they had subsisted on for so long. Maybe they should have been more frugal, but in this weather a man could not keep going for long with an empty belly.

Despite his bone-crushing fatigue, Halsgørd could not sleep. Restless, ill at ease, and plagued with guilt at the secret he was carrying, he stood at the cave entrance staring unseeingly out into the darkness.

'What's going on?' Oldin's quiet voice startled him. 'What are you keeping from us?'

'What makes you think I'm keeping something from you?' There was a challenge in his reply, and a warning, but Oldin ignored it.

'Don't pretend to me, Halsgørd. I've known you far too long.' Relentless. 'I taught you to fight as a boy, and I've stood and fought at your side for the past fifteen years. Something is wrong. What aren't you telling us?'

Halsgørd turned angrily, ready to retaliate, but the steady, concerned look in Oldin's eyes stilled the words on his tongue. The tension and anguish of the last weeks overtook him and he slumped exhaustedly against the cave wall, all resistance draining from him. He had promised himself he would tell them. Well, maybe that time had arrived.

He forced himself to look his oldest friend directly in the eyes. 'We aren't going home, Oldin. We aren't going anywhere, except to our deaths.' Oldin looked at him in disbelief. 'I was ordered never to tell you but... There can be no trace. No-one left who knows where it is, or how to get there. We are to travel as far as we can, leading anyone who is trying to follow us away from that place, until...' His voice tailed off.

'Halsgørd, you know I would follow you into the blackest depths of hell. We all would. You only need to ask. But this? To not tell us? To lie to us? Don't we deserve better than this? Or do we count for nothing? All our years of friendship? Of trust? Of loyalty? We have never questioned your authority, Halsgørd, and this is how you betray us?' Although Oldin's voice was low and measured, Halsgørd could hear the bitter fury in his words. 'We would have come anyway. We would have willingly volunteered our lives for this. But you should have told us.'

'I know.' Halsgørd felt empty, bone weary. He just wanted this to end and end now, but it wouldn't. Not yet. They still had to travel on. Travel on until they could go no further.

'Will you tell them now?' Oldin was remorseless.

Halsgørd nodded. 'Let them sleep. I will tell them when they wake.' He put a hand on his friend's shoulder. 'I'm sorry, Oldin. I was wrong. I should have listened to my feelings and told you.'

'Yes, you should have.' Oldin's reply was as cold as the night air as he shrugged off the gesture and moved back into the cave.

* * * * * * *

It was a resentful, angry group that left the cave several hours later. All were revived and strengthened by the fire that had warmed their bodies, the meat that filled their stomachs and the sleep that had rested their heavy, tired legs. But there was no sense of lightness. No-one spoke. The men were still coming to terms with Halsgørd's recent disclosures. He had given them the choice to continue or not, and even then it never crossed any man's mind to walk away, to turn back and abandon his fate. But a deep sense of betrayal had exploded in each of them. Halsgørd knew he had lost their trust, their respect, and their friendship, perhaps irretrievably.

The wind had eased but the snow still fell heavily, in minutes covering them in a thick, white shroud. It settled ever deeper underfoot so that the simple act of putting one foot in front of the other soon became a challenge. Their feet, even encased in the thick sealskin boots that they wore, quickly grew numb. They trudged onwards through the almost perpetual winter night, each now fully and openly committed to the destiny of which he had so lately learned.

Two days. Three. On and on, each laboured step draining their already failing resources of strength and stamina. They scarcely stopped to rest. What was the point? All knew they were heading to nowhere but their final resting places, wherever that might be. Just keep going. Keep going. They were hungry. There had been no fresh meat since that night in the cave when Halsgørd had spoken. There had been no sign of life, no tracks, nothing to hunt since they had left there. They were subsisting on the tough leathery strips of dried bear meat that they had brought with them for exactly this purpose – emergency rations. There was little left now, however, and they were eating of it sparingly. It would not keep them going for long. In this weather and terrain a man needed a full belly to have even a chance of survival.

On the fifth day they gave in to their exhaustion and rested for several hours, huddled beneath a skin tarpaulin. It protected them from the constantly falling snow but not the penetrating cold, and when it was time to leave one of the men did not awaken. Halsgørd's heart contracted as he looked at the cold, empty body of his friend and comrade in arms, a man he knew almost as well as himself and who was now lying stiff and lifeless in this bleak unforgiving place. The first self-sacrifice of this accursed journey. An almost unbearable wave of sorrow and anger washed over him. Sorrow as he felt his loss and that of the men around him and for the further losses yet to come. Anger at the circumstances that had forced him to be the architect of these events. He uttered a short but heartfelt prayer asking for the gods to care for his companion's soul and then they started walking once more. No-one wanted to linger there.

Over the next three days two more men fell, and they too were left where they lay to be entombed in icy graves by the thick snow. Only Oldin and Halsgørd remained now, and neither had the strength or the heart to do more, knowing that the same fate awaited them too, perhaps within hours.

It was another three torturous days, however, before Oldin stumbled to his knees and did not get up again, three days that had drained every last scrap of strength and will from the two lone travellers. 'You must leave me. Go on alone. I can't go any further.'

Halsgørd sank to the ground beside him. 'No, my old friend. I won't leave you. And in any case, how far do you really think I'd get? I have no more left in me than you do.' Oldin simply nodded, too spent to argue. 'I'm sorry Oldin. Sorry for having dragged you into this. Sorry for not telling you. Sorry for not trusting you enough. I was wrong. Forgive me. Can we not face death together as friends?'

With a considerable effort Oldin raised his head to look at Halsgørd, and reached out to grasp his hand. 'These past few days I have had plenty of time to think. We... I... judged you too harshly, Halsgørd. Yes, you were wrong. You should have told us. You owed us that much. But would any of us acted differently? I cannot say in all honesty that I would have. I just don't know. It wasn't me in that position. Yes, my friend, my chieftain, of course I forgive you. I love you as my brother and will not go to my end with this gulf between us. Now please, just let me sleep.' The long speech had bled dry the last of the warrior's reserves, and he allowed his body to sink to the ground where he curled up against the cold. As he closed his eyes, Halsgørd allowed the tears to come. He knew that this was the end. That Oldin, his friend, his teacher, his mentor and, as Oldin had considered him, his brother would not wake up again. This was his last rest.

'Sleep in peace my friend,' he murmured. 'We have come far enough. We have done all that was asked of us.' The cave and the skull within it were safe and would not be found. Their own bodies now would be buried beneath the winter snows with no chance of discovery until the spring. Fatigue was inexorably claiming him. No, not yet. He felt the weight of his belt bag around his waist. There was still one more thing he had to do.

They had been following a river course for the past two days. While at the edge the stream was frozen over, in the centre a wide, swirling current kept the water ice free as it churned over a swathe of submerged boulders. Stumbling down the shallow beach, Halsgørd fumbled in the bag with cold-deadened fingers and pulled out the small sealskin package. Unwrapping it clumsily, for the final time the contents tumbled out and lay in his palm. The golden key – a glint of warm sunshine in the silver-white expanse of the bitter winter landscape.

With all the strength left in him, Halsgørd drew back his arm and hurled the key towards the channel of flowing water. His aim was true. It hit the water with a soft splash and sank straight to the river bed. Now it is done, he told himself. He lurched painfully back to where Oldin lay and saw that the snow was already beginning to blanket his friend's body in its white softness. Soon nothing would show that they rested there, cocooned beneath the surface in their eternal sleep.

Wearily, with a sense of grateful surrender, Halsgørd lay down beside his comrade and gave himself up to the cold and his exhaustion, allowing it to claim him. As he drifted deeper into the warm, welcoming darkness he thought he heard a soft laugh. Linka? No, it couldn't be. He was dying, he knew that much. And she was... But there she was, walking towards him through the snow, smiling at him, reaching out her hand... No.

His confusion grew, but still she came closer, as real as anyone could be. Her hand touching his cheek, her amber eyes gazing into his. 'Come,' she whispered, her voice low but clear, filling his head. 'Come.' And she took his hand and led him forward...

*   *   *   *   *   *   *

The years, centuries and millennia passed. Earth tremors and rock falls buried the entrance to the cave that had become a tomb. Snows fell and did not melt. Far to the north, Halsgørd and his men lay undisturbed and undiscovered where they had fallen. Glaciers claimed the valleys for their own, submerging the cliffs deep under their slow moving bulk. Inside the cave, ice slowly thickened on the walls, roof and floor, sealing both woman and skull in a frozen shroud. They were inaccessible, untouchable. Lost and forgotten.

GEMMA

Chapter 12

This was really weird. I had no idea what these dreams meant. Maybe they didn't mean anything at all, but a small persistent inner voice murmured repeatedly that something significant was going on. Joe's words replayed themselves to me over and over again. 'I think they have work for you... You're going to be in for one hell of a ride...' How could I find out? Maybe if I explained it all to Joe, this time he would be willing to tell me more.

*   *   *   *   *   *   *

I didn't get a chance to speak to Joe. When I got to the office on Monday morning – late, after a dentist's appointment – his desk had been cleared and he was gone. There was just a brief sticky note on my PC screen: 'First casualty :0(Going away for a while to consider my options. Be in touch when I get back. Hugs, Joe x'. The dark space I was in pressed closer and blacker around me. With Joe gone, it felt like one more nail in my coffin. I was already missing his good-natured leg-pulling and sense of humour.

And then, just when I thought things couldn't get any more complicated, they did. My life was, officially, in meltdown. A couple of weeks previously I had received a letter from Dan's solicitor, threatening action if I didn't put the house on the market immediately. I had been stalling for a few months but now Dan's patience had finally run out. To be honest, I wasn't that worried. I knew the housing market was pretty much dead in the water and that it would take months to find a buyer, if one turned up at all.

I was wrong. Seriously Wrong. To my horrified disbelief the house sold within the fortnight at the asking price. What the hell was I going to do now?

* * * * * * *

That evening I went to the pub with Cathy. Poor woman. All she got was me moaning about how totally crap my life was. For hours. Without a break. Eventually she interrupted me. 'OK Gemma. Enough. Have you ever thought that all this might be happening for a reason?'

I snorted. 'Yeah. And the reason is that life sucks.'

To Cathy's eternal credit, she didn't walk out then and there leaving me to drown in my self-pity. 'That's not what I meant. You know, when you need to make some big changes to get to where you want to be, and you resist making those changes, sooner or later the universe will make them anyway. You can jump – or you can wait to be pushed. And it can be one hell of a hefty shove. It's a lot easier and more comfortable to choose to jump. That way you get to pick the time and place.'

She was pushing her airy-fairy spiritual stuff at me again, only this time I didn't pooh-pooh it completely. Maybe part of me was beginning to wonder if there could be any truth in it. But then again, maybe this business with the dreams and that fact that my life had collapsed around my ears, was scrambling my brain.

'It's already happened once,' she continued. 'And if you don't do something, it'll happen again.'

'What do you mean? None of this was my fault.' I didn't have a clue what she was talking about.

'You were unhappy in your life. Miserable, stuck, limiting yourself. You told me so. But you wouldn't do anything about it so the universe gave you a shove. That's why it all changed.'

'Rubbish!'

65

'You'll see. Don't say I haven't warned you.'

'But what am I going to do?'

'The solution is there. You just have to let it in.' Good god, sometimes Cathy could be so bloody irritating. She caught my look and laughed, although her voice remained earnest. 'Seriously, Gemma. The answer is there. But if you try and work it out you'll tie yourself in knots and never find it. Look, life isn't exactly turning out that well doing it your way, is it? What have you really got to lose by giving my way a go? Just for a little while.'

'Nothing I suppose.' I gave her a hangdog kind of smile. 'Sorry Cathy, I'm being a real whinger, aren't I?'

'Yes, you are.' The kindliness in her face softened her words. 'And not without reason. But you can't go on like this. Oh come on Gemma, what do you say? Try my way. Just take a holiday. Go away for a while, stop thinking and trying to figure it all out, and just see what turns up. The worse that happens is that you have a pleasant break and recharge your batteries.'

Her words came back later as I was getting ready for bed. 'Rubbish!' I said again, out loud to the world at large. A bit more vehemently that I had intended. Who was I trying to convince I wondered?

* * * * * * *

Nevertheless, I took her advice and booked a week's leave and a cottage on the coast. Though it was still only late February, I had the luck of some glorious early spring weather. I walked on the beach, visited local tea shops and museums, and in the evenings curled up with a book in front of a crackling log fire. Gradually I began to feel a little better.

The day before I was due to leave, the weather was beautiful. I sat on the beach, the sun on my face, just listening to the waves lapping the sand. I was, I admit, more contented than I had been in a long time, even faced with the prospect of real life crashing back in on me the next day. A solution would come to me, Cathy had said. I wasn't to go looking for it. Well, it had better hurry up. The clock was ticking and so far not even the tiniest flash of inspiration had hit me.

By the time I went to bed I was still no wiser. Sorry Cathy, I tried. It just doesn't work. Strangely though, I wasn't feeling worried.

* * * * * * *

My eyes flew open and I lay disorientated in the darkness of the still unfamiliar surroundings. It was back. The black skull. Floating there in front of me just as real as that first time. It hadn't appeared so blatantly since. All my subsequent dreams had been like watching a series of stories unfolding. But this was just 'it', huge, clear, unmissable, and unmistakeable. What was it telling me? I didn't have a clue. I shook my head, bringing myself back to reality. What was it telling me, indeed! Get real, girl. It was just a dream. Nothing more.

I was wide awake now and looked at the clock: 1.20am. Its lurid green numbers seemed to mock me. I'd been asleep less than two hours but there was no way I was going to go back to sleep any time soon. Irritably I grabbed a blanket and curled up in the chair in front of the still warm fire, staring into the glowing embers. OK, so what now?

'Read what you have written.' I jumped as if someone had stabbed me with a hot pin. Where the hell had that come from? The voice was as clear as someone speaking beside me – but it had come from inside my head. I did not like this. Could the cottage be haunted? There had been nothing about that in the information pack!

'All is well. You will know what to do by the time you leave here. Just read what you have written.' I was sitting rigid, my hands gripping the chair arms. I could tell the voice was in my head, but it didn't make it any less frightening. I waited... and waited. Nothing. It – whoever or whatever it was – had gone.

Eventually I relaxed – clearly no-one else was going to start talking to me – and considered what I had heard. 'Read what you have written.' What on earth did it mean? I hadn't written anything. Unless... Did they... or he... or whoever it was... mean the notes I had scribbled down about the dreams?

I grabbed my case, dragging it towards the hearth and scrabbling through it in search of my notebook. I couldn't think why I had brought it along, I hadn't added to it in weeks but... I yanked the notebook out, spilling all my carefully packed clothes out onto the floor, threw a couple more logs on the fire – it was pretty chilly and if I was going to be sitting up I would at least do it in comfort – pulled the blanket around me, and opened the notebook.

An hour later I came to the end of the final page. As I had read, a combination of astonishment, puzzlement and incomprehension had built and built within me. All of these nocturnal scribblings had somehow coalesced into a coherent whole. Into several coherent wholes in fact.

For a long while I just sat there, staring into the flames. Remembering. Remembering how I had loved to write when I was a child. Remembering how, back then, I had always dreamed of becoming a 'proper' author and seeing my name alongside all those other 'proper' authors whose books I had loved. Where had that dream disappeared, I wondered?

'Then write. Write this book.' The voice was back, only this time it didn't frighten me at all, the words whispered encouragingly, spiralling through my mind. In that moment I knew exactly what I was going to do. It felt

right. It felt so good. And yet... Oh hell, this was madness.
Sheer reckless madness. And I was going to do it anyway.

Chapter 13

'You're doing WHAT? Gemma, you can't!' Cathy's incredulity and dismay rang out in each word.

'Why not? You told me I had to jump before I was pushed. Well, I'm jumping. And now you're telling me not to do it.'

'I know what I told you, and I still stand by that. Sort of... But this? It doesn't make sense. It's... it's like you leaping out of a plane without a parachute and hoping a passing seagull will be there to catch you. There's jumping – and there is what you're planning to do. Gemma, it's sheer suicide.'

'I know, Cathy.' I spoke gently, knowing that already she was blaming herself for my decision. 'It seems crazy to me too. But at the same time it feels so right, like I'm setting myself free to find out who I really am. I have to do this.'

'Let me get this straight. You are going to quit your job, and use the money from the sale of your house to live on while you take a year out to write a book...'

'That's pretty much it.'

'Which is something you have never done before, never even attempted before. Oh for heaven's sake, never once even mentioned before. You're nuts. What if you can't write it? Or if you do, can't publish it? You'll end up with nothing. No job, no money... and probably no roof over your head either.'

'I know.' I repeated.

'So why? You are either very brave or completely off your trolley! And I know which I'd go for.' She calmed down a little. 'What is this book going to be about anyway?'

'Crystal skulls.' Her disbelieving shriek pretty much said it all. 'But you hate them!'

'I know, but I'm clearly going to have to acquire a liking of them.'

'Why? Why crystal skulls? You don't know anything about them.'

I pulled my notebook from my bag and handed it across to her. 'Take a look at that. Then you'll know why.'

Cathy's face grew more and more incredulous as she turned the pages.

'I..' I wanted to explain, but she held up her hand to stop me.

'Shhh. I'm reading.' At last she reached the final scribbled page and looked across at me with a wary look on her face. 'You dreamed all this?' I nodded. 'When?'

I recounted the whole saga, from the first appearance of the black skull to that final evening in the holiday cottage.

'Why didn't you say anything?'

'Because I had never looked at any of it. I just scribbled it down so I wouldn't forget it and then left it. It was only that evening that something told me to read it,' – even now I couldn't tell Cathy about the voice that had spoken to me – 'and when I did, I knew what I had to do.'

She nodded. 'I understand. At least, I think I do. Yes, you definitely have to do this. And Gemma…'

'Yes?'

'I love it'

'Help me find somewhere wonderful to live?'

Her grin nearly spilt her face in two. 'Try stopping me.'

* * * * * * *

All thought of writing anything vanished for the next few weeks. A completion date had finally been set for the sale of our house so all my attention became focussed on finding myself somewhere to live, packing up nearly thirty years of married life, and moving on.

It was difficult, but cathartic. Little by little I began to feel better. The process of healing the wounds I had received over the last few months, a process kick-started that February night in the holiday cottage, accelerated. As I threw out the debris of so many years, ridding myself of the clutter and the bittersweet memories, the world around me grew lighter and brighter. The pain remained for even now I still loved and missed Dan deeply, but it had transformed into a pain I could handle, a sharp contained pain that broke through from time to time instead of the constant, all-encompassing, crushing anguish that it had been at the beginning.

Cathy was a rock, always there when I needed her. Calming me when I grew panicky. Lifting and carrying me when I tumbled back into depression. Tempering my overexcited enthusiasm when necessary with a gentle reality check. Viewing endless unsuitable properties with endless patience.

'It's there. It's waiting for you,' she would tell me whenever I began to feel despairing. 'Stop worrying. It'll come to you in plenty of time.' To her credit and my utter incredulity, it had. The perfect little house in the perfect spot. I knew it as soon as I saw it. 'So why are you hesitating?' she asked me, as we stood in the garden looking out over the sun-speckled valley. 'Tell them you'll take it before someone else beats you to it.' So I did, there and then. Two weeks later, I had moved in.

GILEADA: The Black Skull

Part 2

THE FLIGHT

Chapter 14

Kahro cautiously approached the door of the skull chamber, his eyes darting this way and that, fearful of being seen. He was jittery. The events of the past few hours had rattled him; his hands shook as his fingertips touched the small illuminated quartz panel on the wall beside him. He was late, very late. It would soon be light and he should have been far away from here by now. It couldn't be helped. When the Shadow Keepers had asked to see him he could not have refused their request without creating suspicion.

Their so-called 'friendly chat' had lasted for several hours. Interrogation would have been a more accurate description, thought Kahro angrily, but the Shadow Chasers were not officially permitted to question the Priests and Priestesses of the Light. Not yet. It was a worrying sign of their growing arrogance and influence that they had dared to summon him at all. He had at times begun to doubt they would ever let him go in time.

It was only a couple of seconds before the heavy wooden door swung smoothly open, but it seemed like an eternity to Kahro who felt exposed and vulnerable in the open corridor. He slipped quickly inside – and pulled up sharply in alarmed surprise. A figure, indistinct in the half-light, was standing beside the centre plinth. Someone else was in the chamber. This wasn't right. He had been told it would be empty, that he would not be seen. But of course, he had been due here hours ago. As the other man stepped forward, Kahro relaxed, recognising him. It was Omar, a senior priest and one of the four architects of this daring, dangerous plan to smuggle the skulls to safety.

'We thought you weren't coming. All the others have long since left. What delayed you?'

'Shadow Chasers.' Kahro's reply was brief. He had no wish to relive the discomfort of his recent experience. He had lied to the Shadow Chasers from start to finish and was certain they had suspected as much, but they had had no proof, and as yet their authority was not great enough to be able to detain him. As it was, the fact that they had questioned a Priest would create wide scale public protest when word got out. To hold one prisoner would be a step too far, and the Shadow Chasers knew it. At the moment. A chill ran down Kahro's spine. Their controlling grip on the people was tightening daily.

'They arrested you?' Kahro shrugged in confirmation as Omar's face betrayed his concern. 'That is not good news. They will not be held in check much longer. Do they know anything?' In his heart Omar was sure they did not, could not, for those involved in the plan were few in number and all had sworn loyalty to the death.

The question pulled Kahro from his thoughts. 'No, but they suspect something is going on, Omar. They don't know what it is, but they are digging seriously for information.'

'Did you stay closed?' Kahro nodded. It had been hard work, for the Shadow Chasers' abilities were well honed and growing stronger all the time. Nonetheless they remained no match for those of a trained Priest and Keeper of the Skulls. He had succeeded in blocking his thoughts against the penetrating tentacles of his interrogator's mind. The concentration it had required had taken a lot out of him but there was no time yet to rest. 'Then take Gileada and go. Quickly now. And be careful. The sun is up. You no longer have the night to help you.' Omar stopped, frowning, as his eyes scanned Kahro. 'Where is the other?'

'Still in my room. I sensed the place was being watched. I couldn't risk going back there to collect it.'

Omar thought quickly. 'No matter. We will deal with that. You must leave now. There is no time to lose.' He turned and left the chamber.

Kahro quickly whispered a blessing, then carefully lifted the skull from its plinth. It had been expertly carved from flawless deep black obsidian and was totally lifelike in appearance. Despite the urgency, he found himself lost for a moment in its mysterious depths, which flashed fire from the reflected lamplight. He had never grown used to the magic of its presence. He shook himself; there was no time for that now. Pulling his attention back to the task in hand, he wrapped the skull safely in his cloak. He carried nothing else. His belongings, everything he had packed in preparation for the days ahead, were still on his bed, and would now remain there. He would be leaving on this perilous journey to who knew where with nothing but the clothes he stood up in. Well, it couldn't be helped. He would just have to trust that the help and guidance he needed would be there for him.

He took a last nostalgic look around the chamber that had been part of his life since he had entered the temple as a child. This was the Skull Chamber in the Temple of the Light, the heart centre of Yo'tlàn and therefore of the whole continent of Atlantis. Twelve perfect carved skulls looked back at him. Everything looked exactly as it always did. Kahro knew, however, that eleven of these skulls were simply dummies, inert lifeless replicas, created to give him and his brother and sister fugitives a head start. Soon another, the one that lay waiting in his room, would join the. The deception would be complete – for as long as it lasted. As for the thirteenth and final skull – The Master – that would be the responsibility of the senior priests to safeguard, but not until the moment of the final reckoning, when the Shadow Chasers finally took control of the Temple. There was no doubt in Kahro's mind that that moment would soon come.

He crossed to the far side of the chamber and exited through a concealed doorway. His heart was racing, his palms clammy with sweat. He wanted to run, as fast and as far as he could, but he forced himself to stop and consider his predicament. He needed clothes, provisions, money, all of which were out of his reach now. Omar had vanished. Who else could he trust to help him?

'Don't try to seek the answer, just allow the solution to present itself to you.' The words of his old teacher rang in his head. 'Allow yourself to know.' Kahro focussed on the words, emptying his mind of all other thought, until the panic and urgency that had begun to take hold of him gradually subsided. A moment's patience and stillness now could be the deciding factor in the success – or failure – of his mission.

The outside world retreated as he listened and waited for an answer to float up from deep within himself, setting firmly to one side the impatience that threatened to swamp him, knowing that a still, receptive and undemanding mind would allow that answer to materialise most quickly. Within a minute or two a woman's face drifted through his thoughts. Dalka. His sister. They had not spoken in over two years, had parted at their last meeting on uncomfortable terms and with bitter words. Intuitively he knew though that despite their quarrel she would help him now. All he had to do was make his way to her home without being caught.

* * * * * * *

Dalka lived a half day's walk from Yo'tlàn, not an arduous trek under normal circumstances, and one he had undertaken many times before. But today was different. The Shadow Chasers were jumpy, highly suspicious of anything out of the ordinary. He would have to be constantly on his guard, all his senses open and alert for

77

danger. He could not risk trusting anyone he met. People were increasingly afraid, intimidated by the aggression and control of the Shadow Chasers. Despite a widespread loathing for these oppressors, there were many who would willingly betray him in order to ensure their own safety. The darkness was spreading rapidly now. The rescue of the skulls was not happening a moment too soon.

By the time Kahro passed through the outer walls of the Temple complex the sun had fully risen, flooding the streets with its fresh, clear light. It was still relatively early and there were few people around, but he was openly visible now with no night or shadows to hide him.

'The safest hiding place is always in full view.' The words leapt unbidden into Kahro's head as he paused to consider his next move. Well, yes. Perhaps that could just work. There were precious few other options. Act with confidence. Act as if he had nothing to hide. Act as if the precious bundle he carried was of no importance at all. So he squared his shoulders, stuffed the package under his arm as if it held no more than a loaf of bread, and stepped boldly out into the street, striding off towards the city's northern boundary, whistling cheerfully as he walked.

If the whistling was at times a little weak, his hands sweating, and his heart pounding, no-one noticed. The few passers-by didn't give him a second glance as he made his way through the city streets. Had they known his identity, Kahro mused, that he was a Priest of the Light and Keeper of the Skulls, had they known that the innocent looking package he carried under his arm was one of their most priceless and important treasures, their response would have been very different. Without his robes and badges of office, he simply melted into anonymity.

*   *   *   *   *   *   *

Once the outermost buildings of the city were behind him, Kahro allowed himself to relax a little. He had, he believed, passed safely through the most dangerous part of his escape, for within the city boundaries the Shadow Chasers frequently patrolled the streets, looking for the least excuse to stop and question a person. From here on it should be quieter, and therefore safer, although he would still have to be on his guard and keep to little used tracks and pathways, avoiding the main thoroughfares. Very soon he would be safely tucked away in his sister's house, preparing for the next stage of this journey into the unknown. The prospect simultaneously both comforted him and filled him with an unease he could not shake off, a dull foreboding that this would not end well.

Chapter 15

Kahro crested the low rise that overlooked Dalka's house. Within a split second, he had dropped to the ground, flattening himself against the rough grass. From his vantage point he had an unobstructed view of both the house and the track that passed by it. Approaching on foot along that track at that moment was a small detachment of Shadow Chasers. Kahro sent up a quick prayer of thanks for his close escape. A minute later, he would have been half way down the exposed hillside and in their clear sights. Cautiously he raised his head and peered through the foliage of a low growing shrub. They had stopped at the house. Were they looking for him? There could be no other reason for their actions. How? Why? Thoughts, panic, jumbled through his mind.

The door opened. He watched the fear creep into Dalka's face as she saw the menacing figures of those standing there. The air was still and the sound of their voices carried distinctly to where Kahro was sprawled. The questions confirmed his suspicions. They were definitely looking for him. Had she seen or heard from Kahro? When was the last time she had had contact with him? Did she know where he was?

Confusion now mingled with the fear in Dalka's eyes. Wasn't he at the temple? She hadn't seen him or heard from him in over two years. Was he in some kind of trouble? She was not even trying to shield her mind in the way that he had taught her to do. She had no need. She was speaking the truth and the Chasers would know that, be able to read it. With luck, they would not detain her further.

'No, no. It's just a minor matter. Something he came to us about. He isn't at the temple so we thought he may have come to pay you a visit. Please let us know if he contacts you. It would be in his best interests to do so.' The insincerity was thick in that voice. Kahro sensed that Dalka was not taken in by his words, and felt her deep mistrust and hostility as she watched them leave. He knew the Shadow Chasers would have picked up on those feelings as well but they were playing the game. It was obvious that they wanted him very badly. Why though? What did they know?

Had he unwittingly given anything away while they were questioning him the night before? He really couldn't see that he had. Or had the deception at the temple been discovered already? If so, then it was all over. With less than a day's head start for any of the fugitives, none of whom were really prepared for the task they were undertaking, there was little chance that they would succeed in evading capture. It was inevitable that at least some of the skulls would fall into the hands of the Chasers, and even one would be too many. No, Kahro felt, that couldn't be it. The alarm couldn't have been raised already. It had to be something else. But what?

* * * * * * *

In truth, the Shadow Chasers were at that moment a long way from discovering what was going on, and remained in total ignorance of the previous night's events at the temple. It was true that they were highly suspicious, certain that they were being duped in some way and intent upon uncovering whatever conspiracy was opposing their authority. They had no idea at all, however, of what that conspiracy comprised, suspecting the involvement of the skull's guardians, the Keepers of the Light, simply because the priests and priestesses of the temple were their fiercest and most powerful opponents. The Chasers therefore had taken the decision to question them illegally, and Kahro had merely been one of those summoned randomly from their ranks. No more than that. He had not been singled out specifically. He had done nothing to give himself away. It had been his misfortune that he was the only one of the twelve future fugitives they had called and, as such, the only one of those questioned who knew anything of what was being planned. He had had no choice but to shield his mind from the intrusive prying, aware even as he did so that it would further fuel their suspicions.

The Shadow Chasers had been unable to learn anything further from him, and without a shred of evidence of his involvement in anything underhand, they had had to let him go. It was a decision that they had quickly regretted. Finally abandoning all pretence of caring either about public reaction, or deference to the authority of the Temple, the order had been given to arrest him. It was too late. By the time the Chasers had come for him, Kahro had disappeared. Now he was a wanted man, to be hunted down and captured at any cost.

*   *   *   *   *   *   *

Dalka's flashing eyes followed the Shadow Chasers a long way along the track before she shut her door with an angry slam. From his hiding place, Kahro waited impatiently for them to disappear from view so that he could make his way down the hillside to the relative safety of the house. He stiffened. To his dismay, two of them slipped away from the group and concealed themselves in a small thicket at the point where the track curved away to the south and vanished from sight. From there they would have a clear view of the track, the house... and of anyone approaching.

All around Kahro the land was open, with very little cover. He would be unlikely to reach the house unseen by the Shadow Keepers' sentries even under the screen of night, for the skies were clear and with the moon only just past full, the land would be bathed in its silver light. He slumped onto the ground as waves of frustration and hopelessness washed over him. What was happening? Why was it all going wrong? So far not one step of his carefully devised strategy had gone to plan. He was in an unenviable situation, his only source of help cut off from him. He could not get to Dalka, would not even try as it would put her in too much danger. Nor was he able return to Yo'tlàn and the Temple. Where else could he go? Who else could he turn to? There was no-one. He tried to think but his mind was in disarray. It was no good. Nothing constructive could come to him while he was in this agitated and negative state of mind.

He concentrated instead on the warmth of the sun on his face, the clear blue of the sky, and the delicate fragrance of the herbs crushed beneath his body, knowing that it would only be when he was clear and open that a solution would bubble to the surface and he could allow in the guidance he needed. Gradually his mind stilled and his thoughts calmed. As they did, exhaustion overtook him – the consequences of his long night and the tension of those past hours – and he drifted into sleep.

*   *   *   *   *   *   *

'Kahro.' The voice in his head was quiet but persistent. Dalka. She had always had strong telepathic abilities and was using them to their full now, breaking into his dreams. How had he not remembered it? Suddenly he was wide awake. 'Kahro!'

'I hear you Dalka.'

'Kahro, you must go to Krista. She will help you. She lives in a cabin on the lakeside by the standing rock. Tell her I sent you.'

'How do you know I can trust her?'

83

'Her son was taken by the Shadow Chasers over half a year ago and has never returned. No-one has seen or heard from him since. Believe me, she has no love for the Dark Ones and is only too willing to help those who are working against them.'

'What makes you think I am working against them?'

'They're looking for you, aren't they? Look, I don't know what you are involved in, and I don't want to know, but I hope for your sake that you know what you are doing.'

He gave a dry laugh. He wished with all his heart he did know. At that moment, however, he felt utterly out of his depth, a drowning man without even a straw to cling to.

'Kahro,' her tone had softened. 'Be careful. Stay safe.' Then she was gone.

Chapter 16

He had been to the lake before. Once. Dalka had taken him there. It had been a long time ago, long before their quarrel. Could he remember the way now, after all this time? At least, he felt, he knew the general direction he had to take – and it was right past the look-outs who had been left to keep watch on Dalka's home. Well, he had little choice. He hoped fervently that their attention would be on anyone approaching the house, not a figure moving away from it.

Keeping low, he followed the brow of the hill as far as he could until it descended steeply towards the track. Fortunately there was more cover here, where a straggling copse overgrown with brambles and ferns twisted alongside the path. He was uncomfortably close to where the Shadow Chasers lay in wait, but he could move unseen, shielded by the thick summer foliage, holding his breath at every step for fear of a cracking twig. Then he was past them, hurrying to put as much space as he could between himself and his hunters, staying off the track in case anyone else came along. It was an easy terrain of low hills and flat meadowlands but Kahro soon began to flag. Lack of food – he had not eaten since early the previous day – and the fear and adrenalin that had been his constant companions since he had left Yo'tlàn, were sapping his energy, his legs growing heavier and heavier as the day progressed. With huge relief, he finally looked down on the vast lake glinting in the evening light. It was a beautiful sight, dark forests stretching down to the shoreline, reflected in the still water which dazzled silver in the sun's dying rays. But today Kahro was too tired to appreciate its wonder.

He made his way wearily down to the shore, which at this point formed a shallow sandy beach that stretched off into the distance in both directions. Where was Krista's cabin – left or right? Instinct told him right, and as he walked he kept his eyes open for anything that resembled a standing rock. This southern shore of the lake was gentle and hospitable; as the view opened out he could see that, further round the shoreline, steep escarpments plunged straight down into the water. He did not relish scaling those in the reduced visibility of night, even with the light of a full moon to guide his steps. Surely the cabin had to be around here somewhere?

There. Ahead. The warm, yellow glow of lamplight through a window. Peering through the dusk, Kahro's eyes could just make out the outline of a small building and behind it, looming out of the shadows, a stone pillar, rising up like a signpost to the stars. This had to be it. Krista's cabin.

As he approached, the door opened. A small plump woman, almost as wide as she was tall, beckoned urgently to him. He quickened his pace, and at the doorway she pulled him unceremoniously inside.

'Dark Ones,' Krista explained. 'They are searching the area.' Kahro's anxiety must have been obvious. 'Oh, don't worry, they've already been here and left empty handed, but it's not a good idea to hang around outside.' She stood back to look at him properly. 'So, you're Kahro. Ha, ha! You've certainly ruffled a few feathers, young man.'

Kahro stared at her. How did she know who he was? Dalka's telepathic ability, though powerful, was limited to connecting with her family. Surely she could not have warned Krista that he was coming?

'I see things that others do not, Kahro.' The warmth of Krista's smile transformed her face, revealing traces of the carefree, vibrant young woman she had once been.

'Now, sit down and make yourself comfortable. You need food and rest.' She bustled away to where a pot of temptingly rich smelling stew was bubbling away on the hearth and came back with a big, steaming bowlful which she handed to him. 'Plenty more where that came from.'

She had asked no questions, sought no explanations, just accepted his presence in her home as natural and expected. He was grateful for her discretion, too worn out to want to relate his story, not knowing whether he should, how much he should share. He finished eating and allowed his gaze to be drawn into the flickering flames of the fire, his mind to quieten...

*   *   *   *   *   *   *

He woke suddenly. The fire had died to a pile of glowing orange-red embers and the first weak light of dawn was filtering into the room.

'Good morning.' Krista's voice made him jump. She was already dressed and preparing breakfast.

'Good morning.' Kahro rose stiffly from the chair where he had fallen asleep, his body protesting at the awkward and unusual position in which it had spent the last few hours. As he stood, a blanket fell from his lap. Krista had at some point tucked it over him, not wanting to disturb him from his much needed rest. Slowly stretching his cramped muscles, he limped to the door. Outside a pale sunlight was struggling to pierce the thick veil of fog that covered the land; it was a chill and uninviting morning. He turned back and watched Krista as she worked.

Her face was lined and drawn this morning, touched by the spectre of an endless and never abating sorrow. He knew of her loss, and this morning its pain was clear to see. But there was also a fire and defiance in her eyes, and he sensed a warmth and powerful compassion in her heart that stemmed from a deep, abiding love for life. It showed in that radiant smile that transformed her appearance. He got the feeling that Krista would not be easily intimidated or subjugated.

She handed him a bowl of something hot, sweet and thick, which tasted delicious although he was at a loss to recognise what it could be,. He ate gratefully, knowing it could be some time before he enjoyed another stomach-filling meal. While he was eating, Krista indicated a pile of items she had gathered together.

'You'll need this. There's some food, money, rope and spare clothes. They belonged to my son...' He caught the waver in her voice but she carried on, ignoring it. '... I think they'll fit you.' She cast her eyes over him and nodded. 'Yes, they'll fit you.' That then had been the cause of her resurfacing pain this morning. She had been going through her son's belongings and preparing to part with them. She began to pack them into a large bag that he could carry on his back.

'Krista, I can't take this. I can't pay you. It...'

'Yes, you can,' she interrupted with an unexpected fierceness. 'You must. You will not get far as you are.' She stepped closer and grasped his hands in her own. 'What you are doing is payment enough. I would give the last piece of roof from over my head to help anyone who is working against the Dark Ones.' Her eyes burned into his, her gaze compelling and unsettling in her passion. Kahro was unable to turn away. Then her focus changed, as if she was looking through him.

'This will not be an easy journey for you. It will test you as nothing has tested you before. You are filled with fear and this blocks from you the words that will help you. You must let go of this fear. You must trust that the way that you follow is the right one. You will lose everything before you find what you are seeking.'

Her voice was deep and resonant, as if coming from a far off place, and at her words he felt that fear rising within him once more. It was a constant companion that from time to time he could ignore, but which reminded him of its presence at every opportunity. Then, as if she had said nothing of importance, Krista released his hands and nodded.

'Time for you to leave.' She handed him the pack she had assembled and led him to the doorway. 'Follow the eastern shore. The Dark Ones are searching to the west. Oh, I nearly forgot...' She shuffled back inside and returned with a second, empty bag. 'Your friend will be safer in here than wrapped in that cloak.'

Kahro stiffened. 'Friend?' he asked warily. Krista looked at him, amusement sparkling in her eyes, bringing back to her face the light of the previous evening.

'The black skull you carry with you. The one from the Temple.'

Kahro looked at her, speechless. 'I...'

'I told you, Kahro, I see the things that others do not. I know you carry it and I know why. Guard it well, young priest. It is precious and must be kept safe. Remember this, though – things are not always what they seem. Now, on your way.'

The door of the cabin closed firmly behind him as Kahro stared open mouthed after her disappearing back. He wanted to ask more, to ask what she meant, what else she could see, but instinctively he knew that she had told him all she was going to tell. So, hoisting his pack more comfortably over his shoulders and stowing Gileada, still wrapped in his cloak, into the other bag, he set off into the mist, not knowing where he was going, only that it was not the way he had planned.

*   *   *   *   *   *   *

The hours of preparation, of finding routes, of studying and memorising maps, meant nothing now. Circumstances had forced him to abandon his carefully worked out plans and head in a completely different direction. He was journeying into uncharted territory, unable to retrace his steps and recover his original course. To do so would mean turning back into the thick of the Shadow Chasers, who he now knew had marked him as a wanted man. The risk of capture, of Gileada falling into their hands, was too great. He would have to take his chances with the unknown.

Try as he might, conscious of Krista's warning, he could not shake off the anxiety and foreboding that had gripped him relentlessly ever since the evening when the Shadow Chasers had summoned him. He knew how unhelpful it was, that to get into the flow and increase his chances of success it would have really been useful to hold an attitude of optimism firmly at the forefront of his thoughts, but he was finding it impossible. Moreover, Gileada had been silent since they had left the temple, his energy dormant, and Kahro had been unable to communicate with him at all. That was ominous. This was the time when he needed the skull's help and guidance most, and it was not forthcoming.

Chapter 17

In stark contrast to the gently rolling countryside he had travelled through on his journey from Yo'tlàn, the land he encountered now was wild and brutal, mostly thick virgin forest devoid of human habitation. He would find no help here should trouble befall him. It was far beyond anything he had ever experienced before, and he did not know how to deal with it.

The land was varied, but persistently difficult. Flat marshy river inlets gave way to steep, craggy tree covered slopes, in places so near vertical that he found himself dragging himself upwards with his arms from trunk to trunk, feet slipping and slithering on the unstable surface. He had sent up more than one prayer of gratitude for the bag that held Gileada. It would have been virtually impossible to ascend those slopes with the skull wrapped precariously and insecurely in nothing but his cloak.

The flat lands were hardly easier; low lying marshlands that sucked at his feet and legs with every step, soaking through so that he walked constantly in sodden boots. Often he had to make long detours inland to find a crossing place for a river, marsh or outcrop.

While no human may have lived here, he was not alone in this wilderness, which was home to countless species of animal, hunter and prey alike. Roaring, howling and shrieking surrounded him at all hours in a disorienting cacophony, so that he could not tell from which direction any danger might appear. It was a terrifying ordeal, especially at night when, thwarted by the darkness, he was forced to stop, and huddled trembling at the mercy of any bear, wolf or lion that may chance upon him – invisible hunters prowling unseen in search of their next meal. He was under no illusion; that meal could easily be him. Fear travelled with him constantly. When he slept, it was briefly and fitfully, waking at every sound, in terror of an attack by one of these creatures. His nerves were worn raw by unimaginable threats that might strike without warning from the blackness.

Kahro did not know where he was or where he was heading, only that he had to put as much distance as possible between himself and the temple, and keep out of the clutches of the Shadow Chasers. He was rationing his food, not knowing how long it would have to last. Already it was diminishing rapidly, for despite the lush vegetation of the forest there was little food to be found, and he was wary of feasting on unfamiliar berries, mindful that many were poisonous. Without Krista's help and generosity he would not have made it this far. Even so, he was growing weaker by the day through lack of food, his meagre rations nowhere near sufficient to meet the needs of the physical demands on his body and lack of sleep. He was cold, wet and tired. The fog that had accompanied him when he had left Krista's cabin all those days ago had been an almost permanent travelling companion, broken only occasionally by a teasing glimpse of blue skies and warm sunshine when the grey shroud momentarily lifted.

He had lost count of the days he had been trudging through the forests and shores of the lake, although when he looked at the moon one night he noticed that it had shrunk from a majestic almost full orb to a mere sliver of silver crescent. He had been toiling through these forests for half its cycle already. The lake was huge, more like an inland sea, and beyond every twist and turn of the shoreline still it stretched into the distance with no sign of a northern shore.

It was many days later when, following the shoreline at the edge of a narrow beach – one of the easier stretches of his journey so far – Kahro rounded a blunt promontory and saw, far in the distance across the wide bay that appeared in front of him, a jumble of buildings stretching along the water's edge. It was the first settlement of any kind he had come across since fleeing Yo'tlàn. He thought at first his eyes were playing tricks on him and he peered intently in temporary disbelief. As he gradually drew nearer, and the buildings became more solid, their outlines sharper, to his hesitant relief it became clear that this was no mirage.

Chapter 18

Kahro was extremely wary of coming into contact with people, but he needed food and somewhere safe to rest. Would it perhaps be possible for him to creep in to the town without being seen? He decided to move closer and assess his chances. It was the only settlement, indeed the only sign of habitation, he had seen since he had left Krista and perhaps his only opportunity to stock up on supplies for a long time to come.

The nearer he drew, the more he realised that far from being a small lakeside hamlet, which had been his first impression, this was a sizeable town that stretched back from the waterfront in a jumble of open squares and twisting alleyways. That brought its own advantages and drawbacks. On the plus side, strangers would be more commonplace in a larger town, so there was less chance of him attracting attention. On the other hand, there was a far greater risk that the Shadow Chasers would be here, perhaps as many as a full complement. They could even be in control of the area.

Approaching the straggling outskirts, it became evident that any thoughts of entering the town itself unobserved were laughable. It was market day and the streets were filled with people. Well, in some ways so much the better. With such crowds everywhere he was unlikely to stand out as a newcomer. He could lose himself, becoming just another faceless visitor. If that was the case though, why was he receiving so many curious stares from those who passed by him? He couldn't work it out at first, but as he glanced down at himself understanding dawned. He was dirty and dishevelled, his clothes stained and torn from his days battling through the forest and sleeping rough. Amongst the well-dressed inhabitants he stood out like a sore thumb. Quickly Kahro left the road and made his way back to the lake shore where, concealed by a thick clump of reeds, he washed and changed into some of the clothes Krista had given him. As he rejoined the highway his new appearance merged easily with that of the people around him. Putting on his best air of confidence and nonchalance, he strode into the town.

After his days of solitude in the wilderness, Kahro felt pummelled by the noise and bustle of the crowds. The town was a busy trading post, filled with vendors who had come from miles around to sell their wares, and with those who had come to buy or simply to gaze at the array of merchandise on offer. Nevertheless, it felt good to be back amongst people again. No-one gave him a second glance as he walked through the streets and he felt his confidence building. Maybe he could discover what was happening in Yo'tlàn. Learn whether the switch of the skulls in the temple had been discovered yet. The inn would probably be the best place to go. He could sit quietly and simply eavesdrop on the chatter of those around him.

Sure enough, as he sat in the busy hostelry keeping himself to himself, a flurry of conversations filled the room. The Temple and the disappearance of the twelve priests seemed to be the only subject. Everyone was talking in hushed voices, fearful of being caught discussing the subject. He had to strain his ears to listen, not wishing to give himself away by mind-probing their thoughts. Random snatches of sentences reached him.

'…stolen by the Priests, can you believe it. They put copies in their place. To think we trusted them…'

'…sixteen of them have disappeared. All priests and priestesses…'

'…vanished without trace. I've heard that the Shadow Chasers have offered a huge reward…'

'…my brother tells me that the Dark Ones have imposed martial law in Yo'tlàn. No-one can get in or out without a permit.'

'…watching the ports… suspect they may try to get away across the ocean…'

'…they're furious apparently. Taking it out on anyone they suspect of opposing them…' Kahro's heart tightened as he thought of Dalka and Krista. He hoped they were safe, and called on the power of the skulls to protect them. There was nothing he could do to help them now.

'…smashed up the Skull Chamber. Not just the skulls but the central crystal plinth as well. From what I've been told, no-one knows what the repercussions of that will be…'

At this last piece of information Kahro's gut clenched. The Shadow Chasers could not even begin to understand what those repercussions might be. He sank his head into his hands with a groan, forgetting where he was and his own predicament, as all the possible consequences played through his imagination. When he raised his head at last, he became aware of several people looking at him intently. His instinct told him it was time to leave. This did not feel a safe place to be any more.

He got up, trying to appear not to rush, and walked briskly back into the main square. He thought he sensed two men get up and follow him, but dared not turn round to check. Come on Kahro, think straight now. Act naturally. You need food. Supplies. He was forcing his mind to think rationally, to hold down the panic that was rising within him. He stopped at a stall to buy bread and fruit, taking the opportunity to throw a quick glance behind him. It confirmed his suspicions. Two men had ducked into a doorway as his head turned, but not quite quickly enough. Kahro's heart was in his mouth. Why were they following him? Had he given himself away? How?

With deliberately casual steps, he moved away from them towards the other side of the square, only to stop dead in his tracks. A second group were closing in on him from that direction. What is more, this group were Shadow Chasers. They were moving towards him with a steady determination, certain they had him cornered. Terror gripped him. It was all he could do not to turn on his heels and run. The two men behind him had given up all pretence, standing now in clear view. Kahro suddenly understood. They were guiding the Shadow Chasers to him telepathically.

*   *   *   *   *   *   *

And then Kahro did run, not knowing where he was going, only that he had to escape from that place. He was trusting in his instinct to lead him but, to his dismay, in his headlong flight all sense of direction abandoned him. He charged blindly up alleys and down stairways, totally lost in the maze of narrow streets and walkways. All the while he could sense them following him, hear their footsteps, unhurried but relentless, no doubt in their minds that they would catch him.

He turned a corner and stopped, almost crashing into the wall that rose in front of him. A dead end! He stared wildly around. The whitewashed wall in front of him was high and featureless. No footholds. To his left, a single doorway led onto the alley. Frantically he tried the latch. It was locked and solid. There was no way out other than the one he had entered by. All the time the ominous footsteps were drawing ever closer. He was trapped.

Someone seized his arm, was jerking him through the doorway and closing it hurriedly behind him. In his panic Kahro lashed out, trying to escape. An iron grip pinned his arms as a strong hand clamped across his mouth. Jet black eyes met his in a reassuring wink, the grip eased and his assailant raised a finger to his lips in an unmistakeable signal to Kahro to remain silent. He was grabbed by the wrist, and pulled along a dark corridor to a small windowless room that was dimly lit by a couple of lamps.

His erstwhile attacker, who Kahro now understood to be his saviour, was a tall, muscular, dark-skinned man whose exotic appearance betrayed the fact that he was not a native Atlantean but a visitor from across the ocean. His dark eyes were warm and kind, and held a ready smile. Kahro nodded his thanks, still wary of making any sound.

A slight, pale-skinned woman now stepped forward, resting a hand on Kahro's shoulder in a mute, friendly greeting, indicating for him to sit as the dark man disappeared into the corridor once more. Despite the Shadow Chasers searching for him outside, just yards from where he sat, Kahro suddenly felt inexplicably safe. He curled up on the floor and, eventually, slept.When, much later, he opened his eyes, the man had returned.

'Good evening.' His voice was rich and melodious. 'You must be one of the priests the Dark Ones are hunting. My name is Hajui. Welcome to our humble abode.' He laughed at the dazed look on Kahro's face. 'It's alright. They've left. Someone started a rumour that you'd been seen heading down the lake shore. One of our group is even now leading them a merry dance as they chase him through the forest.' His mellow laugh rumbled out again.

'Who are you?' Kahro instinctively liked this friendly giant with his amused laugh and twinkling eyes.

'We are a band of... Well, we like to call ourselves guardians of freedom. The Dark Ones prefer to call us outlaws. We work to the best of our abilities to undermine their power and authority. I recognised you in the inn earlier and thought you might need some help. Your description was widely circulated once the skulls' disappearance was discovered,' he explained.

The woman Kahro had seen earlier appeared in the doorway. 'I thought I heard you, Hajui. Was there any trouble?'

He shook his head. 'No. They fell for it completely.'

'Will Jak be alright?' Kahro picked up on the anxiety in her voice.

'Don't worry, Rosa. He's good. He knows what he's doing. He'll be safely back home by now, leaving the Dark Ones scrabbling around for his trail.' Hajui's words seemed to reassure her, for she nodded and turned to Kahro with a welcoming smile.

'My name is Rosa. Tomorrow evening when night has fallen and the town sleeps, I will guide you to the valley by the mountains. From there you should be able to lose the Dark Ones once and for all, and make your way to safety.'

'Do you have any news of the others?' Kahro was desperate to know if his fellow fugitives had so far also managed to evade the clutches of the Shadow Chasers.

'As far as we know, they are all still at liberty. That is one of the reasons why the Dark Ones are so angry. Apparently they are taking that anger out on anyone who gets in their way.'

'So I overheard in the inn. Is it true that the Skull Chamber has been destroyed?'

'Yes, I'm afraid so. When the Dark Ones found out that the real skulls had gone, they were furious, and took that rage out on the temple.' This came from Hajui. He looked concerned. 'All the remaining priests were taken away for questioning.'

Kahro felt sick to his stomach. He had a good idea of how that questioning might go. He forced himself to push away the thoughts that battered him. Those they had arrested knew nothing, were the innocent parties in all of this.

The hour had finally come then. The Shadow Chasers, the Dark Ones of the people, had finally overcome the last bastion of light: the temple and priesthood of the skulls. The future would be dark for the people of Atlantis. Kahro could not bring himself to contemplate the possible cataclysmic consequences of the power that had been unleashed by the destruction of the Skull Chamber.

Chapter 19

For the remainder of the evening and the following day, as Rosa and Hajui went about their business, Kahro drifted in and out of sleep, for the first time in a long while able to relax and enjoy the luxury of an unaccustomed feeling of security. Slowly the debilitating fatigue brought about by the past days eased. Late in the evening, a light touch on his arm roused him from some uncomfortable dreams. As he opened his eyes, Rosa held out a plate, speaking in a low voice. 'It's almost nightfall. We shall be leaving shortly.'

Kahro quickly ate the food he was offered, feeling its warm nourishment strengthening his body with every mouthful. When he had finished he stood up, stretching stiffly. His body had suffered through the recent demands placed on it. Although he had always maintained a good level of fitness, he was a priest, not an athlete, and his joints and muscles groaned at the prospect of more exertion to come. Rosa came back into the room and motioned for him to follow her, a finger to her lips warning him to silence. He hoisted his pack back onto his shoulders and picked up the smaller bag containing Gileada, noticing as he did so Rosa's eyes, which were fixed on the bag in awe and not a little fear. She felt Gileada's power, even in his concealment.

They left the town through a labyrinth of narrow alleys and rooftop walkways, not speaking for fear of being discovered. Rosa led the way with assurance, constantly checking the path ahead was clear before leading him forward. They had several close calls as a patrol of Shadow Chasers or a vigilante group unexpectedly appeared around a corner, pressing themselves into shadowy doorways or crouching behind abutments or barrels, not daring to breathe until the danger had passed. Kahro had been recognised, and the Shadow Chasers knew he had to be nearby. They were determined to take him and retrieve the black skull.

After what seemed a lifetime they reached the northern outskirts of the town, which here drifted away into the surrounding forest. Rosa stopped. 'I can guide you as far as the foothills, but from there you will be on your own. I must leave you then and return to the town before I am missed. I have important work to do, and I cannot risk suspicion falling on me. But you should be safe. The Dark Ones are unlikely to follow you there.' Her voice was still barely above a whisper.

They entered the cover of the trees, where visibility fell immediately to almost nothing, the dense summer canopy shielding the moonlight. Rosa led the way confidently and sure-footedly, unlike Kahro who constantly stumbled over the rough ground, catching his clothes in the brambles and thorn-laden branches, tripping over twisted jutting roots. She was setting a rapid pace, and Kahro was finding it hard to keep up with her.

When at last the forest finally thinned and disappeared behind them, they were standing on the edge of a wide, shallow valley. Opposite them its gentle slopes gradually climbed to a towering mountain range. To the east, the head of the valley was lost in the foothills of the same mountains while open meadowland, dissected by a meandering, idly flowing river, led off to the west. Rosa pointed in the direction of the river's flow.

'If you follow the river it will eventually take you to the coast, where you will be able to find transport overseas. Look for the double spiral symbol. The people that carry it are our allies and will help you. It will be a long journey of many moons' walk. Keep to the higher part of the slopes where you can, there is more tree cover there so you'll be less conspicuous. Blessings, Kahro, and good luck.' Rosa hugged him and pressed a heavy bag of supplies into his hand before disappearing back into the shadows of the forest once more.

*   *   *   *   *   *   *

Kahro surveyed the terrain in front of him, his spirits high for the first time in many days. It would be much easier going here, and he felt he had finally left the Shadow Chasers behind. The way was easy to see in the moonlight. Revived by his lengthy rest, and fortified by the food inside him, it was all he could do to prevent himself whistling as he strode along keeping, as Rosa had advised, under the cover of the trees that grew just below the ridge line.

Towards noon of the following day he stopped to eat and drink at one of the many small streams that tumbled down the valley slope. For the first time he took the opportunity to properly survey the landscape around him in daylight. The going looked easier on the far side, despite the rising foothills that edged it, so he decided to cross over, wading cautiously through the river that seemed to be rising quickly, despite the sunshine and blue skies around him.

Over the course of the afternoon, heavy clouds that threatened imminent rain slowly overtook the sun so that by the time night had settled over the valley all moonlight was totally obscured. Despite his desire to put as much distance between himself and the town as possible, Kahro decided to stop for the night. He was tired, in need of rest and unwilling to continue in the dark, when he risked stumbling over unseen obstacles. In the shelter of a shallow hollow that hid him from view from the opposite ridge he stretched a canvas sheet between two saplings to protect himself from the thick drizzle that had now started to fall and crawled underneath it to sleep, confident that he had at last shaken his pursuers from his tail.

*   *   *   *   *   *   *

Voices! Kahro lay motionless in his makeshift tent, immediately wide awake and alert, listening hard. Yes, there they were again. They were what had woken him, and they sounded close. Cautiously he peeped out from his shelter, crawled nervously to the lip of the bowl and peered over. He ducked his head immediately back down again. There was a string of lights across the valley bottom, trailing all the way up the slope to where he was hiding – lights that were heading his way. They would be on him in a matter of minutes. Shadow Chasers. He could tell by the heavy energy that was pervading the area. How had they picked up his trail so quickly? Had Rosa been caught? Had he been betrayed? There was no time to think about that now. He had to leave, and quickly.

He did not stop to gather his belongings, grabbing only the bag containing Gileada. He peered again over the edge of the hollow. They were heading up the slope, straight towards him. The only direction that was open to him led towards the foothills behind. He slipped over the rim and ran as fast as he could, the grass underfoot deadening the sound of his footsteps in his crashing, headlong flight. Running blind in the pitch dark night, breath gasping, mind in turmoil. He had believed himself safe, and he had been wrong. Kahro did not slow until he reached the first of the rock faces where he slumped down, trying to draw air into his tortured lungs. He allowed himself to rest only a few moments before he dragged himself once more to his feet, skirting the wall, looking for a way through, all the time trying to control the panic that once more threatened to engulf him. To his relief the stone barricade gradually gave way to a narrow pass that led the way across into the next valley.

Far behind him he heard a shout; they had discovered his camp. So they would know he was close by, but hopefully not the direction he had taken. He had to keep moving, even though his legs were burning and his lungs bursting. He scrambled as quickly as he could over the steep stony ground, risking a fall at any moment but not daring to slow his pace. The clouds were clearing but the moonlight was still intermittent which, while it gave him concealment, also frequently hid his footing from sight. Although the route was a continual up and down, he could tell that he was climbing ever higher.

*　　*　　*　　*　　*　　*　　*

As dawn broke he was standing on the edge of a deep, wide canyon that ran like a giant scar through the mountain range. Its sheer, squared sides were in sharp contrast to the pitched mountain slopes that surrounded it. Which way? He looked around. Behind him the canyon disappeared into the mountains; in front it was brought to an abrupt halt by massive overshadowing cliffs. Kahro could see no possible way out in that direction and yet some irresistible force within him was telling him that was the way he should go. Well, he couldn't return the way he had come, and he couldn't cross the canyon – the far wall was too high and too sheer to climb even if he could descend to its floor. He had to make a decision. The instinct inside him urging him forward was getting stronger and eventually he gave into it.

The further he walked, the more he questioned his choice. The rock loomed above him, grey and ominous. The closer he got, the more he realised that there was no way of scaling those cliffs. Finding a route past them seemed an increasingly impossible feat. But then, as the sun lifted higher and shone directly onto the rock face, a dark line appeared, a thin jagged crack, running vertically upwards from centre of the canyon floor, splitting the cliff in two. Could that be his way out? He didn't know, but he no longer had a choice. He had come too far to turn back. There was no doubt in his mind that the Shadow Chasers would have picked up his scent by now. Somewhere deep within him he could sense that they were determinedly on his trail. He didn't know how far behind him they might be but he had to keep moving. He was a sitting target on the exposed canyon lip and needed to get out of sight, to somehow find his way down to the canyon floor.

The walls were a little more forgiving here and he could just discern a possible path down. It was steep, narrow and treacherous, little more than an animal track; still, it was his only option. The descent was slow, difficult and terrifying, and at times it felt like it would never end, but eventually he set foot on the solid floor of the canyon.

As he neared the fissure, doubts once more assailed him from all sides. It was dark, gloomy and improbably narrow. Would it just close in on itself after a few paces and leave him trapped? Maybe he could find a way up the other side of the canyon after all? The more he looked the more unlikely that escape route showed itself to be. No, he had made his choice earlier standing on the canyon rim, and now he had to abide by it. It was not an enticing prospect but there was no longer any alternative. Fear and foreboding grew in him even as the voice inside him was telling him it was the right path to take. Reluctantly, hesitantly, he stepped into the dark chasm and was swallowed up in its shadows.

Chapter 20

Kahro scrambled as quickly as he could over the uneven, rocky floor of the narrow, dank ravine. The gap between its jagged walls was barely an arm span across, closing here and there to a scant shoulders' width. Despite the urgency that clamoured within him he was making slow progress as his feet slipped constantly on the damp, mossy stones. One careless step here could easily result in a twisted – or worse still, broken – ankle. Sure and steady, sure and steady, Kahro told himself over and over again, forcing down the almost uncontrollable urge to run that threatened at every moment to overpower him.

Sunlight rarely touched this place. The sheer rock walls towered above him on both sides, the opening at the top barely wider than the base, as if a giant axe had fallen on the Earth, splitting it in two. Only in midsummer, for a few hours each day when the sun was at its highest, could the warming rays penetrate these furthest depths. This was not midsummer. This dismal, gloomy place had not been touched by direct sunlight for several weeks. Moss and ferns soaked up the moisture that dripped relentlessly from the walls, puddling underfoot, and the stench of stagnation, stale air and rotting vegetation lay heavily in the chill air.

Kahro was quickly exhausted by the difficult progress but he dared not rest. The Shadow Chasers had to be close behind him, catching up with him slowly and inexorably. He prayed that this gorge had an exit and would not end in a cul-de-sac from where he would have no escape. If they caught him... He pushed the idea from his mind, refusing to allow it to take root, knowing that if he did, fear would overwhelm him completely, stealing the last vestiges of his rational thought and with it his chances of survival.

The ravine twisted and turned, the result of a fierce and sudden land shift in the far distant past that had torn the very fabric of the Earth apart, a monumental scar threading through the land. This was one of the major fault lines that ran through the continent, still waiting to rip it asunder. It had happened many times in the past and Kahro had listened to the words of the skulls as they informed the Keepers of further cataclysmic quakes that before long would again rock Atlantis.

On and on he walked, struggling on for hour after hour through this nightmarish underworld, the bag slung on his shoulder hampering his progress even more, threatening to throw him off balance at every step. Growing heavier with every move he made. His breath was laboured, exertion and adrenalin both taking their toll on his body. The sun had begun to set on the land above. The murkiness that surrounded him grew deeper; making headway was almost impossible. No longer able to see the ground beneath his feet, he stumbled and tripped continually. He was grateful for a waxing moon whose pale silvery glow, faint though it was in the bowels of the chasm, still gave some glimmer of light that allowed him to see at least the silhouette of the cliffs that surrounded him.

Several times, the debris from a long-ago cliff fall forced him to scrabble over mounds of loose rock that threatened to come crashing down at any false move, taking him with it. They brought him an additional challenge as he sought to protect Gileada from swinging against the rocks and shattering.

All at once he could go no further. A flat slab of rock blocked his path. More than twenty feet high, weighing he could not even begin to guess how much, at some point in the distant past it had sheared away from the cliff face and fallen to wedge itself across the base of the ravine. Looking up to his right, in the dim light Kahro could just make out where it had once rested. Refusing to let his exhaustion give birth to despair, he peered at the obstacle that blocked his path. He could see almost nothing in the darkness so he allowed his hands to show it to him. The surface, on this side at least, was nearly vertical and completely smooth. He could feel no possible handholds, no crevices or ledges that would provide leverage or support. Just for a moment, allowing the tiredness and hopelessness to wash over him, he rested against it, feeling its chill on his back, and closed his eyes. Surely he had not come this far to fail now. There had to be a way.

'Please,' he prayed. 'Please, show me.' He opened his eyes, his mind turning over every possible option – and froze. There… Was that…? As he watched, the moon peeked over the edge of the ravine's lip. It was now directly overhead, illuminating the wall of the ravine as clearly as if it was daytime, and in that moment his eyes caught a glimpse of a narrow ledge that ran along it. It would be highly dangerous, but he was out of options. He couldn't stay here. He would be sitting prey for the Shadow Chasers. It was a risk he would have to take.

How could he get to it? It was way above his head, perhaps thirty feet up from the base of the ravine. He would have to try and climb up. He didn't relish the prospect at all. It would have been a difficult and perilous enough challenge in daylight and unburdened. Attempting it in the dark, unbalanced by the weight of the black skull, it bordered on the suicidal, but he could see no other choice. The moon was still shining down into the chasm and as quickly as he could, fearing that the light would disappear again at any moment, Kahro retraced his steps, searching for a route up the rock face to the ledge.

There. It might just be possible to find a way up there. In a moment of inspiration, he stuffed the bag inside the front of his tunic. It would mean he had to climb at an awkward angle, his torso arched out from the cliff wall, but it would give him both hands free.

Kahro took a couple of deep slow breaths to steady his nerves, and set about the climb. It was painfully slow going that sapped his already depleted energy mercilessly. The damp cliff face was as slippery as the path, and the rock was weak and unstable. After a couple of close calls as a seemingly firm handhold unexpectedly broke away, he began to test every move fully before committing his weight to it. Inch by inch, with muscle-punishing deliberation, his spine protesting at every tortuous twist, he crawled up the cliff.

There it was at last: the ledge, running away from him along the cliff. His heart sank as he examined it. It was less than a foot's length wide. He would have to edge along it sideways, his back against the cliff. One wrong step, one crumbling section of rock, would plunge him back down to the path below. He was still near enough to the ground that a fall would be unlikely to kill him but, short of a miracle, crashing onto that stony ground would certainly cause serious injury. His heart pounding as if it would leap from his chest, Kahro gingerly twisted his body and sidled one foot onto the precarious foothold, then the other. He stood trembling, pressed against the rough stone behind him, waiting for his breathing to steady and slow. Waiting for the shaking in his legs to subside so that he could move without them giving way beneath him. Creeping his way then in tiny movements along the narrow lip, the weight of the bundle that was still tucked into the front of his tunic threatening to throw him off balance and pull him forwards over the edge.

He did not know how long he spent, inching along that ledge. The moon's light had once more vanished and in the darkness he dared not look down, unable to see the floor below him. His focus was simply and only on shifting one foot sideways, testing the stability of his foothold, then bringing the other foot to it, aware of nothing but feeling his way along the interminable blind traverse, the treacherously meagre path beneath his feet and the hard jagged rock digging into the flesh of his back.

He recoiled, startled, his mind brought roughly back to the ravine as his foot dislodged some loose pebbles that clattered down the cliff like machine gun fire in the silence. The sudden, unexpected noise exploded in his heart as if it would burst from his chest, and he clung desperately to the rock face behind him with his fingertips, recovering his balance and calming his jangled nerves. For the first time since he had begun this desperate climb he looked down. Relief flooded through him; in the strengthening light of early morning, he saw that he was perched directly above the giant slab of rock that blocked the path. Unnoticed by him as he had edged his way blindly along, the ledge had been descending almost imperceptibly so that it now ran barely a foot above the top of the massive boulder. To his joy he could just about make out that this side of the rock, unlike the vertical face that had previously confronted him on the other side, sloped out and downwards towards the base. It was a steep incline, but if he could climb down onto it then with care he should be able to slide down safely to the ground.

Carefully, his exhaustion weakened muscles shaking with the effort, Kahro lowered himself until he was sitting on the ledge, where he allowed himself to relax for a moment. His eyes closed and he rested his head against the cliff face behind him. How much more would he have to endure? He wasn't sure he could go on much longer. His body was unused to this punishing action and was telling him so in no uncertain terms. Every part of him ached, and he knew that the unremitting strain was slowing his mental processes and dulling his senses. But he could not allow himself the luxury of rest. Not now. He set his feet onto the sharp apex, eased himself across into a crouched position and cautiously slithered the first few feet, braking his descent with his heels. Slowly, slowly. All was well and the ground not far below now. But the rock was more slippery that he had anticipated. All at once he lost control and crashed heavily the last few feet to the ground, losing consciousness as the air was punched from his lungs.

*   *   *   *   *   *   *

When he came to, he knew he was still alive. His body would not feel pain like this if he had died. Every inch throbbed and burned where it had smashed into the rock-strewn ground. Gileada? Was he still safe? Concern for the black skull temporarily pulled Kahro's thoughts from his own uncomfortable situation. He realised he was lying on his back, the bundle still safely tucked into the front of his tunic. It had been a lucky break. His body had cushioned it from the impact of the fall. If he had landed face down, Gileada would have shattered.

As it was, the skull was unharmed. But what about himself? He tested his body, gingerly moving his limbs. His arms and legs worked; they were battered and bruised but unbroken. His head ached where it had hit the floor, but luckily he had avoided the sharp rocks that littered the area. Except for a huge lump on the back of his own skull, it seemed undamaged. When he tried to sit up, however, it was a different story. The extent of his injuries immediately revealed themselves. He had cracked a rib or two on landing, and every movement sent an agonising shaft of pain through his chest.

Painfully he pulled himself to his feet and stumbled onwards. He could not stay here. He had to keep moving. Had to keep Gileada from the clutches of the Shadow Chasers. To find somewhere safe to hide and recover. He did not know this land, was travelling blind, not knowing how much further this ravine would go or where it would lead him. Not knowing where or when he would find the shelter he needed. He had to trust now, more than ever, where he was being led. His pace had slowed even more; each step sent white hot knives slicing through his ribcage. How long had he been lying unconscious? He didn't know. Couldn't know. It was full daylight now but was it still morning or late afternoon? However long it had been, the Shadow Chasers would have made up ground on him. The question was, how much? How close behind him were they now?

On he limped, the pain that assaulted his body weakening him with every movement. He knew a cracked rib or two would not be fatal, and that in time they would heal, but their constant onslaught was draining the last dregs of his already empty endurance. If they caught him now, he would not have the strength to defend himself. Or Gileada.

The chasm seemed endless. He was staggering now, his bruised and exhausted legs buckling beneath him at every step. Then, unexpectedly, as he rounded a craggy spur, the path opened out in front of him onto a wide expanse of grassy, sunlit plateau. The warm sunshine brought him renewed strength and vigour as he emerged from the tomblike gloom of the ravine. The air was fresh and clean, the soft breeze like a caress on his skin. He breathed as deeply as his damaged ribs would allow, drinking in the light and air like a starving man.

Chapter 21

Kahro surveyed the scene that lay before him. The sun was almost right above him; it was early afternoon, he estimated, so he could have only been out for a few minutes at most following his fall. He was still high in the mountains; snow-capped peaks encircled the plateau, their lower slopes thickly forested. Which direction now? There did not appear to be any way off the plateau behind him, where the stark cliffs of the ravine reached up into the clouds. There was no obvious route to their summit and, other than that through which he had come, no break in their towering walls, which curved around in an arc to frame the rear of the plateau. He would have to go forwards then.

He crossed the meadow, little by little his premature optimism dissolving in the face of a growing misgiving. The muffled roar that he had ignored in his initial delight at being back out in the open air was growing louder with every step. And the far edge of the plateau was looking more and more like a cliff edge. He had to go that way, he had no other option, but Kahro was beginning to fear that he would be trapped here.

The closer he drew, the more his suspicions were confirmed. The roar had become the deafening thunder of a mighty cataract that pierced the cliff walls and plummeted to the gorge below, invisible through clouds of spray that rose from its foot. The plateau dropped away too in a near vertical fall to the river far below. There was no possibility of climbing down there, even for a mountain goat. He turned his attention back to the falls and skirted the rim of the gorge to take a closer look at the cliff face through which it flowed. Yes, maybe he could make his way down here. Over time rock falls and huge boulders carried by the torrent had piled up one over the other and the powerful currents, aided by the weather, had carved giant steps out of the rock face. It would be difficult but not impossible. A sharp stab in his side was a cruel reminder. No, with these damaged ribs it would be impossible. There was no way he would be able to undertake that descent with his injuries. He sank wearily to the soft grass as pain and exhaustion finally claimed him, and drifted into a welcome oblivion.

*   *   *   *   *   *   *

It was several hours before he regained consciousness, and the sun was sinking towards the mountain peaks as his eyes opened. He sat up stiffly, feeling stronger and rested. His spirit had returned. Maybe he couldn't manage that climb, but maybe, just maybe, he could. Of one thing he was certain: he wasn't going to just stay here and wait for capture. If he died trying it would be better than dying at the hands of the Shadow Chasers. He got painfully to his feet, stowed the precious bundle down the front of his tunic once more, and began to make his way to the cliff edge.

'STOP!' The imperious voice was distant but clearly audible. Kahro wheeled around in dismay. Shadow Chasers. They had been closer than he had realised. Well, if they wanted him, they would have to catch him. He hadn't come this far to now give up without a fight. Resolutely he turned on his heels and walked as quickly as he could towards the falls.

'STOP!' They were closer now and gaining. The Shadow Chasers were all fit, strong and well-trained. Even uninjured it would have been unlikely that Kahro could have outrun them. With his cracked ribs it would be impossible. But he was at the lip of the cataract already, and they were still only half way across the meadow. If they drew close enough, they would be able to use their weapons; he wasn't prepared to let that happen. He had to keep some distance between himself and his pursuers.

Awkwardly he climbed down the first few feet of the cliff, gasping at the agonised protests of his damaged body. There was a clear trail here that under normal circumstances Kahro would have found relatively easy to negotiate; with a sinking heart he quickly realised that today it would be far beyond him to manage the descent. Searing pain was wracking through his chest and back, stealing his breath and what was left of his energy reserves. He thought quickly. They must not capture Gileada. That was crucial, whatever his own fate. What could he do?

'Destroy me.' The order rang out in his head. 'Better I am destroyed than fall into the hands of darkness. Destroy me!' Gileada had taken the decision for him. Could he do it? He would have to summon the strength, however difficult he found it, however wrong it felt to extinguish such a beacon of knowledge and wisdom. He would do it because he understood the fateful consequences of not doing so.

'Where are you going to run now, Priest?' The Shadow Chaser was staring down at him, his face a mask of scorn and contempt. 'Where is the skull?' The voice was sharper now, colder. 'Give it to me.'

Kahro had closed his mind to the Dark Ones' mind probing as soon as he had seen them on the plateau. They could not suspect his intention. Surprise was essential to its success. He looked up at them feigning fear, his body cowering in defeat and compliance. He reached inside his tunic and withdrew Gileada, leaving the wrapping behind, sensing that many of the Shadow Chasers stepped back uneasily as the black skull appeared before them. None of them would have ever seen one of the sacred skulls before, and in the evening sunlight Gileada's inky blackness shone

116

with an eerie otherworldliness. His malevolent appearance was deceptive; nonetheless, it had the required effect in unsettling the Chasers and breaking their focus.

'This skull?' Kahro asked, feigning innocence.

'Give it to me now, or you will suffer the consequences.' The cruelty in the Chaser's voice was tangible.

Kahro drew a shuddering breath, fearful of what he was about to do; knowing he had no choice. The Chaser's patience ran out. 'Get it,' he growled.

'NO!' Kahro's arm no longer belonged to him. Before he had a chance to act, an impulse outside of himself drew it back and hurled Gileada without a moment's hesitation into the chasm below. The decision had been taken out of his hands; Gileada had acted as the force behind his own sacrifice. He watched as the skull tumbled through the air and with a muffled crack shattered into a million tiny coal black shards on the rocks below. A sudden violent nausea threatened to overwhelm Kahro as the magnitude of what had just happened sank into his consciousness.

The Chasers too were stunned, caught off guard by this unimaginable act of desecration. Whatever else they had been expecting, it was not this. They had not believed that a Priest of the Light, a Keeper of the Skulls, would deliberately destroy one of his sacred charges.

'GET HIM!' The order, screamed in a red fury, came too late. Kahro had already followed Gileada, launching himself over the precipice to disappear in the clouds of vapour that shrouded the base of the falls. The Chasers stood staring after him, incensed that their prey had once more evaded them, this time, it seemed, forever.

'Get down there and see what you can find. If by some miracle he's still alive, I want him... And he'll soon wish he wasn't.'

One by one they descended the perilous route to the base of the waterfall. Gileada had shattered into razor sharp splinters that dusted the rocks over a wide area. He was finished, could never be retrieved. But they did not find Kahro, whose body had been carried far downstream by the fast-flowing current. The Shadow Chasers searched for days, unwilling to give up until they found his broken corpse to prove his death. Eventually, however, they had to resign themselves to the bitter fact that with his last breath, he had beaten them.

GEMMA

Chapter 22

Within a couple of weeks of arriving in my new home I had settled in completely. It was a tiny, ancient cottage with thick walls and draughty windows – and I loved it. I felt at home straight away, like I had been living there my whole lifetime. My neighbours were sheep along with the other wildlife – foxes, deer, badgers, rabbits and owls – that freely roamed the fields and woods that surrounded it. It was a far cry from the soulless, if comfortable, cloned suburban box I had shared with Dan.

It was peaceful, tranquil, after the emotional roller-coaster of the previous few months. A healing place, Cathy called it, a place where I could regain my balance and rediscover myself. It began to work its magic almost immediately. I became aware of an unfamiliar sense of freedom within myself. Freedom from the restrictions and habits of a predictable and uninspiring life, and a marriage that had long since lost its sparkle. Freedom from the demands and expectations of anyone else. Freedom from my own long-established ideas about who I was. Despite the uncertainty and chaos of the recent changes that had been thrust upon me and turned my world upside down, the realisation slowly filtered into my consciousness that I was actually happy. Happy and content. Feelings I hadn't experienced for a long time.

My only disappointment was that I hadn't heard from Joe. Not a word since that day when he'd been made redundant and left before I had arrived at the office. I was a bit surprised. I thought he would have been in touch at some point before now, but my texts and emails remained unanswered. I hoped he was OK. Now that everything in my life was settling down I realised that I missed him.

Missed his gentle teasing and his ready laugh. Missed the easy, relaxed friendship that we had always enjoyed.

*　*　*　*　*　*　*

I began to write. There was a rickety old summerhouse in the garden and I made it my study, wandering out there every morning with my notepad, laptop and coffee – for as long as it remained warm and sunny. It leaked like a sieve in bad weather.

The dreams had given me the storylines. It was up to me now to turn them into something that would seize a reader's imagination. I didn't have to think too hard. The words were crowding into my head, tumbling over themselves as soon as I picked up the pen. The moment it touched the paper, there they were, filling themselves out – characters, descriptions, emotions – giving themselves depth and realism with little input from me. Where was all this coming from? I didn't know and, frankly, I didn't care. It was coming and I was loving every moment of this birthing.

I needed a break though. I had locked myself away from the outside world for too long, paying little heed to the days that were passing, so absorbed was I in my new passion. It was too easy to do, but I was starting to feel distanced and disengaged. I needed company, trivial girlie chat, and to get back into real life before my friends and family thought I'd been kidnapped or something. Cathy was first on the list.

I had promised her a sneak preview and could practically hear her bouncing up and down with excitement as I spoke to her on the phone.

'Gemma! Hello stranger. You haven't finished it? Not already?'

'No, don't be daft. Just the first small bit. But I did promise to show it to you as soon as I'd done it. Fancy going for a coffee?'

Silly question. An hour later we were sitting in the café of our local garden centre. It was a bit mundane perhaps for such an auspicious occasion but was one of our favourite haunts for a meet-up, due largely to their selection of unbelievably good home-made cakes. Cathy shook her head in amazement as she looked across the table at me.

'What's up?' I asked her. I couldn't help smiling at the bemused look on her face.

'I can't believe you're the same woman. You look incredible, so happy and contented. Younger. And, well, maybe its sounds odd, but there's a kind of glow about you. To think I said you were crazy to even think about doing this.'

'It's how I feel, Cathy. I am happy. I love what I'm doing. I can write for hours and it doesn't feel like work at all. I love my home. What more can I ask for? Well, except maybe to have a publisher lined up...'

'Patience, dear girl, patience. Now, hand it over and go get us some coffee. Oh, and a slice of coffee and walnut please.' Cathy thrust her hand out over the table and I placed in it those first few precious pages. She perched her glasses on her nose, settled herself, and began to read. At last she leant back in her chair and looked at me long and hard over the top of her spectacles. 'This is good. Really good. You know that don't you?'

I shrugged. 'I think so, but then I wrote it. I've hardly got an objective viewpoint, have I?'

'It is good,' Cathy repeated firmly. 'What happens at the end?'

'I don't know.'

'You don't know? How can you not know?'

'It's just like I told you. The storylines come to me when I dream. So, OK, I have a rough idea but as for the rest of it... Until I start writing I don't know for sure. I have to wait and see what comes out of the pen.'

'Well, hurry up and get on with it. I'm dying to find out what happens next.' She grinned. 'You have changed so much you know. There is no way you would have been talking like this before all this stuff happened.' She leaned forward and took my hand. 'I'm sorry, Gemma. I was so wrong. This is exactly what you are meant to be doing. Now, let's eat cake and celebrate.'

* * * * * * *

'You know dad thinks you've lost the plot.' At twenty six my son Jamie still hung on to the casual attitude and habits of his student years. At this moment he was sprawled on the low stone wall that divided the patio from the herb garden where I was pottering away.

'Any reason in particular?'

'Oh, pretty much everything.' Jamie threw me a mischievous grin. 'Chucking in your job. Thinking you can write a book – his words, not mine mum. I know you can,' he quickly reassured me. 'Living out here in the wilderness.' 'The wilderness' was a tiny dilapidated farm cottage at the end of a rough track, a mile or so from the nearest village.

'What do you think, Jamie?'

'Oh, I agree with him, you have lost the plot, and I think it's fantastic. I can't ever remember seeing you this happy. If this is what losing the plot does for people, it should happen much more often.' We both burst out laughing. 'No, honestly mum, you are following your dreams and that has to be a great thing, whatever the outcome.'

I leant over and gave him a hug. 'I never realised I had raised a philosopher,' I teased. Then I grew serious. 'Was I really that grumpy?'

'Grumpy? No, you were never grumpy. Not that I remember. But you didn't ever really seem happy either, not the way you do now.' Then, in the way of most sons, he changed the subject to something more pressing. 'Now, where's lunch? I'm getting hungry.'

His arm around my shoulder – when did he get to grow so tall? – we wandered back to the kitchen. 'Mum, do you think your book will ever be made into a film?' There was a definite twinkle in his eye.

'It would be great to think so, wouldn't it? I suppose anything is possible, though I find it hard to imagine. Anyway it's not even a book yet. There's a long way to go before it'll be finished and then I have to find a publisher and...' I stopped, looking at him quizzically. 'Why?'

'Just thinking. Could you write in a part for a tall, good-looking young man who rescues a beautiful, sexy woman from a horrible fate?' He winked.

'I suppose you would be cast in the hero's role?' He nodded. 'I always fancied being a movie star, ever since I got that job as an extra when I was a student. And if you could arrange for someone like Natalie Portman to be the damsel in distress, it would be perfect.'

'I'll see what I can do,' I promised, the twinkle in my eye matching his own.

*   *   *   *   *   *   *

They may have been said jokingly, but Jamie's words started me thinking – daydreaming really, I suppose – about how fabulous it would be if it did happen. I wasted a very pleasant couple of hours that afternoon after he left, allowing my imagination carry me into all realms of wonderful possibilities before I dragged myself out of my little fantasy cloud and back down to earth. Like I had said to Jamie earlier, I hadn't even finished the book yet. Nowhere near it. To tell the truth I still wasn't convinced I had the talent to make it as a 'proper' writer. But even as the doubts nagged me, I knew that I had been called to do this for a reason, and I didn't believe that it was going to stop at just this one book.

Chapter 23

The next thing I knew, I'd bought myself a skull. Not a real skull, of course. One that had been carved from stone. Don't ask me why, because I have no idea what made me do it. I certainly had no intention of buying one. While I continued to dream about skulls a couple of times a month, and was writing a book about them, I still found them – well, if no longer actually repulsive, certainly ugly and off-putting. Not something I would choose to come face to face with every day.

But there I was, marching out of the shop with one, wrapped carefully in white tissue paper and tucked into a small brown paper bag. I had only gone in because a bracelet in the window had caught my eye. From the outside I had thought it to be a normal gift shop but as I walked through the door, beautifully arranged shelves of weird and wonderful objects surrounded me, objects I had only ever heard of in fairy tales and in my ignorance didn't really believe were sold openly in shops: wands, staffs, silver pentagrams; Tarot cards and rune stones; silver pendants and velvet robes. The powerful but beautiful fragrance of what I later discovered to be incense permeated every nook and cranny.

Tucked away in an alcove at the back was a crowded display of crystals of every size, shape and colour, all glittering like precious jewels in the artificial downlight. And there, right in front of me, sat a collection of carved skulls. Some were almost life-size, others no bigger than a sparrow's egg. Again I felt the old familiar fascinated repulsion, not wanting to linger but reluctant to pull myself away. I turned to go back to the jewellery, which after all was the reason I had come in, when a flash of light on glassy black caught my eye. I hadn't seen it at first but now it grabbed my full attention, standing out from all the others, which had faded into a hazy blur on the edges of my vision. It was about the size of a hen's egg and the deepest blackest black, the colour of the night sky behind the stars, polished to a mirror finish that gleamed softly as it reflected the harsh glare of the fluorescent bulbs overhead. It drew me like a magnet and I stretched my fingers out to touch it. Picked it up and carried it to the cash desk, as inevitably and irresistibly as I had that painting all those months ago. Any thought of the bracelet had vanished completely from my mind.

I left the shop, and within a moment had totally forgotten about the skull in my hand too. Joe was walking down the street some way ahead of me. At least, I was pretty sure it was Joe. He looked different – slimmer, longer hair – but, yes. I was certain it was him. That relaxed loping gait, the way his head was always tilted slightly to one side, as if he was listening for something.

'Joe! JOE!' He clearly couldn't hear me, and his long, easy stride was quickly carrying him further away. I started after him – and nearly fell flat on my face, stumbling into a woman coming towards me. Blasted heels! Why, today of all days, had I decided to go all girly and glamorous and stick on a pair of high heels instead of the comfy flat boots that I usually wore?

By the time I'd regained my balance, and apologised to the woman I'd almost squashed, Joe had disappeared from sight. I was puzzled. If it had been Joe – and I was convinced it was – he was clearly back in the area. So why hadn't he called to say hello?

*   *   *   *   *   *   *

'Maybe because it wasn't him? Oh for heaven's sake Gemma, even if it was there could be any number of explanations. Why is it so important anyway?'

127

'Oh I don't know Cathy. I suppose I'm a bit worried about him. I'd really thought he'd have been in touch by now. And... Well, more than anything I was hoping he might be able to shed some light on this skull stuff. I know he was really interested in it all.'

'That's all?'

'Of course that's all. What else would there be?'

'Mmmm.' She changed the subject. 'How's the book coming along?' I slumped back in my chair, feeling thoroughly dejected.

'It's not. I've come to a complete standstill. It's just not happening. Writer's block I think they call it.' I wasn't joking. Over the last two weeks I'd managed precisely half a page. And even that half a page wasn't particularly good. At this rate I'd still be writing it when I was a hundred.

'That's why you bought the skull,' she burst out triumphantly. 'To get it flowing again. Have you got it with you?' I nodded. I had forgotten to take it out of my handbag the previous day, my thoughts so preoccupied as they were by the mysterious Joe sighting.

'Well, show me then.' I unwrapped it and put it in her hand. 'Yeuww! Creepy. That black colour doesn't help either. Makes it look even more sinister.' She paused and briefly closed her eyes. 'Mind you, there's a pretty powerful energy firing out from it.'

Cathy spoke about energy with the same easy understanding that other people spoke about the weather or cricket. It was part and parcel of her life. She'd tried to explain it to me on several occasions but it had just gone over my head. 'You'll know what I mean when you feel it for yourself,' she had told me. But I didn't feel it and I didn't believe I ever would.

'This will talk to you. You'll feel this. Give it a chance.' She'd pretty much read my mind again. Before I could reply she was standing up, grabbing her coat. 'Come on, the film starts in ten minutes.' At the door she stopped and turned to me, the hint of a frown wrinkling her forehead. 'You know, I have a feeling you are going to see Joe again a lot sooner than you think.'

*　　*　　*　　*　　*　　*　　*

When I got home late that evening I began to think again about what Cathy had said, both about Joe and about the skull that still sat in my bag. Joe I could do little about. I couldn't make him get in touch with me and that was that, and he obviously had his reasons for not doing so. Which left the little black skull. Had it really come to me to help me move forward with the book? The whole idea seemed ludicrously far-fetched. But then again, everything that had happened over the past year had been ludicrously far-fetched too. What was plain as the nose on my face was that I needed something to give me a hefty kick up the backside. Not only had the writing dried up – the words and ideas stubbornly refusing to come forth – so had the dreams. It had been nearly six weeks now since I'd had the last one. They were the source of all the stories, all the words I'd been writing – no dreams equalled no book. What's more, strange though it may sound, I missed them.

OK, so even if I accepted (with difficulty, I admit) that the skull had come to help – how would it? How could it? Did I need to do anything, and if so what? I hadn't thought to ask Cathy earlier, and by the time we left the cinema our heads were so full of the film we had just seen that everything else had vanished from our minds. It was too late to text her but, now that I had the bit between my teeth, I didn't want to wait until the following day. I'd just have to work it out for myself.

I sat down and took out the brown paper bag, once more unwrapping the tissue paper that cushioned the skull. It emerged in striking contrast, jet black against pure white. I looked more closely at it. It was just like opaque

129

black glass. There was a tiny label on its base that I hadn't noticed before: 'obsidian'. Well, at least I knew what that was. I had been watching a history programme on television just a few nights earlier in which obsidian had been mentioned. From what I could recall, it was indeed a form of glass, occurring naturally as a result of volcanic activity. Right, so I knew what obsidian was. Now what? Knowing the skull was made from obsidian didn't help at all. I still didn't know what to do with it.

In that moment I remembered what Cathy had done, my mind seeing her sitting there just holding it in her hands, so I decided I would do the same. I cupped it in my hands and waited… and waited… and waited. Nothing! And still nothing. This was ridiculous. Here I was, holding a lump of rock and waiting for it to talk to me when all I really wanted to do was go to bed. Maybe Dan was right. Maybe I was completely losing the plot?

I was so tired, yet still I sat there. My eyelids began to close. I felt myself drifting off to sleep.

'What the…?' A powerful burst of energy had jolted right through me, jarring me back to full wakefulness. At the same time I felt myself falling…falling…

I flung the skull to the floor and the room immediately stabilised around me. My breath was coming in rapid gulps, my heart was racing. What the hell was going on? I looked at the skull. It had rolled into the dark shadows under the front of the bookcase from where it stared out at me, malevolent and menacing. It had scared the wits out of me and I didn't want it anywhere near me. If this is what energy felt like, Cathy was welcome to it. I didn't want to know. I grabbed a tea-towel from the kitchen and, using it to pick up the skull gingerly with my fingertips, ran out into the garden and dumped it under the lavender bush.

GILEADA: The Black Skull

Part 3

REVELATION

Chapter 24

Flickering lights drifted across the inside of Kahro's eyelids. Orange. Red. Yellow. Dancing and twisting in the darkness, fading and then expanding once more. Was this how death was? A never-ending kaleidoscope of shifting colours and patterns in a field of nothingness?

But if he was dead, why was his whole body encased in a cocoon of aching discomfort? From his head to his feet every muscle, every bone, every nerve ending throbbed and burned. Distant sounds slowly penetrated his fog-bound mind, waking him further. Reluctantly he fought his way to the surface of his consciousness. The sounds, though still muted, became clearer: voices speaking in low whispers, a baby crying, rustling movement, the thundering roar of water. A waterfall...

Kahro started with a wrenching jolt that seared through his battered body, fully conscious now as memory surged back to him. The waterfall. Gileada. His own desperate plunge into the seething cauldron at the fall's base, a plunge to what should have been certain death. He was not dead, but Gileada was, destroyed as he exploded into a million inky splinters on the jagged rocks at the cliff base. He had heard him shatter, felt the energy shock of his destruction even as he himself was falling. A sorrow and loss, more agonising and intense than any pain his physical body was experiencing, clutched at his heart, and a creeping cold took hold of him. His mind was still reeling, still trying to accept the reality of what had happened, but the deeper part of him was already grieving.

A cool hand brushed his forehead, calming and soothing him, bringing him back to where he lay. 'Welcome back, stranger. We were afraid you would not

132

return to us.' Soft grey eyes searched his own. 'You have been gone a long time.'

'How long?' He felt as weak as if it had been a year.

'Seven days.' Her voice was low and velvety, as soothing as honey on a wound. 'We found you washed up on the river bank more dead than alive and brought you here to care for you. Rest now. We can talk later when you are stronger.'

*   *   *   *   *   *   *

Piece by piece, he learned of his good luck in being found in this virtually uninhabited landscape. Two young men from the village out on a fishing expedition had come across him, broken and barely alive, sprawled across a boulder at the river's edge. The river, in spate after days of storms and heavy rain higher up in the mountain range, had carried him far downstream in its rushing fury, tossing him through rapids like a rag doll, finally flipping him onto this rock. It was a stroke of good fortune which had undoubtedly saved his life. If surviving the plunge down the waterfall had been miraculous, then surviving the river's rage was no less so. He could remember nothing after hitting the water so hard it had knocked every ounce of breath from his body, the crushing agony from his damaged ribs tipping him into a welcome oblivion.

He had lain senseless for seven days until he had woken to those incredible grey eyes. He learned that they belonged to Malika, daughter of the village healer and she herself highly skilled in the healing arts. Malika was gentle, kind and gifted, and nursed Kahro through the long, difficult days and months that followed his return to the world. Many of his bones had been fractured and as they healed she was constantly at his side. Incredibly, his injuries, though serious and sometimes slow to mend, had not resulted in any permanent disability. His lapses into unconsciousness gradually eased.

His mind and heart were slower to heal, however. Night after night the voice of Gileada called to him in his dreams. Night after night he woke shaking, guilt overwhelming him, reliving the moment he had hurled Gileada to obliteration. Part of him, the rational, logical part, knew that he had had no choice. It had been that or let the skull fall into the clutches of the Shadow Chasers. Knew, moreover, that Gileada himself had orchestrated those events and controlled his actions, and that he had been powerless to resist the command. But another, louder part constantly berated him – for not having anticipated the eventuality, for not having acted differently, even though he did not know what else he could have done. For not having found another solution. Try as he might, he could not rid himself of that gnawing, all-consuming remorse.

Malika was concerned. He saw it in her eyes, felt it in her touch, although she never said anything, never questioned him. She simply sat with him through the night, soothing his nightmares with her light touch on his brow and her quiet words of reassurance. He could not bring himself to speak of it, to share his burden with her. They were growing closer by the day and he knew he was falling in love with her. He hated keeping his secrets from her, wanted to tell her who he was, but something always stopped him. She would be curious as to what a Priest of the Light was doing out here in the wilderness, so far from the Temple in Yo'tlàn. How could he admit to having destroyed one of the thirteen sacred skulls? They were beyond value, irreplaceable, central to the life of Atlantis. He feared that even Malika would not understand why he had acted as he had. That she would condemn him and walk away.

* * * * * * *

134

Kahro was living with a small group of former Yo'tlàn residents who had left the city many years previously in order to establish their own community far away from the pollution that was even then being created by the Shadow Chasers, a pollution of greed, separation and fear. These were all highly conscious and awakened Atlanteans who still remembered and held fast to their true origins as children of the light. Unhappy at the spreading darkness and fear that was taking hold of the land, understanding that it would only increase, they had left the city, in ones and twos so that their exodus would go unnoticed. Distancing themselves from the control and aggression of the Dark Ones, they had re-established themselves as a self-contained society hidden away within the uninhabited forests and mountains of the heartlands. They were able to shield their existence from detection and lived peacefully and undisturbed, in harmony with the land around them.

Kahro quickly grew to love these people for their openness and kindness, their willingness to welcome him into their hearts and their homes. They were warm and generous, sharing all they had with him without a thought, treating him as a friend and brother rather than a stranger who had fallen into their midst by chance. As his body healed, he began to feel increasingly uncomfortable and deceitful. No-one in the small settlement knew his true identity and no-one had asked, trusting totally their intuitive feelings about him. To them, he was simply Kahro, an unfortunate traveller who had lost his footing and fallen into the river.

But Kahro knew he was no innocent wayfarer. He was a Priest and a fugitive whose presence could endanger the hidden world of these kindly people. Threaten their peace and seclusion, and possibly even their lives. He could not stay and bring that upon them. He would leave as soon as he was strong enough to travel, he decided, forcing himself to ignore the pain that gripped his heart at the thought of walking away from Malika. Under any other circumstances he would have willingly stayed and taken her as his wife, but his heartache at leaving her was dwarfed by his fear that staying could bring about her death and that of everyone else in this idyllic place.

Chapter 25

He was strong enough. He would leave tonight. He did not know where he would go, but it didn't matter. In his heart of hearts he realised that he would be unlikely to stay alive for long in this wild country in any case. He was a Priest, a Keeper of the Skulls – a former Keeper of the Skulls he reminded himself sadly – not a mountain dweller who knew how to survive in this land. Well, so be it. Better him than the people who had innocently taken him in and befriended him. His heart contracted cruelly as Malika's smiling face appeared in his mind; his decision though was firm.

*   *   *   *   *   *   *

It was time. Night had just fallen and surrounded him with those few darkest minutes that come after the sun has set but before the moon has risen. Kahro glanced cautiously around as he crept silently past the outermost homes of the settlement and headed towards the cover of the nearby forest. No-one was about. As he reached the first of the trees, he allowed himself to breathe more easily. He had not been seen.

'Kahro?' Malika's low voice came from behind him, faltering, confused. He turned, just able to see her silhouette approaching him along the path. 'Kahro? Where are you going?'

No. Anything but this. He could handle anything but this. He could feel his heart starting to tear, his resolve evaporating.

Malika's eyes fell on the bag he carried over his shoulder. 'You're leaving?' She took a step closer, lifting her face to look at him. He could see the hurt, the

137

hesitation and the incomprehension etched upon it. He had to walk away. NOW. He did not have the strength to stand here and endure that gaze. 'Why?'

'I can't tell you why.' His voice was rough; the only way he could get through this was to pretend to himself that he didn't care. To turn his back on her and walk away, his heart falling to pieces. Still her footsteps were there, running after him.

'Kahro.' He could hear the tears in her bewildered voice as she hesitantly placed a hand on his arm, desperate to hold him back. He turned to her once more, unable to bear her anguish, allowing himself to look this time into her face, into those incredible grey eyes. Her unruly curly brown hair, usually firmly secured, now tumbled uncombed around her face. Malika was not pretty in any accepted sense, but the glow of effortless natural love and warmth that flowed from deep within her brought to her features a gentle serenity and beauty, which Kahro had found irresistible from the first.

Tonight that glow had faded in the misery that overwhelmed her, leaving her standing adrift in a mist of heart-melting vulnerability. And he loved her even more for it. His resistance crumpled in an instant. Love overcame him and he lost himself in her tear-stained face. He pulled her into his arms, holding her tightly as she melted into him.

'Please. Don't go, Kahro. Don't leave me.' Her whispered appeal tore further at the raw, open wound of his breaking heart.

'I have to.' His lips moved against her soft curls. 'I can't stay here. If I do, your life and the lives of everyone here will be in danger. I couldn't bear it if anything happened to you because of me.'

'I don't understand, Kahro. How could you ever be the cause of anything bad happening? What are you so afraid of? What can't you tell me?'

Her gentleness and compassion at last broke down the floodgates and Kahro sank to the floor in despair. All the pain, all the fear, all the misery he had been holding back burst from him then like a ruptured dam. The story poured from him in an unstoppable flow: his identity and the mission he had taken on; the flight from Yo'tlàn with Gileada; the Shadow Chasers hunting him down; those final wretched moments when he had destroyed the black skull.

Malika listened in silence as the story tumbled from his lips in an at times almost incoherent stream, hardly able to take in what she was hearing. Gradually his words, and the understanding of what he was telling her, filtered through to her stunned mind. Watching him, never taking her eyes from his face as his words spilled out, tripping over themselves in their desire to be heard. Surrounding him with her love as he spewed out his torment.

Eventually the torrent slowed and stopped. Kahro slumped drained and exhausted, Malika dazed and bewildered by his revelations. After a long time, Kahro took her hand. 'Now you know why I have to leave.' The hopelessness in his voice was tangible.

Wordlessly Malika rose and moved closer to him, taking him in her arms and holding him so tightly that he knew she would never let him go. His arms wrapped around her like a drowning man grasping a lifeline. They stayed that way for what seemed a lifetime, her love enfolding him, healing him. Love so strong it would not be denied its future. She finally pulled back a little, her hand gently touching his face. 'Why didn't you tell me? All these months you've been carrying this burden by yourself. Blamed yourself when there was no cause for blame. I love you Kahro and I won't let you just walk away from me.'

'I...'

'Come with me.' An enigmatic smile shone through her tear-streaked face as she rose, pulling him to his feet. 'There is someone I want you to meet. I think he can help you.'

Mystified but unquestioning, Kahro allowed her to lead him further into the forest, the silvery light of the now-risen moon guiding their way. He had never been this far into the forest before. Malika obviously knew the path well. After perhaps an hour's walk, a dim yellowish glow pierced the gloom ahead of them. It was the light from the window of a small log cabin that nestled isolated and hidden amongst the trees.

'This is where he lives.'

'Who?' Kahro was still as puzzled as when they had started out.

'Johr'an.' Nothing was any clearer. Kahro thought that he had met everyone in the small community, but he had never heard of Johr'an.

*   *   *   *   *   *   *

Malika knocked on the door. After much shuffling inside, and a stifled oath as something heavy was knocked over with an echoing crash, it opened. A tall, very thin old man stood before them peering at him curiously.

'Good evening, Johr'an.' There was a deep affection in Malika's voice as she addressed the old man. 'I hope you don't mind me disturbing you, but we need your help.'

'Welcome, Malika, I have been expecting you. I know why you have come here and yes, I think I can help.' Warm brown eyes bored into Kahro, as if reaching deep into every cell of his body. A strange sensation began to build within him – a distant recognition or familiarity that he could not place and which came from far beyond his conscious mind. At length the old man nodded.

'You were right to bring him. Leave us now. All will be well.' He smiled reassuringly at her as she turned to leave.

'I...' Kahro hesitated.

'She will return in the morning. For now, you and I have work to do, young Priest.' Kahro stared at him in confusion. His mental shields were still strong and he had sensed no attempt to breach them. How did this man know...?

'Don't worry, Kahro, you haven't given yourself away.' Johr'an's eyes twinkled in amusement. 'No one else would be able to tell, but I knew you to be a Priest the moment I saw you. I always recognise one of my own kind.' Kahro stared. Surely he had misheard, or misunderstood.

'No, you heard me correctly. I too was a Priest of the Light at the Temple of the Skulls in Yo'tlàn.' He chuckled. 'Oh, that was many years ago now. When these people left to build a new life here, I was guided to come with them. To bring what wisdom and knowledge the skulls had given me so that I could share it with them and help them build the community they dreamed of. I was given dispensation to leave the Priesthood and I have been here ever since.'

Kahro understood then. Understood the recognition he had felt at Johr'an's scrutiny. It was a sense of deep connection and brotherhood forged through the energy of the skulls.

Johr'an placed his hands on Kahro's shoulders, facing him square on. Once more his caramel eyes gazed deeply into Kahro's own, seeing the battle going on within.

'Are you going to heal me?' Kahro was still unsure why Malika had brought him here. Did she know of Johr'an's past?

'Heal?' The old man chuckled again. 'No, Kahro. At least not in the way you mean. I am simply going to show

141

you the truth so that you may let go of your guilt and despair once and for all. I am going to take your consciousness on a journey that will allow you to see what you do not yet know, and in doing so reveal the whole picture to you.'

It was only then that Kahro noticed a low couch in the centre of the room. It had been covered in a soft fabric and was surrounded by crystals – some natural points, some carved into sacred geometric shapes. All gleamed in the firelight, casting flickering rainbows across the walls and ceiling.

Kahro had been on many of these journeys on his way to priesthood, inner quests into the infinite source of knowledge that lies within every human being. They were an integral part of his training and subsequent practice. In that instant he realised that, since the day he had fled Yo'tlàn carrying Gileada under his arm wrapped only in his cloak, virtually all thought of inner enquiry had evaporated. He had allowed his fear, the panic and urgency of his flight, to mask his hard-earned wisdom, stealing away clear thought and inspiration. Allowed it to hide the light and understanding that had shone so brightly from him while he had remained closeted in the Temple at Yo'tlàn. That was why Gileada had remained so silent and inert. Not because he had been taken from the Temple but because he, Kahro, had closed himself down. Shut himself off from the guidance that could have made his escape so much easier – until that final fatal moment when the black skull's voice had finally penetrated the shields of his consciousness and compelled his body to act. It must have taken every last shred of Gileada's power.

'Do not judge yourself too harshly, Kahro.' Johr'an's words were kindly. 'When fear and darkness take over, the voice of love and guidance cannot be easily heard. Then is the moment we must make the deliberate choice to listen for it, and that is not an easy task.

'Now come, it is time to begin. Allow yourself to be led to wherever you need to go, to see whatever you need to see. I will remain here at your side and watch over you for as long as it must take.'

Chapter 26

Johr'an's mellow voice was soothing. Kahro lay back, closed his eyes, and began to breathe deeply and slowly as he had been taught. Immediately he felt himself sinking, descending into the warm heart of the Earth. As if on a screen in front of him, he saw a cave. A small, dark cave with a huge square block of stone in its centre. And lying on the stone... Kahro jolted. It was a woman. Or rather the body of a woman, lying as peacefully as if she simply slept. With difficulty he pulled his attention from her and looked around the rest of the cave, sensing there was more here for him to see. There. An alcove had been chipped out of the wall behind her, and in it rested... Gileada?

No. There was something not quite right about him. The energy didn't feel the same. Not by much, but enough for Kahro to notice. He had known the skulls long enough to recognise immediately each of their energy signatures, and this one was subtly different. This was not the Gileada he had known

It seemed this revelation was a catalyst, for he now found himself rising up through the roof of the cave and hovering above the landscape. A white, frozen landscape of snow and ice. Below him, a huge glacier, hundreds of feet in depth, inched down the valley carrying away everything in its path. When he looked down though, he could also still see into the cave, was able to see straight through the tons of rock that separated them. The cave was buried, inaccessible under the ice. What did it mean?

In an instant, Kahro was transported to a completely new location. It appeared to some kind of council chamber, empty apart from two men engaged in an earnest discussion. He was drawn closer. One of the men was small, slightly built and dark – exactly the same colouring

144

as the woman in the cave, Kahro noticed, puzzled by the coincidence. The other was tall and blond, dressed in robes of electric blue. Kahro recognised him immediately. He was one of the Visitors who had occasionally come to the Temple to meet with the senior priests and priestesses. He had never been able to discover who the Visitors were or where they came from, but they were evidently well-liked and respected and they carried an air of peace and serenity around them wherever they went. The voices became clearer; Kahro was able to pick up some of the conversation.

'We cannot access the skull. It is lost to us, at least until the ice recedes, and we do not know when that will be.' The smaller man paced anxiously.

'We cannot wait that long.' The taller man spoke with a calm authority. 'The time will soon be upon us when the skulls must once more be brought to the knowledge of the humans. They are ready to hear.'

A long pause followed, both men deep in thought, seeking a solution. The blond man suddenly looked up. 'Can you create a duplicate?'

His companion looked at him in questioningly. 'A duplicate?'

'Yes. We need all thirteen of the skulls in order for them to function as the unity that was planned. If we cannot retrieve Gileada, can we not create a twin to take his place?'

'It just may be possible.' The small, dark-haired man considered the suggestion, deep in thought. 'Yes, it could work. It would not be exactly the same, for those ancient craftsmen who created the original have long departed our world. But we could programme it in the same way and imbue it with a similar consciousness.'

'Then that is what we must do.'

*   *   *   *   *   *   *

145

A series of scenes flickered past Kahro: craftsmen carving and polishing a skull of the purest black obsidian. A silver ship moving effortlessly through space A black skull being brought to a newly constructed temple. All the while, in the background, the faint image of a cave, a woman, and a black skull resting in an alcove.

Kahro finally understood. The Gileada he had destroyed was not the only Gileada. He was a duplicate, a twin. The original still waited patiently in a cave under the ice for the day when he would once more come to the light. And come to the light he would. Kahro saw that clearly. At a future time when the skulls were once more reunited for the purpose for which they were intended: to guide humankind forward into the next step of its evolution. It would not happen until the world was ready and willing to hear their wisdom, open and aware enough to truly understand it. He saw that clearly too. Only when humankind chose to set fear aside, to no longer allow it to dominate its existence, would they be able to see the way of the skulls: the way of love, unity and co-operation.

It would be a strange world they would return to. A hellish world, to Kahro's eyes. A world filled with noise and teeming with people. A world where so much of the water, air and soil were dirty and lifeless, where natural resources were running out, and no-one seemed to see it or to care. A world where fear reigned. But Kahro also saw that only then, when it seemed almost too late, would humankind open its eyes to new possibilities. The vision faded and Kahro felt himself rising upwards once more.

*　　*　　*　　*　　*　　*　　*

As if waking from a dream, Kahro opened his eyes cautiously. He was back in Johr'an's cabin with the pale light of early morning peeking in through the window. For the first time since he had left Yo'tlàn he was fully at peace. He understood now why the black skull had called to him in his dreams. All those times he had pushed him away, fearing his reproach. But Gileada had not been calling to him in reproach, rather as a reassurance that he survived.

He became aware of Johr'an's dark eyes upon him. 'You must speak of this to no-one,' the old priest warned. 'No-one must know that Gileada still lives. Not even Malika.'

'You saw?'

Johr'an nodded. 'I watched with you.'

Kahro's head dropped as his fear-filled thoughts once more crowded in, his elation that Gileada lived on quickly overtaken once more by his anxiety for Malika and her people.

'It doesn't solve the problem of the danger I pose though, does it?' he said bitterly. 'I am still a fugitive from the Shadow Chasers, and for as long as I am here you are all at risk.'

Johr'an sat beside him, placing a fatherly arm across his shoulders. 'The Shadow Chasers believe you are dead, Kahro. They are no longer looking for you. They have more important quarry to chase now that Gileada is beyond their reach. They are putting all their resources into tracking the other skulls.'

'How do you know?'

'I know.' Johr'an's certainty left Kahro in no doubt that he spoke the truth. 'Besides,' he continued with a grin, 'do you think we would not have protected ourselves from unwelcome intruders? I have been here thirty years and they have not found me yet. Why then should they be able to find you? Believe me, we are in no more danger with you here than without you.'

Kahro looked at him, reassured by the old man's words. Johr'an laughed and clapped him on the back.

147

'So you'll be staying then. Good. It'll be pleasant to have someone to talk with about the old days. I love my life here, but part of me still misses those times.' Kahro hugged him in gratitude, a growing bond of warmth and affection building between them.

A knock on the door told them that Malika had returned.

'Should I tell people who I am, Johr'an?'

'Only if you want to. It isn't necessary. They are more concerned with how you are than who or what you are. They have accepted you based on their feelings about you. Let that be enough. Go now and tell Malika you are staying. I have a feeling she wants to know.'

Kahro blinked as he stepped out of the cabin into the bright morning sunlight. Malika's anxious eyes met his.

'It's alright. Everything is alright. I'm going to stay.' He had no chance to say more as Malika wrapped her arms around him and kissed him deeply and passionately. Her soft lips and searching tongue, her warm yielding body pressed hard against his, woke in him a desire and urgency he had never felt before. It was some time before they once more became aware of the world around them. They pulled apart, breathless and laughing.

'Now,' Kahro grinned, 'if you agree, shall we go back to the village and plan a wedding?'

From the cabin window, Johr'an watched them walk off into the forest. He smiled. Yes, everything was going to be alright.

GEMMA

Chapter 27

The dreams returned…

So did Joe.

He knocked on my door, completely out of the blue, just over a week later whilst I was in the middle of tussling with my latest chapters. Now that the dreams were back, just as Cathy had predicted, I had something to work with and the words were flowing again.

As I opened the door my heart, it has to be said, somersaulted. Not only because I was absolutely NOT expecting to see him standing there on the door mat, but also because this was a very different Joe to the man who had walked out of the office on that Monday morning nearly a year before. This Joe had lost weight and toned up. This Joe was lean, suntanned and, damn it, looking incredibly sexy. It threw me completely. I had never seen him that way before. Then again, he'd never actually looked that way before! The pale-faced, pudgy man I had known had disappeared. This new version Joe was relaxed, a picture of health. He was wearing his hair much longer too. It curled down over his collar and into the nape of his neck. I felt an almost irresistible urge to put my hand up and curl it round my fingers. 'Don't be ridiculous!' I told myself sharply. 'This is Joe.'

'Where the hell have you been?' I hadn't meant it to come out as harshly as it did but I was totally thrown by his unannounced reappearance – and by the sudden and unexpected feeling of attraction that was coursing through me.

'Hi Gemma, it's good to see you too. Going to invite me in?' His mischievous grin reassured me. It was every bit the Joe I had known. 'You look amazing.' He had taken the words right out of my mouth.

'Well, you don't look so bad yourself.' THAT was the understatement of the year. 'So what's been going on with you?' I ploughed on, talking partly to calm my confusion but also giving vent to the frustration and anxiety I'd been feeling at not having had any word from him for so long. 'Where did you disappear to? Wherever it was, it's obviously done you the world of good, but why didn't you email or anything? I was worried about you. You could have been kidnapped or murdered or anything.'

'That's my girl, Gemma. Always looking on the bright side.' His eyes twinkled, but as he noticed the genuine concern on my face he became serious. 'Look, I really am sorry I didn't get in touch to let you know I was OK, but so much started happening, and I just needed time to get my head around it all. I've been all over the place in the last twelve months but for most of the time I was in South America...'

'South America?' I interrupted. 'What on earth for?'

'It's a very long story. Put the kettle on and I'll give you all the gory details. Although I warn you, I doubt it'll make much sense to you.' He stopped and looked around him. 'On the other hand,' he said thoughtfully. 'Maybe it will... There's been a lot going on for you as well, hasn't there?'

Ten minutes later armed with a full teapot and the biscuit tin, we were settled at the kitchen table, swapping stories. As we talked, I forgot about how good-looking he was now, forgot about the attraction I had felt, and we fell back into our old familiar, easy friendship.

*   *   *   *   *   *   *

Joe told me how, when he had turned up at the office that morning to be informed that there was no longer a job for

151

him, his world had pretty much collapsed around him. How he had become so firmly ensconced in what he called the 'wage slave mentality' that the unanticipated bombshell of finding himself with no employment and no steady secure income had sent him into free-fall. Not only had his 'job for life' and therefore his 'salary for life' been swept away, with it had gone the bedrock of everything he had ever learned was important. What was more, in the current job market he could see that his prospects for finding another position quickly looked more than bleak.

His initial reaction had been to take some time out alone, to find some thinking space in which to pick up the pieces and consider his future so, still reeling from the shock, he had packed a bag and driven down to Cornwall the very same morning, ending up in Tintagel, a village on its beautiful rocky north coast. There, he had spent a few days walking, worrying, and generally wallowing in his misery and misfortune. Until the day he met the person who was going to change the course of his whole life.

Crow was a young sculptor, maybe thirty years old, into whose gallery Joe walked one wet Cornish afternoon. Joe was the only customer and the two started chatting. Before he could stop himself, Joe was pouring out all his woes to this generous, warm-hearted man. When he finally ran out of steam, Crow simply looked at him steadily and in a voice filled with compassion asked, 'But what is the problem?' Joe stared. Hadn't he just spent the last twenty minutes telling him?

'What is the problem?' Crow repeated. 'I hear what you've just said, but I'm asking you a serious question. It doesn't sound to me like you have any problem at all, just a huge opportunity. Look, you've already said your life wasn't particularly fulfilling, and that you didn't really enjoy your job. That your heart wasn't in it, and that you only stuck at it because it gave you a decent wage. To me, that really doesn't sound a great reason for doing anything.

You have no ties, no obligations. The world is yours to grab hold of with both hands. Can you see that? See it as perhaps the biggest and most important opportunity that life will ever bring you. The opportunity for you to get off that hamster wheel we're all conditioned to believe is the right way, the only way, to live and to follow your heart.'

'But my house... the mortgage?'

'Sell your house. Get rid of everything that is tying you to a way of life that is killing your joy and suffocating your soul. Set yourself free. Live your passions and your dreams rather than your fears. I've discovered that when you start to do that, life has a funny way of providing for you. Look at this.' Crow waved his arms at the gallery around them. 'I did it. Gave up my nice, safe, secure prison cell in order to forge my own path. And there is no way I would ever willingly lock myself back up in it again.' He smiled. 'Think about it. No, forget that. Don't think. Feel about it. You'll find you'll know exactly what you want to do.'

* * * * * * *

'Well, Crow's words did get me thinking – thinking hard – and the more I thought, the more I saw how grey and empty my life really was. I'd got pretty good at glossing over my dissatisfaction and learning to look on the bright side, but the truth was that underneath it all my life didn't reflect the person I really was, and it certainly wasn't the life I'd have chosen to lead. Except of course that I *had* chosen it...

'I started to question everything I'd ever believed. Suddenly I saw how well I had been taken in by all the conditioning I had been taught: be sensible, get a proper job with the security of a steady income, play it safe. I had been well and truly caught up in the illusion of it all, believed it to be the right way and the responsible way to live, regardless of how unfulfilling and stifling that way was.

'Well, here I was, having played the game all my adult life, pushing forty five years old, stressed, overweight, and probably heading for an early heart-attack. What else did I have to show for it? A crippling mortgage, a failed marriage and no job. Could this really be what life was all about?

'Of course it's not! When we're living according to how we are told we should live we are trying to fit into someone else's mould, and it will never be a good fit, even if we can manage to squeeze ourselves in. It can never work.

'The light came on. Life isn't about some false illusion of security and permanence. Life is about getting out there and living it, taking chances, doing the things that feel right for you in the ways that feel right for you. Not allowing anyone else to tell you how that should be.

'Don't get me wrong, Gemma. I can see that for many people that might still be the nine to five job, two point four children and suburban semi. If that's what makes them feel alive then it's great. But it wasn't right for me. I was single and free with no-one to answer to other than myself. The world was my oyster and I wasn't going to play the game any longer.'

Was this really Joe talking? He was so animated, so intense, so alive. I had not once seen this side of him in the eight years we had worked together. Then again, there would have been no cause for it to surface, buried as we all were under years of conventionality and the – what had he called it? – 'wage slave mentality'.

'So, come on. Tell me. What did you decide to do?' I was hooked on his story, eager to hear more.

'I did what Crow suggested. I listened to my heart. When Crow started talking to me about feeling rather than thinking I didn't know what he was going on about; As soon as I started mulling over ideas though, it all became obvious. You don't decide with your head. If you do that all sorts of crap kicks in: I can't because... What if... Yes, but... When you look at how a decision *feels* there's never any doubt. You can just feel what's right. So that's what I did. I've wanted to visit Nepal for years and I always found some excuse not to. Could never justify the expense I suppose. As soon as I listened to my heart rather than my head all those doubts disappeared. An old friend of mine from university now runs a travel company out there. One phone call later, he'd fixed me up with an itinerary and a guide... and off I went, without a second thought. I wanted to go and so I went. I had absolutely no other agenda other than to enjoy myself and see a part of the world I had always wanted to see. That was my plan – but, well, that's when stuff really started to happen.'

If I was hooked before, now I was being well and truly reeled into the net, leaning forward in my chair, hanging on Joe's every word.

'What sort of 'stuff'?' Clearly important stuff, perhaps extraordinary stuff... But WHAT?

'My guide, Taiki, took me up to a monastery high in the mountains. Honestly Gemma it was unbelievable. Absolutely breath-taking, and so remote from anywhere. It blew me away. Steve – the travel guy – had set it up as part of my itinerary. This particular monastery is rarely visited by outsiders but he'd met the monks a few years earlier and struck up a close friendship with them, so I was granted permission to visit. I couldn't get over how friendly and welcoming they were. Anyway, to cut a long story short, inside the central room of the monastery they showed me a crystal skull sitting on a big, ornately carved stone altar. It was pretty amazing I can tell you. I could tell there was something really special about it, even though I didn't know what. Taiki told me it was extremely ancient, at least two thousand years old, and had been in the

155

monks' care for at least one thousand of those years. No-one knew where it had originated but the local people believed it brought peace and prosperity to their community.

'Through Taiki, the senior monk told me that there are many such skulls scattered around the world, protected by the ancient cultures and their descendants. That's the reason I went to Nepal, Gemma!' Joe's voice was triumphant. 'To find out about them. I left that monastery knowing exactly what I would do. Learn as much as I could about the ancient skulls. Meet them and those who watched over them as often as I could. I had no idea why but I was in no doubt that it was my way forward.'

Listening to his words my spine tingled and goose bumps shivered over my skin as my mind flew to the stories that covered the countless sheets of A4 stacked on the desk upstairs. Was it just coincidence? That we had both become so deeply involved with these peculiar objects at more or less the same moment? That for both of us, events had conspired to bring this about, as if some great, carefully orchestrated plan was being set into motion? And that it had all happened following a massive upheaval that had completely overturned our former individual lives? It had to be coincidence, anything else was unthinkable. Impossible. Nonetheless the nagging suspicion refused to be silenced.

Joe was still speaking, recounting how his quest had taken him all over the world, from the Himalayas and China, to Mongolia, Russia and Scandinavia and back to Europe, before crossing the Atlantic to South America where he had spent the last seven months. In those months he had spoken with countless shamans and tribal elders, travelled from the Andes to the Amazon Basin and on to Mexico. Come into direct contact with some very old and powerfully energetic skulls and their keepers.

'How did you find all these people? How did you know where to look?'

'That was the strangest part of all. I didn't have to find them. They found me. I can't really explain it because I don't know how it happened; it was almost like everything was being lined up for me. I'd take one step and the next became obvious.' His voice became animated. 'I've still only scratched the surface, Gemma.' He was excited, impassioned. 'These people have so much knowledge that they are not yet ready to share. Knowledge about the skulls. Why they exist, what they mean. I'm certain the skulls have a crucial message and purpose, if only we could find out how to access it. Something huge and incredible is about to happen. I can feel it. Maybe not today, or tomorrow, but soon...'

He gave a wry smile. 'OK, you think I'm crazy. I know you Gemma, feet on the floor and head firmly in the material world. To be honest, sometimes I think I'm crazy too.'

*   *   *   *   *   *   *

I looked at Joe steadily, feeling his infectious excitement and sense of anticipation touch me too. 'Actually Joe, I don't think you're crazy at all.'

Now it was his turn to look at me as if I'd grown an extra head. I bustled around refilling the kettle to hide my hesitation. Come on, Gemma. Say it and be done. OK. I took a deep breath and sat back down opposite him.

'I don't really understand where you are coming from with all of this, but I definitely do NOT think that you are crazy. Some pretty unusual things have been going on in my life too.' I paused, half wanting Joe to say something. He remained silent, giving me a questioning glance, waiting for me to continue. 'You remember that hideous painting I bought with the indians and the skull?' He nodded. 'Well…'

Over our second pot of tea, I related the whole story from the evening that the painting had crashed to the floor to the moment I'd thrown the little black skull out into the garden. I left nothing out – the dreams, the writing, even the voice in the cottage. I hadn't ever mentioned that part to a living soul, and that included Cathy. Joe watched me with growing incredulity, staying silent until I'd finished speaking.

'Bloody hell, Gemma, you've been on one hell of a roller-coaster ride too, haven't you? There is something important going on here, something we should be taking note of. We both head off in the same direction at the same time, pretty much. That is seriously weird!'

'Coincidence, that's all Joe.' Even if I wasn't sure I believed that, I was certainly not going to allow myself to consider the alternative. It was too scary.

'If there's one thing I've learned above anything else over the last year, it's that there is no such thing as coincidence. Synchronicity, yes. Coincidence, no!'

'What's the difference?' I was getting a bit lost.

'Coincidence is meaningless. Synchronicity is meaningful. With synchronicity, if you look deeper into those apparently 'coincidental' events, you find that there is always either a message or something else – information, people to help you, resources, for example – that will lead you further forward towards something important.'

'Mmm.' I wasn't convinced but I let it go. I didn't want to get into a discussion that would pull Joe's thoughts away from his story. 'Tell me what you learned about the skulls.'

'No, not yet. I was going to, but after what you've told me I feel that if I did it would influence what you are writing and I don't want to do that. What you are putting

158

onto paper has to be untainted by anyone else's ideas or experiences. That's why you were chosen, I think. You knew nothing about the skulls, so didn't have any preconceived ideas that would colour what you are getting through. I will tell you soon, when you've finished the book. I promise.'

I can honestly say I had no real idea of what he was going on about, but knowing that once Joe had made his mind up, that was it, I didn't push him. To tell the truth I could sort of see some reasoning in his words. What was more, I didn't really want any literary criticism until I had polished it up a bit. Cathy was different. She insisted on reading every page pretty much as it was coming out of the printer, but as she was always full of praise there was little chance of my confidence being knocked. I had a feeling Joe would be a bit more honest and I wasn't quite ready for that yet, so I told him so. Besides, two could play at his game.

'No problem. When you're ready. You do promise to let me see it at some point though?' I promised. 'Good. Now, can I see this skull you said you'd bought?'

'It's in the front garden under the lavender bush.' I felt pretty sheepish even as I said it. I assumed it was still there; I hadn't looked since I'd thrown it out. To his credit, Joe said nothing, simply disappeared out through the door. He came back a couple of minutes later with a very muddy, very sorry looking object in his hand. I shuddered at the sight of it. 'Ugghh! Keep it away from me.'

'It's a beauty, Gemma. At least it will be after a good wash. Pretty powerful too. Why don't you like it?'

I related the tale of that evening when it had frightened me half to death. 'If you like it so much, you keep it.' I told him. 'I don't want it anywhere near me.'

'I'll tell you what. This is definitely your skull, not mine, but it doesn't deserve to live under a lavender bush, lovely though lavender bushes are. How about I just look after it for you until you're ready to make friends with it?'

My dry laugh said it all. 'OK. Be warned though. It might be staying with you for a very long time.'

Chapter 28

Joe became a regular visitor after that first evening, frequently dropping in for a quick chat that often stretched to several hours and way into the night. Sometimes I'd open a bottle of wine and he'd end up sleeping on the couch, not wishing to drive after drinking. It got to the point where I kept a spare pillow and duvet in the downstairs cupboard, ready for his overnight stays. He was easy company and our friendship grew.

* * * * * * *

What did Joe and I find to talk about for hour after hour? Pretty much anything and everything, really. It felt so good to be with someone with whom I could just ramble. We chatted about the changes in my life and the book I was writing, although I still hadn't shown Joe any of it. We speculated about ancient mysteries, which was an area he was becoming more and more excited about, and he told me about his travels. I loved to hear Joe talk. He had a way of making even the most ordinary experiences sound fun and exciting. To my intense frustration though, he still wouldn't tell me anything much about the skulls.

'There are some things you have to discover for yourself, Gemma,' he would say every time I pushed him for more information. 'It's the only way to really understand.' I could have Googled some things I suppose, but I didn't. I wanted to hear what Joe had found out, based on his own first-hand research. Clearly I wasn't going to get it. Not yet anyway.

One evening he came in, bright eyed and bushy tailed, bursting to share his latest new-found knowledge. 'Atlantis and Lemuria,' he announced. 'Ancient highly advanced civilisations that simply vanished without a trace.'

'Atlantis? I've written something about that.' I was puzzled. 'Did it really exist then? I thought it was just a myth.'

'That's how most people consider it. Plato wrote about it and since then it's been the stuff of legends. Historians, archaeologists, almost all the scientific community reckon it's all a load of nonsense. I'm beginning to wonder though…' He halted mid-sentence as my first words belatedly sunk in. 'You've written about it? How?'

'You tell me!' I stated flatly. 'All I know about Atlantis comes from that cheesy nineteen seventies TV series about a man with gills. I don't know how I've written about it, but I have. I try not to think about where I'm making this stuff up from. Sometimes it gives me the creeps.'

'Can I see it?' So far I had managed to avoid showing Joe the manuscript; maybe now it was time to show him just a small bit of it. I brought the relevant pages downstairs and dropped them in his lap. 'You read, I'm going to make dinner. Do you want some?'

Joe's head moved in an almost imperceptible nod. He was already engrossed.

* * * * * * *

'I don't think you are making this up at all.' It was an hour later. Joe hadn't spoken a word until now, his full attention on the words in front of him, which he had read through slowly at least twice before he looked up. He had even eaten his dinner with one eye on the food and the other glued firmly to the manuscript. I frowned. If I wasn't making it up, how was I writing it? Joe wouldn't elaborate.

'It's no good me trying to explain, I don't think you'd believe me. You need to experience it for yourself.' I swear I could scream with frustration when he started getting all cryptic like this.

'Experience what? Joe, what on earth are you talking about?'

'I'd like to take you to meet a friend of mine. I feel it would really help you understand these skulls a bit better.'

'What friend? And how exactly would it help?'

'Duncan Standish. I met him when I was out in South America. What he doesn't know about skulls isn't worth knowing. He'll be able to explain all this to you much better than I can.'

I hesitated. At present I was, more or less and most of the time, snug in my comfort zone and able to ignore anything that impinged on that. I'd reconciled myself to what was going on. More than that. I was actually enjoying it, loving my writing and, in general, happy with the way my life was unfolding. I wasn't sure I wanted to step out of that safe, comfortable little box to meet the unknown head on. I told Joe as much.

Chapter 29

I managed to find enough excuses to put off meeting Joe's friend for quite some time, but Joe was not going to be thwarted forever. They were pretty underhand tactics of his, I thought, but they worked. He walked into my kitchen at around seven o'clock one evening just as I was clearing away my supper dishes, a picture of innocence. Although it was an unexpected visit, I wasn't surprised to see him as he quite often turned up unannounced.

'Hi Gemma, how's it going?' Maybe I should have guessed he was up to something from his over-the-top cheeriness. 'Busy?' Oh, he was good. Said so nonchalantly. I didn't suspect a thing.

'Hi Joe, no. I'm going to have a quiet evening in front of the TV, that's all.' Big mistake! I'd just leapt headlong into his trap.

'Good,' he said triumphantly. 'If you haven't got anything planned, it means you're free to come out with me. Get your bag.' Before I'd had time to gather my thoughts, let alone raise any objection, he'd bundled me out of the house and into the passenger seat of his car. 'Here, door keys.' They dropped into my lap. He was so determined to get me to go with him that he'd even locked up for me.

We were half way down the lane before I found my voice. 'Where are we going? Why the rush? Why all this cloak and dagger stuff?' The ominous thought entered my brain even as the words were coming out of my mouth. He hadn't... He wouldn't...

'Joe,' I said steadily, 'where are we going? Are you taking me to see that that friend of yours?'

He turned to me and smiled that beautiful mischievous boyish grin of his. 'Would I have ever got you there any other way?'

I was furious. At least the biggest part of me was. Irritatingly, the other part was filled with a thoroughly unexpected rush of anticipation as if it knew something the rest of me didn't. I refused to speak to Joe for the rest of the journey. The anger in me was slowly abating but I wasn't going to let him off the hook that easily. Bloody cheek! He'd practically kidnapped me just to get me to see these blasted skulls.

'This is it. We're here.' My stony silence wasn't fazing him in the least. He seemed totally immune to it. 'Come on.'

'This is it?' We had stopped in front of a rather run down block of modern flats, all concrete block and plastic windows. It wasn't quite what I had been expecting. What had I been expecting? A gloomy, gothic manor house with creaking floorboards and resident spooks? Oh Gemma, you have one hell of an imagination.

Neither did the man who opened the door in any way resemble the mental picture I had built of him, which had been some weird and wonderful wild-haired fusion between Indiana Jones and Nicolas Cage. Instead I was faced with a short, neatly dressed man in his early thirties, wearing a grey wool suit, with a carefully trimmed moustache and his hair combed tidily back.

'Joe, it's good to see you again.' The two men hugged, the warmth and friendship between them clear to see. 'This must be Gemma. Welcome, Gemma. Come on in.'

I followed Joe along the dark narrow hallway into the living room – and stopped in amazement. Every surface in this small room was tightly packed with skulls of all sizes, shapes and colours. I was in my worst nightmare. Joe noticed my expression and squeezed my hand, leading me to a comfortable looking armchair.

'Don't freak out on me, Gemma. They can't hurt you. Hear Duncan out. I really think you'll change your mind about them after this evening. If you don't, I promise never to bring the subject up again. Deal?'

I nodded. I was here now. I might as well listen to what Duncan had to say. And at this moment Duncan was standing in the doorway with a thoroughly bewildered look on his face.

'I more or less kidnapped her to get her here,' Joe explained. 'She isn't all that happy about being surrounded by all these skulls.'

'Well, let's see what we can do to change that.' Duncan's expression was sympathetic as he took a seat on the shabby sofa opposite me. Joe perched next to him.

Duncan related how his skulls had come from all over the world. Many were ancient, relics of long-forgotten civilisations and cultures, though some were very new. All had been given to him freely and all had stories to tell and information to share. I listened to this last part with determined scepticism, pointedly ignoring my own experience with the black skull that Joe now held in safe-keeping. It had been too real, too frightening, for me to be able to convince myself that I had imagined it all, but I had become very good at pretending I had.

Duncan and Joe talked about the skulls as though they were old friends or family members, their conversation from time to time veering off into subjects that went completely over my head. At those times, I let my gaze wander around the room. To my astonishment I realised that I wasn't feeling at all uncomfortable, despite the countless sightless eyes that stared back at me. In fact, I felt strangely cared for and peaceful.

'Well, I always say the best way to learn about something is to actually experience it.' Duncan had stood up and was fiddling around on one of the shelves that lined the far wall of the room. 'How about we try a meditation? What do you think, Joe?'

'Great idea. It'll give Gemma a much better idea of what these lovelies are all about.'

The next thing I knew, Duncan had dumped one of his skulls in my lap – and I didn't flinch. It was big, life-sized I guessed, although I didn't really know how big a human skull actually was, and heavy, carved from a pale aquamarine coloured stone. I touched it warily. It was rough, like the bits of glass you find on a beach that have been tumbled in the sea and scoured by the sand and the tides. There was something unexpectedly calming and soothing about it.

'What are we going to do?' I asked.

'Meditate.' Duncan broke into an amused laugh at the blank look on my face. 'So can I take it then that you've never meditated before? Well you're in for an interesting experience. There's nothing to it. All you have to do is close your eyes, focus your attention on your breathing to help you clear your mind... and let yourself be taken to wherever the skull leads you. Just remember, there isn't anything to be scared of.' Just like there wasn't anything to be scared of with the little black skull, I supposed. Duncan saw my misgivings. 'It's safe, Gemma. I promise. Nothing bad can possibly happen to you.' I still had some big doubts but was reassured by his and Joe's presence.

'Yes, OK.' I said reluctantly. I was about to take another huge step forward in my learning.

*   *   *   *   *   *   *

I closed my eyes and somehow, despite my anxiety and by putting all my attention on my breathing as Duncan had told me, managed to bring my racing mind to some semblance of calm. Breathing in, breathing out. Breathing

167

in, breathing out. In a little while I had forgotten where I was. My whole world was concentrated on the process. Everything around me had receded far into the background. My eyes were closed, but I could see images slowly coming into focus.

I was in a jungle. All around me was lush and green, and vibrant exotic flowers hung from the trees. In front of me was a large clearing and people were moving around, exactly like in the painting... that painting. I was walking around freely and no-one was paying any attention to me. It was as if they couldn't see me. I wasn't just watching though, like it was on a TV screen; I was participating. I could choose where to go and what to look at, peer around corners and into huts.

A strange looking pyramid towered over the whole scene, stretching high into the cloudless sky. It wasn't like the pyramids I'd seen in Egypt, with their smooth sides and definite pointed apex. This one had clearly defined stepped sides – it had obviously been built that way – and at its peak was a flat platform. Every part of it was decorated with images and symbols, some of which, like the snakes and leopards I recognised. Others were totally alien to me, mysterious and indecipherable. Suddenly I knew where I was. Mexico, or somewhere like that. I had seen a building very similar to this recently in a travel supplement.

Tucked away at the side of the huge external staircase was a small low doorway that led into the interior of the pyramid. I wondered if I could go in; I had a really strong desire to do so despite its spooky darkness. Tentatively, I walked forward, stepping over the threshold out of the fierce heat of the sun. Right, I was inside. What now? There was something there, right down at the far end, something I couldn't quite make out. As I moved closer it materialised like magic out of the gloom. A skull. A skull identical to the one Duncan had dropped into my lap. I...

*　　*　　*　　*　　*　　*　　*

Duncan's voice broke into my fantasy world, forcing me back to reality. I slowly opened my eyes to see the two of them staring at me intently.

'Well...?' Joe was almost clambering out of his seat in his impatience to hear what had happened.

I couldn't get the words out fast enough. It had been my painting, almost down to the last detail – except that the skull had been deep in the bowels of the pyramid and not on an altar out in the daylight. The people were dressed exactly the same, the clearing was identical, the skull... I stopped and looked down at the one I was holding. What did it all mean? Was it just my imagination going into overdrive and dredging up old memories to merge with newer ones? I couldn't work it out.

Both Duncan and Joe began to speak at once, until Joe fell silent to let Duncan tell the story. The skull he had passed to me was an ancient Mayan relic given to him out of the blue one day as he sat outside a café on one of his frequent trips to Guatamala. An old indigenous woman had simply walked up to him, peered penetratingly into his eyes and, presumably having been satisfied with what she saw there, pressed it into his hands. 'You are its Keeper now. Use it wisely, treat it with respect and let it teach you what you need to know.' With those words she had turned and vanished into the crowd, before he had really understood what was happening.

'What did it teach you?' I couldn't quite believe I was asking the question. It was just a lump of carved rock, nothing more. Or so my rational, logical mind was asserting adamantly. That firm-set scepticism was no longer sitting quite as comfortably with me as it had, though. Hovering elusively somewhere behind it was a burgeoning understanding that there was so much more to this than I could possibly conceive. And whatever that

169

'much more' was, it was way beyond the grasp of my rational mind, lurking somewhere in the obscure fringes of fantasy and magic.

'Information.' Duncan's voice intruded into my mental wanderings. 'It has taken me to view their ceremonies and rituals, some of which I'd really rather not have witnessed, to tell the truth.' He shuddered. 'Understanding of their belief systems, technology, knowledge of the cosmos. Things they knew as second nature that we today are only just beginning to catch up with.'

A low chuckle came from Joe. He had been watching me and now indicated the skull I was holding. Without being aware of my actions, I was cradling it as tenderly as a baby, my fingers lightly caressing its lines and curves.

'Didn't I tell you that you'd change your mind about them? It appears that you have.'

'Yes, it does, doesn't it?' I didn't know why, what had brought it about, but my feelings towards them had changed.

'The skulls have work for you, Gemma. There is a purpose in their contact with you.' Duncan's tone was light but his words were earnest. 'I believe they wish you to introduce them to the world once more. That is why they have come to you.'

'What...? I had taken a step forward tonight but this was too much for me to accept. 'That's nonsense. It's just a story.'

'Let it happen, Gemma. Just let it happen.'

*   *   *   *   *   *   *

Later, as Joe drew the car to a halt outside my cottage, he turned to me. 'I think it's time you had this back.' He put his hand in his pocket and pulled out the little black skull he'd rescued from under the lavender bush. I hesitated.

170

Gently he took my hand and placed the skull in the palm, curling my fingers closed around it. 'Take it.'

With a wave and a flash of his headlights he drove away. I looked at the shiny black object in my hand. No. Whatever Joe thought, I didn't feel ready to get up close and personal again with it again quite yet. I would compromise. I would set it in full view in the centre of the mantelpiece. To my surprise, within a day or two I discovered I welcomed its presence. I found it comforting, like having an old friend always around for company. What was going on?

Chapter 30

I had made a decision. To anyone else it may not have appeared particularly momentous but to me it was. I was going to sit with Tim again. (Tim was the name I'd given to the little black skull. I have no idea why I called him Tim, it just suited him. And he was a him, although I couldn't explain my logic behind that either). Tim had been sitting happily on the mantelpiece for a couple of weeks now and over the last few days I had been consumed with a powerful desire to pick him up and hold him, just like I'd done on that first – and for all the wrong reasons, unforgettable – occasion. I hadn't given in to it. I was too scared.

Was still scared, even now that I had made the decision. If I was going to do this, though, and I was determined to, I had no intention of doing it sitting there all by myself, quaking in my shoes. I needed to have someone with me to hold my hand, act as my safety net. For reassurance I suppose. Joe was the obvious person for me to ask, but for some reason I couldn't, I didn't want to. Didn't want him to be part of this at all. So I asked Cathy instead. I felt confident with Cathy. She would understand my fears, and was used to working with all sorts of weird and wonderful energies. Needless to say, she leapt at the chance.

*   *   *   *   *   *   *

Cathy was sitting curled up comfortably on the sofa while I sat upright in the armchair, my feet firmly planted flat on the floor, holding Tim in both hands, which were resting lightly in my lap exactly as Cathy had instructed me to do. Just like on the previous occasion in Duncan's flat, I was focussing all my attention on my breathing in order to try and calm my mind which, it has to be said, was firing off all over the place because I was feeling so tense and anxious.

'Just breathe.' Cathy was there with me, supporting and leading me. 'Nice and steady, Gemma. That's it. Let yourself relax.' To my heartfelt relief, the intense bolt of energy I had been expecting did not materialise. Instead, a comforting, pulsing warmth slowly enveloped me, relaxing my entire body as if I was floating into nothingness. This was turning out to be a very different experience to that first time.

I drifted easily in this somewhere-that-was-nowhere-state. Slowly but surely an image began to form in my mind until it crystallised into a clear picture in which I could see myself standing on a high cliff, with the wind blowing my hair across my face. I was on a rocky bluff that overlooked a narrow canyon. My overriding impression was of red earth and red sandstone, cacti and scrub. As I watched, I became aware of a far-off rumbling that quickly grew to an earth-rattling crescendo of countless hoof beats as a herd of wild horses swept through the gulley below me. I could actually feel the earth shake under my feet as they passed by. From my vantage point, the setting looked like something out of a cowboy film: desert, strange wind-carved rock formations, endless skies. Somehow I knew I was in America. As if to confirm it, a little way off a group of five or six people appeared, talking together – all wearing cowboy hats.

This was a very different vision to the one I had experienced at Duncan's. There I had been me, inside my own body, seeing through my own eyes. Here though I was standing outside of me, as if I had stepped out of my physical body and was watching myself as a separate observer. It felt odd but I didn't feel at all afraid or threatened.

173

The image in front of me dissolved and reformed. It had changed. Now we were on horseback, ambling leisurely through this stark, beautiful landscape. Me? On a horse? The nearest I'd ever got to riding a horse was a donkey ride on the beach. All these thoughts raced through my mind even as the scene played out in front of me. It was the same group of people as before and we all appeared to know each other well. One of them, a man, was riding alongside me. He was tall, dark-haired, slim – verging on skinny really – but wiry. I couldn't see his face, no matter how hard I tried to focus. It was just a blur. Why was that? I wondered. He helped me dismount, was standing with his arm around my shoulders as if... Were we together?

I jerked back in alarm, that image vanishing instantaneously, as a skull flashed right in front of my face, extinguishing everything else from my vision. A skull, appearing just as it had the very first time. But this was not that first skull. Instead of deep inky black, this one was a pale sea-green. And as it sat there, hovering there just in front of my face, a hazy background began to form around it, a background the colour of the desert I had just left.

Then rapidly, one after the other, another skull, and another, and another, all different, appearing and disappearing so quickly that I could not register any of them clearly. I thought I counted thirteen in all but I couldn't be sure. My mind began to spin and everything went black.

'Gemma. Gemma.' I became aware gradually of Cathy's slow, firm words, the concerned note they held. 'Gemma, listen to my voice. Follow it. Let it bring you back. It's time to come back now, Gemma.'

Slowly I opened my eyes, feeling dazed and disorientated. Cathy's anxious face was looking down at me. Gently she took the skull from my lap where it had fallen from my fingers and placed it back on the mantelpiece.

'Wow, that must have been one hell of a trip. You were well away and you really didn't want to come back. What happened?' She tried to make light of it but I could see her concern. I had been gone a long time and, experienced as she was, she had found it difficult to pull me back to reality.

I was still feeling extremely light headed but little by little described what I had seen. 'I don't have any idea what it means though.'

Cathy was lost in thought. 'It feels important. The first part might be some kind of prediction. You know, a hint at what is coming your way in the future.' That I found very hard to believe. 'The other part, those other skulls coming in… It feels to me like that is the really important bit. And like they weren't going to allow you to come back until you'd seen their message.' I couldn't follow her train of thought and said so. 'Look, your dreams have only shown you skull one so far, haven't they?' I nodded. 'Well then, maybe this is to show you that there is a long way to go with this still. More books to write. Maybe these other skulls are going to start appearing in your dreams too.'

She was right. That night, for the first time, I dreamed about the blue skull.

175

GAL-ATHIEL: The Blue Skull

Part 1

THE GIFT

Chapter 31

The boy wandered easily through the damp, lush undergrowth, even though the forest was at its thickest here. Ferns and thorns smothered the ground, obliterating any trace of a possible path, while around and above him sturdy creepers, some as thick as a man's forearm, clambered and tangled to the canopy far above. Every size and form of bird fluttered through the scramble of branches, their brilliant plumage flashing neon jewels through the sun-dappled shadows in a mosaic of colour. Some were as small as bumble bees, others with wingspans as wide as a man's reach. The boy loved the birds, envied them their ability to free themselves from the limitations of an Earth-bound life and soar unhindered into the skies.

He sat to watch them as they soared and swooped around him, resting his back against a moss-covered tree. The air was filled with their music: warbling trills, waterfalls of song in impossible combinations of harmonies, punctuated by the jarringly harsh screeches and caws of warning cries.

The forest could be a dangerous place. Predators, large and small, ruthlessly hunted both man and beast, able to steal undetected through the dense vegetation. Many could kill with one blow of their huge claws or powerful jaws and few they set their sights on could outrun them. Beneath the leaves and stones, venomous snakes and lizards lay in wait. The boy, though wary and alert, was not afraid. He knew the whereabouts of each bird, each animal, each reptile and insect for an hour's walk in every direction. He would sense if danger was heading his way and be able to move out of its path long before it arrived.

He had been born and had grown up in this place, as had everyone in his village for countless generations before him. All possessed the same extrasensory awareness as the boy, an array of seemingly supernatural mental abilities. They were an integral and natural part of each man, woman and child of his people, although his were perhaps stronger than most. One thing he knew well, for it was recounted over and over by the story keepers – these abilities had grown and developed to their current level since She had appeared in their midst so far back in those early times.

The boy had learned that these powers were not commonplace, or at least not commonly recognised. Travellers who passed through their village did not share or understand them, often becoming afraid and hostile. He smiled knowingly. Of course those travellers possessed them; every human who walked the earth possessed them. They just didn't know it. Didn't know either how to access or use them. Gal-Athiel had shown them this one evening as they sat in communion with her. The People were already aware of their skills, were using them the best they could. Very few others on the Earth had learned to do the same.

Gal-Athiel's presence had somehow strengthened and enhanced all of these natural skills, taught the People how to use them wisely and effectively. But She had also given them so much more. She had entered their minds to show them images of distant fantastical worlds; of huge glistening silver vessels that travelled between the stars; of races and beings unknown on Earth; of technologies that provided unlimited and unimaginable power through harnessing the sun and other natural energies; of craft that flew in the skies and beneath the waters, and of cities built from gold and lace-delicate stonework. She had offered them tantalising glimpses into the secrets of creation.

* * * * * * *

The People had never used speech as their main form of communication, 'speaking' instead through their thoughts. It was so much easier that way. People shared what they meant. There could be no misunderstanding. Because when another touches your thoughts at their origin, they also understand the feelings, meanings and deeper concepts that accompany them. The spoken word, however beautiful its form, was incomplete at best. At worst it could be twisted, misinterpreted and falsified.

But when the story tellers told of how Gal-Athiel had come to them, the stories were narrated aloud in words and phrases of deep poetic beauty, accompanied by the low hypnotic songs of the Singing Voices that brought forth the harmonies and melodies of the first creation.

'In the time of our distant fathers,' they told, *'A time lost in the wandering mists of the past, a stranger from the stars came amongst us, bringing to our People a gift beyond value. The gift of Gal-Athiel.*

'The stranger was tall, standing at least a head above the tallest of our own kind, with long flowing hair and a beard the colour of ripe malucca blossom. He walked out of the forest and into our world just as the first sunlight brushed the uppermost tips of the highest trees on the morning of the longest day. The pale blushing rays of this dawning sun turned his white gold hair to fire, bathing him in a glowing halo of unearthly light.

'In his hands he carried a small box, the like of which none had ever set eyes on before. A box of dull, metallic grey, a little under two hand spans in length, inscribed with mysterious and magical symbols'.

The storytellers would recount how the People came from their huts to greet him, this visitor from so far away, in his

180

robes of deep turquoise blue and gold. How, though they were still mere infants in the mastery of their skills in those times, immature and untrained, their senses told them that he came in peace and friendship. They were curious yes, but at ease with his presence in their midst, intuiting nothing ill-intentioned or untrustworthy about him. On the contrary, his entire being emanated a deep, almost tangible, serenity and benevolence.

'Greetings, friend.' The senior village Elder, Darsh, approached the newcomer. 'What brings you to our village?'

'Greetings. My name is Ashar and I come to you with a gift. A gift we know you will use wisely.' A ripple of confusion ran through those who had gathered to see what was happening. A gift? Why? Who from? Although none could detect any element of threat from this golden man, puzzlement and uncertainty began to spread.

'What gift? And who sends it?' The first seeds of suspicion were plain to hear in the Elder's voice.

'From those of us who would be your friends. Who would see you grow and flourish, living in peace and harmony with your world and those upon it. A gift to you from those who come from beyond the stars.'

A hushed whisper of bewilderment and incredulity ran through the gathering. These were impossible words yet, in their hearts, none doubted their sincerity. All could feel the truth that they held. Nonetheless, the uncertainty remained, for while their instincts told them this stranger was speaking the truth, their minds were mistrustful of his words, and they doubted the knowing of their hearts.

'I understand your hesitation. I am not known to you and you are right to be cautious. And yet you all know the integrity of my intentions for I know that you can sense it in your deepest being.' The group stared at him in yet greater astonishment, for he had conveyed these latest words to them through thought, not speech. No-one outside their village had ever done such a thing. What is more, he had done so as easily and naturally as they did.

He waited calmly and patiently. There was no hurry. He already knew their answer.

'Come, Ashar. You are welcome. Join us. Show to us your gift and tell us why you have brought it here.' Darsh bowed his head in a gesture of respect and welcome, and the people parted to allow the two men through, following on behind them as the Elder led the tall, radiant stranger through the clearing to the great stone circle beyond.

$$* \quad * \quad * \quad * \quad * \quad * \quad *$$

The stranger bowed to the gathering. The whole village was present. No-one wished to miss this moment.

'Thank you. Thank you for welcoming me and allowing me to speak with you. I am Ashar, emissary of the Thetan council and I have come... But no, first let me show you what I bring to you.'

He carefully set the strange grey box on a flat tree stump. Viewed more closely the colour was a dark matt silver and the symbols appeared to be a combination of star constellations and geometric shapes. But only the wisest of the village seers would recognise any of these markings. There did not appear to be a clasp or any other obvious way of opening it. From beneath his long robes Ashar had withdrawn a small golden object that resembled a key of sorts. Two curved arms, one shaped like a 'j' and one like an 'f', came off a small centre circle at 180° to each other. It fitted easily into the palm of his hand. As the gathered villagers watched in growing anticipation he fitted it into a matching impression on the side of the box and with an almost imperceptible click, the lid slid aside. Reached into the box he slowly, carefully, withdrew the contents. As it emerged into the daylight those nearest

182

took an involuntary step backwards, and a gasp of wonder and reverence burst from everyone present.

It was beautiful: a life-sized skull, carved from a single chunk of pale sea blue obsidian, a mineral unknown on Earth at that time and rare even in the distant corners of the galaxy. As its mirror-like surface reflected the soft early morning sunlight, the magical effects deep within enchanted all of those close enough to it to be able to see it clearly. Ripples and shadows of every shade of blue, from palest aquamarine to deepest sapphire, pulsed and danced through the interior of the skull, bringing it to life. Ashar held it up so all could see.

'This is Gal-Athiel. She is a gift to the Earth from the people of Theta. You have been chosen as her keepers. She is here to teach and guide you and She will share much if you learn to hear Her knowledge and listen to Her wisdom. Use Her gifts wisely and you will prosper.' And so it had begun.

*   *   *   *   *   *   *

In the generations that followed, the People flourished in Gal-Athiel's presence. They learned how to harness the power of wind and water to ease the heavy labour of their day-to-day existence; to strengthen still further their natural abilities and sensitivities; to heal sickness and disease; to master their thoughts and emotions in order to bring about a desired outcome. They communicated with the animals, birds and plants, with the energies of the natural world around them, both seen and unseen, and heard their own special wisdom. Learned too how to foretell weather, threat, where to hunt, and the most beneficial times to plant and harvest.

The People lived peacefully and compassionately, in tune with each other and in complete harmony with the world around them. Life was good and the village flourished.

Chapter 32

It hadn't stayed that way, the boy thought with sadness. He allowed his consciousness to drift through time and to sense this change, this departure from the true purpose of Gal-Athiel's presence. Sense its beginnings.

He could see how in those first days, way back in time, She stood as the focal point of village life, honoured and respected certainly, but seen for what She was: a sacred friend and counsellor, to be used with reverence, freely available to all who sought Her guidance. Her home was a small shrine at the centre of the village, where She was greeted with an easy hello by all who passed by. There was almost always someone with the blue skull, communicating with Her, seeking Her wisdom, for She was a guide and confidante to everyone. People spoke to Her as they would their close friends and family members, with complete love and respect, and She answered them always in the same way. It had been so for many years and many generations.

As he continued to watch, the boy saw this pure connection become distorted. Saw how over time the People had gradually turned Her into an object of worship and ritual in Her own right. Building Her up into an all-powerful and unassailable god figure. No longer seeing Her as the loving adviser but instead as a binding oracle, infallible and never to be questioned, to whose word their own deep inner knowing must now be subjugated. The People's need to find answers and authority outside of themselves, to be told what to do, subverted Her messages and the truth of Her purpose.

He saw how, at some point in the more recent past, a small group had assembled around the blue skull, proclaiming themselves Her chosen guardians. They were strong and determined, but cunning in their pursuit of their goals, and the village elders of the time had not challenged them, perceiving no threat. How mistaken they had been. These self-appointed guardians were ambitious, hungry for control of Gal-Athiel, and ruthless in satisfying that hunger. From his heightened perspective the boy could see clearly how it had unfolded, a subtle and almost imperceptible gradual shift in the balance of power as, little by little, the new 'guardians' had distanced Her ever further from the villagers. The elders had not realised anything was amiss until it was too late. It was a patient and deliberate ploy, calculatingly and skilfully executed by those who were seduced by Gal-Athiel's power and sought to hold it for themselves. They called themselves The Enlightened Ones. The boy snorted in disgust. The Enlightened Ones. Nothing could be further from the truth.

Recently this deification and disconnection had accelerated rapidly. Even in his own short lifetime of twelve summers, the Enlightened Ones had grown in power so that the elders themselves now bowed to their command. Access to the blue skull's wisdom had become even more restricted, limited to those few who claimed to be Her mouthpiece. No-one else any longer had the right to communicate directly with Her, on penalty of severe punishment. The boy could not understand why the villagers had accepted this without objection, but such was the influence now of the Enlightened Ones that it seemed none dared go against their word. The boy's own mother and father, fearful of his rebellious streak, had elicited from him a solemn oath that he would not attempt to connect with Her in defiance of the law. He had sulked and fumed but, feeling the strength of the genuine fear that was drawn on his parents' faces and held in their hearts, he had eventually conceded and given them his word.

His village, once and for so long a peaceful and welcoming home, was becoming an uncomfortable and oppressive place to live, ruled by those who professed to speak the blue skull's truth. Where once love and co-operation had reigned, the chill fingers of suspicion and separation now brushed. If not stopped, they would take hold completely. The tide had to be turned, but how?

Chapter 33.

The boy's eyes flew open. For a moment, he was completely disorientated. He had heard clearly his name being called, it had woken him from a deep, dreamless sleep, but around him nothing stirred. The village was silent in these early hours, save for the occasional screech of an animal or bird in the surrounding forest. At that moment a deep roar sounded nearby. That must have been what had woken him, his mind playing tricks, translating it to his name in his subconscious.

He closed his eyes and rolled over, quickly falling asleep once more. Again the sound of his name woke him. This time he was more alert. It had been distinct, unmistakeable. He looked around; his family were all sleeping peacefully. And again. This time he recognised that it was coming from within his mind. He sat up quietly so as not to wake those around him and opened up his awareness to better receive the message. Immediately he was connected to a strong yet gentle energy, an energy that was filled with light, with love and compassion. He thought that he recognised it, had felt it somewhere before, but he was unable to remember when or where.

'Zim, I need your help.' The voice was back. In a heartbeat, the boy knew. This was Gal-Athiel; She was speaking to him. The urgency in Her voice was palpable and all thoughts of the promise he had made to his parents vanished at Her cry for help.

'How? How can I help?' The boy was puzzled. He was still just a child. How could he do anything, how could he challenge those who now held the village and the skull?

'No, I do not wish you to fight, Zim. That is not the way.' Gal-Athiel had heard his thoughts. 'I must contact those who brought me here but I am not strong enough. Those who imprison me also block my power. I need your help to contact them for me.'

'Me? How? I-I can't... I don't know how.' The boy struggled to understand what She was asking of him.

'You are still young, Zim; even so your power, your abilities, are strong. Stronger than anyone else in the village. What is more, you see clearly the danger that threatens you all. I know you can do this. That is why I am asking you.' The boy swallowed down the fear that was rising in his throat. If he was caught...

'This is not the purpose for which I was brought here. I know you understand that. If I remain amongst you, life will only become harder for your people. Their fear will grow and because of it they will allow themselves to become ever more enslaved to the will of those who seek to control you.'

'What must I do?' The boy would do as She asked. He was still afraid but he would not let that stand in his way. Things could not continue as they were and, young though he was, this was his chance to do something that would bring about that change. For the rest of that night Gal-Athiel taught him how to reach out his mind and his thoughts across the emptiness of space, to communicate with the golden-haired people from the sky who had brought Her to Earth so long before.

*   *   *   *   *   *   *

Two nights later, when the moon was at its darkest, the boy crept out of his village and into the forest, as Gal-Athiel had requested him to do. It was a dangerous time to be out roaming this place where the dark shadows hid countless invisible dangers. His nerves were taut and he held all of his senses fully open and alert for any threat until he safely reached the spot that She had shown to him.

189

He was in a small clearing around which stood a circle of small standing stones, none higher than a man's thigh. At the northern side, three larger stones formed a trilithon. The boy knew of this place. It was already standing when his people had first come to settle here so long ago, its origins and purpose a mystery even then. He walked to the centre, sat cross-legged on the grass-covered ground as he had been instructed, and in his mind he saw an imaginary stream of bright white light connecting all of the stones, creating a protective barrier against the creatures of the forest. Once he had done so, he drew his attention back into his body, feeling the ground beneath him, and allowed his energy field to expand. Immediately he was enveloped in a warm, dark void, and from this safe nowhere place he focussed his thoughts on that far distant world and sent out his message to the people from the stars. Gal-Athiel's people. 'Please help us. Help Gal-Athiel. We need you. Please, come now.'

He did not know whether they had heard him, had no way of knowing, but he did not stop. On and on, over and over again, he sent out his cry for help, totally absorbed in his plea and oblivious to the passage of time. It wasn't until the dawning sun rose over the tree tops, its brightness dazzling him through his closed eyelids, that he shook his head and remembered where he was. Had he succeeded? Only time would tell.

Chapter 34

Before another moon's cycle had passed, the whole village was called upon to attend a meeting, 'at Gal-Athiel's request'. Ordered to attend would be a better description, the boy thought resentfully. The summons came from Pili, self-appointed leader of the group of self-appointed skull guardians. Everyone would be present. They dared not do otherwise. The guardians would note any absence and punish it as contempt, citing disrespect of Gal-Athiel's word. And Her word was inviolable, according to her spokespeople, the guardians. What was so frightening was that the People had started to believe it, to give their power away to these usurpers. Allowed themselves to be controlled and restricted by them. He could see what was happening. Why couldn't anyone else?

Pili was charismatic and forceful, able to get his own way through intimidation and the strength of his will, overwhelming and bending that of others to his own. Few were able to stand up to him and those who did quickly learned the perils of doing so, for he was quick to anger and carried within him a cruel, cold streak that set him apart from the other villagers. He was young, strong and good looking but his eyes bore no hint of warmth or compassion and the young women of the village shied away from him, avoiding his company, repelled on a deep level by this emptiness. It was an antipathy that had not gone unnoticed by him and it further fuelled his already strong desire for absolute control. The people of the village may have feared Pili but he knew they did not respect him, and this angered him greatly.

As always when he addressed any of the villagers, he spoke out loud, blocking his mind to those of the People, refusing to allow them to see further than his uttered words. It was a skill he and his fellow guardians had learned from Gal-Athiel; one they were not prepared to share. The People's open minds and his ability to read their thoughts whilst shielding his own gave Pili a crucial advantage that permitted him to always stay one step ahead, to be forewarned of any potential unrest.

The announcement he was to make at that meeting went further than he had ever gone before and plunged his reluctant audience into a state of bitter incredulity. The blue skull, he told them, had commanded that he take a wife. The chosen one could not refuse him, for this was the will of Gal-Athiel, and to disobey would be heresy, punishable by death. A swelling wave of outrage and rippling unrest ran through the gathering. This was unheard of. Pili had gone too far this time. A man and a woman married in free will, for love. There was no other reason. To force someone into marriage with another who was not of their choosing… it could not be.

The guardians bristled menacingly as Pili stepped forward, his cold eyes scanning the gathered crowd until they settled on the one he was looking for. Lela, the boy's sister. No, it couldn't be. The boy looked around, desperate for someone to say something. No-one did, although every face betrayed its fury and loathing. Lela was young, barely seventeen summers, and stunningly beautiful, a beauty that was at this moment clouded by the terror that marked her face. No, not her. She was vibrant and alive, deeply in love and already promised to another.

His stride arrogant, as if inviting a challenge from the onlookers, Pili walked up to Lela and seized her wrist, pulling her towards him. 'No!' She was spirited and courageous. She would not submit to this like a lamb to the slaughter. Her eyes flashed rebellion as she twisted vigorously in an attempt to escape his vicelike hold.

Pili's grip did not loosen. He wrenched her closer and looked down at her with his cruel eyes, his voice almost mocking in its insolence. 'You cannot refuse, Lela. It is the will of Gal-Athiel.'

With a howl of rage, a young man darted out of the crowd, lunging at Pili. It was Kori, Lela's fiancé, incensed at the outrage that was being committed, refusing to allow his love to be stolen from him. Hands grabbed at him desperately as his friends tried to hold him back but Kori avoided them all, twisting out of their reach, blind to everything but the furious emotion burning within him. He did not get far. A fleeting flash of metal in the morning sunlight, a gasp, and with a look of surprise he collapsed, blood pouring from a wound in his side. He had been struck down by one of Pili's henchman wielding one of the long knives that was normally used to clear the forest – a knife that had now become a weapon.

The crowd was stunned into a ghastly silence that seemed endless but in reality lasted only a fraction of a second before Lela's raw scream filled the air. Wrenching herself free from Pili's grasp, she ran to Kori, throwing her body over his in protection, eyes flashing fires of hatred at her tormentor. Pili acted as if nothing had happened, stepping forward and dragging her roughly to her feet. 'The wedding will take place at first light. Prepare the celebrations.'

He turned and walked away, pulling a suddenly limp and defeated Lela after him. Her gaze never left the body of the man she loved. All defiance had left her now that he was gone. There was no use any more in fighting the inevitable.

The crowd were still motionless. Violence on this scale was virtually unknown in the village. Slowly their simmering anger and revulsion at the atrocity they had just witnessed began to surface within them. Several of the women knelt at Kori's side trying to stem the flow of blood as his life gushed from him. He was not dead, as Lela believed, but his wounds were severe, and even with their enhanced healing skills he was unlikely to survive. They lifted him gently and carried him to the shelter of the nearest hut.

Sensing the unrest, aware of a potential uprising, the guardians stepped forward, raising their weapons menacingly. Each of them carried a knife identical to the one that had struck down Kiro. The villagers hesitated. They had no experience of fighting and were unsure of themselves, unsure of what to do. Faced with armed adversaries the mutinous rumble gradually subsided into a sullen muttering and they backed away, shaken by the events of the day but believing themselves powerless to act.

*　　*　　*　　*　　*　　*　　*

The boy had watched helplessly, barely able to believe what was happening, frozen with horror at the events he had just witnessed. Kori, his future brother-in-law, was more like a true brother to him. Now he lay dying, if not already dead, and the boy's sister was in Pili's clutches. Where were the sky people? Why hadn't they come? Were they going to come at all? And if so, when?

That night he went to the clearing again, and again he sent out his message. This time, it was even more heartfelt, filled with his desperation and sadness. He did not return to the village until the following morning, just as the first rays of the sun were rising above the forest.

Chapter 35

The villagers had already begun to assemble for the wedding celebrations as they had been commanded although there was no joy in this crowd as they waited for the ceremony to begin. All were grim-faced, angrily and openly defiant, summoned to attend against their will, their hearts weeping at the sight of the small, crushed figure of Lela who stood facing them, her pale face puffed and tear-stained. Two guardians held her firmly by the arms in case she tried to run, but the subdued and despairing demeanour of this usually feisty young woman told its own story. She could see no hope, and it showed.

The angry muttering of the crowd grew louder as Pili came from his hut, carrying Gal-Athiel, whom he set on a raised stone slab. The boy watched helplessly. There was nothing he could do to save his sister. Kori, though still somehow clinging on to life, lay unconscious, mercifully unaware of what was about to occur.

A sudden warm wave of reassurance washed over him, so unexpectedly and so forcibly that he almost staggered. His eyes flew to the blue skull even as Her voice reached him. 'Do not worry, Zim. All will be well.'

He did not know how that could be but in that moment he trusted Her completely and allowed the wave to hold him in its embrace, even as the obscene events played out in front of his eyes. Time seemed to stand still around him.

A shuffling in the crowd broke the spell; the boy turned to see what was causing the disturbance. A group of five people were walking unhurriedly towards the centre of the circle, moving through the gathered villagers who parted silently before them. Five people unlike any the boy had seen before, three men and two women, all dressed in flowing robes of electric blue. They were tall, very tall – the boy would have barely reached the chest of even the shortest – and slender, with long, white-gold hair, the men with beards of the same colour. They appeared calm, relaxed, and at the same time quietly, confidently, determined.

A short distance from the wedding party the strangers paused. 'We cannot allow this.' Although the voice was quiet, it carried clearly to those looking on, pulsing with an authority that brooked no argument. In his arrogance Pili did not hear its soft warning.

'And who are you to say so? Mind your own business stranger and leave here while you still can. You are not welcome.' His face betrayed his fury at this interruption.

The newcomers did not move. The one who had addressed the gathering, clearly the group's leader, continued as if Pili had not spoken. 'I am Karnata, elected leader of the Thetan high council. Gal-Athiel was our gift to the human race, entrusted to the care of the People. But you misuse Her power and bring darkness upon yourself and your kind. We cannot allow this to be. We have come to take Her to a place of safety until such time as humankind can use Her wisely and for the good of all.' The blue skull seemed to blaze golden at his words.

'Kill them.' The fury in Pili's words was echoed in his actions as he and his supporters charged, weapons flashing. The five stood motionless and unharmed as the blows simply glanced off them, as if from an unseen shield. Their attackers dropped back, fear and doubt appearing on their faces for the first time. Were these men... or ghosts?

Before anyone could react, Pili had his knife at Lela's throat, was backing away towards where the forest grew thick at the edge of the village, dragging her with him. 'Leave now or she dies. Know the truth in my words.' He was deadly serious, his threat real; still the calm, peaceful bearing of the tall stranger did not change.

'No, she will not,' Karnata replied. 'You do not really wish to harm her. You will put your weapon down and let her go.' Terror mixed with disbelief washed over Pili's face; he watched his arm lower as if it possessed a will of its own. He was fighting it with the full force of his willpower and yet he was unable to resist. The knife dropped to the ground as he released Lela and took several juddering steps backwards, his will unable to match that of his opponent. Around him his supporters stood paralysed with fear, not making any attempt to stop Lela as she ran to the safety of the crowd.

Unhurriedly Karnata stepped forward and lifted Gal-Athiel from the stone slab as one of his companions ducked into the Pili's hut and brought out the dull silver-grey box. The crowd remained silent, uncertain, trying to make sense of what was going on. Karnata turned to Lela. 'You are safe now. He will not trouble you again. Nor anyone else. Now, where is your man?'

Lela's face crumpled. 'Dead,' she whispered, tears filling her eyes.

'No, he lives, though barely. In here.' The woman who had spoken pointed to a hut nearby. Scarcely were the words out of her mouth than Lela was racing towards it, followed closely by one of the tall, blond haired men.

Karnata turned now to the gathered villagers. 'We must return Gal-Athiel to Her home. You are not yet ready for Her to live amongst you. You worshipped Her as a god and in doing so distorted Her purpose and allowed fear to gain a foothold.' His voice, though kind and compassionate, also held power and authority. 'You have learned much. Use that knowledge wisely. When you are ready, She will return to you.'

And then, walking into their midst, supported by a tearfully joyful Lela, was Kori, deathly pale but alive, and growing stronger by the minute.

'Thank you.' Lela took Karnata's hand in her own and held it tightly. 'Thank you.'

'What about Pili?' Kori's voice was weak but audible.

'He will not trouble you. He has learned his lesson as you have learned yours. In future, give your power away to no-one and no thing. Stand firm in your own truth and your own hearts. That way you stay strong. Fear creates control, control creates more fear and ever onwards in a downward spiral. But where love and truth hold sway, fear cannot take hold. Return to your former ways, to the ways in which you have lived for generations, return to peace, co-operation and unity, and all will be well.'

*   *   *   *   *   *   *

With those words Karnata and his companions turned and walked out of the village, carrying Gal-Athiel with them. The boy followed. They knew he was there but they did not try to stop him. Did not even acknowledge his presence until they arrived at the forest clearing from where he had called on them so fervently to come, first to Gal-Athiel's aid and later to Lela's. Once within the circle of stones, they turned and smiled at him.

'Who are you?' he asked.

'We have told you.' The voice was patient and kindly. 'We are Thetans. We come from a world beyond the stars. Many thousands of years ago we created Gal-Athiel and brought Her to Earth to assist in humankind's evolution and the awakening of its consciousness. More recently we brought Her to your people believing you were ready to welcome Her and use Her gifts wisely. We were wrong. But you will grow and She will return.'

'How did you do it? You know, with Pili?'

'We have means that are not of this world. We also have the power of our minds, which can create what you would consider miracles. I must tell you now that we broke our own rules – to not interfere in the affairs of your world. Whilst we regret that, on this occasion it was right for us to do so. You must understand though that what we did is no more than you are capable of doing. The power is within you, within all of you, you just haven't learned to access it yet.

We are saddened because this will not happen for a long time now that Gal-Athiel is leaving you. Will not happen until She returns. Slowly you will forget what She has taught you and your abilities will fall dormant until the time of the final awakening.'

'When will that be?'

Karnata smiled. 'Far in the future. Many, many lifetimes ahead.'

'Will you come back then?'

'No, not in the way you see us now. You see, we too are evolving and growing, moving into a higher dimension. From there we will not be able to visit this world in our physical form, although we may return in other ways. Others will come in our place.'

'I want to come with you.'

'That is not possible, little one.'

'Why not? You can come here so why can I not come with you? I want to learn to do what you can do.'

The Thetans exchanged glances as they looked at this boy, still only a child, yet who had had the ability to reach them across the vastness of space. 'What about your life here? Your parents?'

The boy looked sorrowful for a moment as he considered what he would be leaving behind. 'I'll miss them,' he admitted. 'A lot. But I still want to come. They'll understand.'

Karnata shook his head. 'I'm sorry. We would like you to come with us very much. You are gifted, your abilities are strong, and it would be our delight to teach you all that we are able. But we cannot. You are just a child. We cannot take you away from your family and your people. We cannot leave them not knowing what has happened to you. That is a suffering we will not inflict.'

'Let him go with you.' The boy whirled around. On the edge of the clearing stood his mother and father. It had been they who had spoken, as one voice. 'Let him go with you if that is what he wishes,' they repeated. 'We have seen that it was he who called you here and in doing so he became Lela's saviour. We will miss him more than we can ever express, but his heart and his destiny is with you.'

'Mother? Father?' The boy's heart trembled as he understood what their words were costing them, felt the sadness and loss that filled them.

His mother smiled through the tears that had begun to flow unchecked. 'You will never be content here now, Zim. Not now that you have seen what lies out there. Go, and go with our blessings and all of our love.'

He ran to them then, holding them as if he would never let them go, in his turn being held so tightly in this last goodbye, each needing to imprint this embrace forever on his memory.

'Stay safe.' With those last whispered words, they released him.

'Are you sure?' Karnata was beside him.

The boy nodded, sadness and apprehension mingling within his body with a heady excitement and anticipation. 'I'm sure.'

They returned to the centre of the clearing and Karnata took his hand. And then he was dissolving into a swirling mist of energy, so that he no longer knew where he ended and everything else began, spiralling upwards in a column of golden light. Upwards to a new life on a new world.

GEMMA

Chapter 36

I loved the new way of life I was leading. Loved the freedom it brought, the satisfaction I felt in every word that I put onto paper, the tranquillity of the natural environment that surrounded me. And, perhaps more than anything, I loved the transformation it was evoking in me. Increasingly I found myself overflowing with an unaccustomed sense of peace and contentment, and filled with more energy and enthusiasm for life than I could remember having since I was a child. I lost count of the times I caught myself singing and dancing around my little cottage for no real reason. I felt (and Cathy told me I looked – I love that woman!) ten years younger.

I loved being able to walk out of my gate straight onto fields and open countryside. I would sit for hours in the woods amongst the trees and ferns, allowing its sights and sounds to simply wash through me, becoming part of it, feeling its heartbeat. Every day it changed, and the steady rhythm of its cycles inspired and nourished me. When the words I sought eluded me, I learned that if I wandered off to my favourite spot – a fallen log in a fern-filled hollow deep amongst the undergrowth – and just sat, did. At that moment I would take the pen and notepad from my pocket and begin to write.

I could no longer imagine being anywhere else, doing anything else. For the first time in my life I was finding out who I really was, and finding out that I wouldn't have wanted to be anyone else. I liked the me I was discovering.

Chapter 37

'So?' Cathy's voice bubbled on the other end of the phone. 'Come on, spill the beans. What's going on between you and Joe? A little bird told me he didn't go home on Saturday night.'

I sighed. Cathy was always up for a juicy bit of gossip. Today however I was going to disappoint her. Who on earth had found out Joe had stayed over anyway? I was hardly on the beaten track out here. 'Nothing, Cathy. We were chatting till the early hours, he had a couple of glasses of wine and wasn't prepared to drive, so he stopped over – ON THE SOFA. It's no big deal. He's done it loads of times before.'

'Oh.' I could hear her exhilaration tumble, but she didn't stay down for long. 'You're seeing a lot of each other though, aren't you? Getting on really well, that's what you told me. Isn't it about time you two did get it together?'

'Cathy, how many times do I have to tell you? He's just a friend. Yes, he's gorgeous, I'll give you that, but there is nothing between us.'

'Well there bloody well should be! How many dates have you been on since you and Dan split up?'

'Er, not many?'

'And just how many is not many?'

'NONE, Cathy, as you well know!' I burst out. 'I've been just a bit busy.'

'Well now that you are coming to the end of the book, you'll have much more time on your hands that you are going to have to fill. Don't you ever get lonely hidden away up out there on your own?'

'No, of course not. I haven't got time to be lonely.' It was a lie. I did get lonely. Yes, I had Jamie and Cathy and plenty of other friends, and now Joe was becoming an important part of my life too, but I did miss having a man in my life. To coin a cheesy phrase, 'that special someone'.

'Liar!' Unfortunately for me, Cathy could read me like a book.

'OK, OK.' I conceded. 'Maybe I do get lonely sometimes. Maybe I am ready to hand in my BAVC membership...'

'BAVC? What on earth is that?'

'Born Again Virgins Club!' I ploughed on, determined to make my point. 'But not with Joe. I don't feel that way about him and he doesn't feel that way about me. Full stop.'

'If you say so.' I could tell she was humouring me, but didn't pursue it. The phone went quiet for a moment; I could tell Cathy was thinking. 'OK then,' she said at last, 'why not manifest a man? Set your intent, write up your wish list and send your request out to the Universe.'

'Do what? My what?'

'Your wish list. You know, the things you're looking for in a guy – tall, dark and handsome. Tasty cute bum. Antonio Banderas look-alike. Own teeth and hair. That sort of thing. Everything that's important to you.'

'Does that really work?' She couldn't be serious, could she?

'Of course it does. How do you think I found Tony?' Tony was her new boyfriend and, it has to be said, he was adorable. If she really had – what did she call it? – manifested this Tony, it was certainly worth giving it a try.

'But Gemma...'

'Hmmm?' Now I was lost in thought.

'Don't overlook what's standing right in front of you. Joe is a man that any woman would give the world to be with.'

'Cathy...'

'OK, OK.' She'd taken note of the warning tone in my voice. 'I'll shut up. I was just saying, that's all.'

*   *   *   *   *   *   *

'What exactly do I put on this list, Cathy?' We were both curled up on my sofa in our pyjamas in front of the roaring fire, having a girlie sleepover. It wasn't quite the sort of sleepover Jamie used to have – we had swapped the fizzy drinks, pizza and ice cream for a couple of bottles of red wine, smoked salmon and Belgian chocolates – but a sleepover is still a sleepover, however you do it. We had a couple of light-hearted DVDs ready to go, a crackling fire in the grate, and with Cathy's help I was writing out my wish list. My 'man order'.

It had been her suggestion originally and I had jumped at the idea. I really didn't believe it would work but it had sounded fun, if a bit silly.

'Like I said, there are two ways you can go about it. Either leave it open so that it's very general, you know 'sane, single and solvent'. Or you can be really detailed. My view is that if you are going to order a bloke, you might as well ask for exactly what you want. That's what I did.'

I thought hard. 'I don't really have any idea of what my ideal man would be like. I've never really considered it. Oh c'mon, Cathy. Please. Help me out here.'

'OK. Well, is he going to be tall or short?'

'Taller than me.'

'Right, put that down. Now what else? Dark hair? Blond?'

The phone interrupted us. It was Jamie. 'Hi mum, what are you up to?'

'Hello Jamie. At this moment I'm about to curl up on the sofa with a fruity little Australian. Oh, and order a man.'

There was a momentary silence. 'Have you been drinking, mum?'

'No, not yet. But Cathy's here, so chances are that I'll have had a couple of glasses by the end of the evening.' There was a satisfying plop from behind me as Cathy pulled the cork from the first bottle.

'Having a girlie night then?'

'Yes'

'And... ordering a man?'

'Yes.'

'I'm not even going to ask, mum. I was going to pop over but I think I'll leave you and Cathy to it – whatever it is that you're up to. I'll see you at the weekend.'

When Cathy and I finally stopped giggling we got down to the serious business of the list once more. 'Adventurous.' I stated firmly. 'Someone whose idea of an exciting life runs to more than football on Saturday and the Sunday papers.' Aided by the rest of the bottle, by the time we'd finished, my list was several pages long. I read it through; it seemed a bit ambitious. I wasn't sure a man like this existed anywhere on the planet. 'Am I asking too much?'

'Of course not.' Cathy was tipsily adamant. 'Look, say you have a website or a kitchen or even a house custom built, you state exactly what you want and it is delivered to you. This is absolutely the same thing.'

'Except that we are talking about a real person who is already in existence. Not someone who is being put together from a selection of separate components' I retorted.

'You'll see.' Cathy was reading through the list. 'You know Gemma, this could easily be Joe. Fits him to a tee.' She ducked as I hurled the nearest cushion across the room at her.

*   *   *   *   *   *   *

208

I neatly folded the sheets of paper then tucked them safely away at the back of the top drawer of the bedroom dresser, as Cathy had instructed. 'Then forget about it,' she had said. I did forget about it. I forgot about it completely.

GAL-ATHIEL: The Blue Skull

Part 2

LEAVING YO'TLÀN

Chapter 38

Thula looked around. There was no-one in sight in the wide brightly lit corridor. She pressed her hand onto the small clear panel set into the wall beside the heavy wooden door and anxiously waited for her identity to be verified. Hurry up. It didn't usually take so long, did it? Someone could come along at any moment. Once inside the chamber she would be safe but out here... Her presence here at this late hour risked provoking suspicion and questions. Questions she would find it hard to answer.

With a soft click the door opened. At last. She darted inside and pushed the door closed behind her, leaning against it for a brief moment, surprised by her long sigh of relief. She hadn't realised she had been holding her breath. In here she was protected from any curious or hostile eyes, for only the Priests and Priestesses of the Skulls were allowed to enter this place. The others would certainly be unable to cross its thresholds. For how long though, she wondered?

There was no time to waste. Even so, Thula took a few moments as she always did to look and feel the beauty and spiritual force of this sacred place. Breathing in, absorbing its powerful energy, allowing it to flow through every cell of her body.

She was in the circular chamber, the heart of the Pyramid Temple that stood in the centre of Yo'tlàn, first city of the continent of Atlantis. It was a chamber unlike any that had existed previously or has existed since. The floor was of glossy black granite and the curving walls were lined with highly polished panels of multi-hued amethyst. Around the outside of this space, a good pace in from the outer perimeter, were arranged twelve quartz pedestals, each standing as high as a man's solar plexus and measuring a hand span across, evenly spaced one from another. They were hexagonal in shape and as clear as glass, formed from the purest of rock crystal. On top of each, facing inwards, rested a carved skull, each one of a different colour and mineral. In the centre of this circle stood an immense square block of opaque white quartz, as tall as the pedestals and topped with a majestic quartz crystal cluster on which sat a thirteenth skull. The Master.

Thula crossed purposefully to one of the pedestals, her lips moving soundlessly in the necessary invocation. Her hands shook a little as she lifted the glassy sea blue skull from it, feeling the energy that surged up her arms as she did so. This was Gal-Athiel, one of the most powerful of the skulls, the one to whom she had been appointed guardian on her initiation into the priesthood only three years previously. To all intents and purposes, Thula was here tonight to steal Her. No, Thula corrected herself, that wasn't true, she wasn't stealing. There was no doubt however that it was how the Shadow Chasers would view her actions if she was caught. She paused for a moment, steadying her nerves and her hands.

No, she wasn't stealing the blue skull; she was taking Her to safety. Thula knew that totally and in every part of her being. As the Shadow Chasers had grown in power and influence, their intentions had become evident: to overthrow the Light Keepers, the priests and priestesses of the temple who watched over and protected the skulls, and to use the skulls' power for their own purposes. Purposes that involved the control and domination of the people of Atlantis through fear and division, the headlong pursuit of ever greater power and wealth at the expense of those unable to defend themselves, an irreparable exploitation of the land and its resources and, ultimately and inescapably, a descent into a way of life that was the antithesis of what the skulls had come here to create. A way of life where competition, fear and separation would gradually replace the unity, co-operation and peace that Atlantis had always stood for. Was already replacing it. It was an uninviting picture.

These dark times would happen in any case, she understood that. Humankind was still vulnerable to the power of fear and the current tide would not be turned. The Atlantean people were becoming so caught up in its illusion that they could no longer believe there was an alternative. But abusing and misusing the power of the skulls would hasten and worsen the situation until it threatened not only Atlantis but the whole future of humankind. The skulls had spoken of this, had warned the priests of what was approaching and asked for their help.

That was why she was here tonight, creeping furtively into this, the most sacred of spaces, to fulfil her role in this conspiracy. Why her? She didn't really know, other than that the skulls had appointed their own guardians in this, and for this sole reason perhaps it hadn't completely surprised her. She had always had a deep connection to Gal-Athiel, right from the beginning, ever since she had entered the temple as nervous twelve year old intern. On her initiation eight years later, she had become one of the blue skull's appointed guardians. Why though, when there were so many others more qualified, more suited, had Gal-Athiel chosen her for this particular task?

At this time of night, when the city slept, the chamber was only dimly lit, the panels around the walls emitting a soft glow. The skulls were not active – some she knew never could be for they were fakes, created to replace those who had already fled – and the centre column stood dormant, the Master skull that rested on it reflecting back the eerie lilac glow of the walls, so that its empty eye sockets blazed as though alive.

She looked down at Gal-Athiel lying in her hands, feeling Her polished glassy surface in contact with her own skin for the first time. Although Thula had been one of Her guardians for several years, she had never before touched Her. To her knowledge, no-one had. She didn't really know why, it was just the way. But now, holding Her, gazing into Her, she felt herself being drawn into the pulsing sea-green depths, losing herself in its shimmering mists. With an effort of will she forced her attention back to her situation. She had little time to lose. From the woollen bag that was slung over her shoulder Thula pulled out a second skull and stowed Gal-Athiel carefully in its place. This duplicate skull, though expertly carved, was a pale imitation of the original. It would though be enough to fool the Shadow Chasers for a while should they penetrate this sanctuary, to give the fugitives some additional time. The Shadow Chasers would not be fooled for long, but maybe for long enough.

With a last look around the chamber she knew and loved so well, and a sad recognition that this would be the last time she would ever set foot here, she walked out of the door.

* * * * * * *

Thula's plan was to return home, to not leave until the morning. She had arranged to travel the following day with a small group who were on their way to Carn'gà, a city far to the west. Her hope was that the Shadow Chasers would not consider that anyone trying to hide anything precious or incriminating would stride out brazenly in broad daylight. Please Sirius that they had not discovered the switch by then, she prayed, or it would all be over. She would have virtually no hope of success. It would be difficult enough as it was to avoid their interest and suspicions. From Carn'gà, she did not know where her path would lead; nonetheless she had complete faith that, once she arrived, her next move would be revealed to her. She trusted Gal-Athiel implicitly to guide and protect her.

* * * * * * *

Making her way through the dark empty streets, Thula was anxious. In many ways this was perhaps the most dangerous stage; if she was stopped now, she could give no viable explanation for being out and about at this time. The curfew may not yet have been official, but no-one in the city doubted that if you were out after dark and were caught, you would be searched and questioned at length. Unless your reason was watertight and convincing, it was an unwise risk to take. Should Gal-Athiel be discovered – and if she was stopped that would be inevitable – the blue skull would fall irretrievably into the hands of the Shadow Chasers. Thula's stomach lurched at the thought, not just at what her own unpleasant fate would be but also because the whole plan would be discovered and bound for failure. That must not, could not, happen.

It was with a heartfelt prayer of thanks that Thula closed the door of her room and waited for the trembling that filled her body to quieten. Reaction to the tension of the past hours was making itself felt. Until this moment, now that she had reached comparative safety, she had been unaware of how scared she had actually been, the adrenalin that coursed through her body masking it from her. When she felt she could move without her legs giving way she crossed to her bed, on which a large pack was lying ready, pushed the pack aside and collapsed onto the soft mattress, allowing the reaction to take its course, knowing that she had to allow it to move through her and dissipate.

As Thula reached to switch on the light, she wondered how long the power supply would hold without the skulls' input. They were not the power source itself –

that came from the people, from the focus of their minds linking to the quartz generators that were in every home – but the skulls gathered, amplified and focused this energy into the massive quartz cells that stored and released the power for the whole continent. Without their presence, the levels available would fall to but a fraction of what they had been – and that decline would have already started. The Master skull could keep the energy up for a while, but without the support of Her brothers and sisters She could not sustain it for more than a few days, and even then it would be at a reduced level. Sooner rather than later the Shadow Chasers would notice something was wrong and discover the switch. She – and Gal-Athiel – had to be as far away as possible by the time that happened.

Shaking her head to clear her mind, Thula reached into the bag and drew out the blue skull. Carved by master craftsmen thousands, if not tens of thousands of years before, using techniques that were still beyond Atlantean understanding, She was as perfect and unmarked as the day She had been completed, an object of breathtaking beauty and mystery, created from flawless, pale ocean blue obsidian. Falling once more into Her pulsing marine core, Thula felt the familiar comfortable sensation of losing her own form and becoming one with the skull. As always, powerful waves of peace, serenity and protection enveloped her, permeating her entire body. 'Why me?' she asked. 'I have so little experience of the world. I am no hero. Why me?'

Gal-Athiel's sweet, melodic voice filled her being, speaking not in words but in feelings and sensations. 'You are strong, you are brave, and you are young. All of which are essential to your success. You are intuitive and intelligent, and our connection is deep and powerful. Listen to me and I will guide you. Know that I chose you because it is you who will be successful in completing the journey that lies ahead. It is your destiny. Trust in me, and trust in yourself.' Energy crackled like golden lightning through the blue and Thula felt her courage and determination return. Gal-Athiel had chosen her, as each had chosen its own guardian. She would not fail the blue skull. She wrapped the precious object back in its woollen sack and pushed Her to the bottom of the large pack that still lay on the bed. Then she closed her eyes and slept.

Chapter 39

It was a long and tiring three day journey to Carn'gà, even
travelling by the solar-powered shuttle that connected all
the main cities of Atlantis. To Thula's relief and heartfelt
gratitude, it passed without incident. She caught her first
glimpse of the city as its distant rooftops caught the late
afternoon sun, glinting gold and red in its rays. It was very
different to Yo'tlàn, whose golden domes and pyramids
she had said a sad and silent farewell to those three days
earlier. By contrast, this was a city of spires and minarets
that thrust up into the deep blue of the summer sky. As the
shuttle grew nearer, the delicate tracery of its stonework
lent it an unreal, almost ethereal quality.

It had been a tense three days for Thula. There were
seven of them in total travelling in the little shuttle group
and her fellow passengers were, without exception,
friendly and good natured. But she feared giving herself
away at any moment with a careless word so, as far as she
could without raising suspicion, she kept herself to herself
and limited her conversation to generalities and small talk.
If her companions found her a little strange and reserved
they said nothing, accepting her without judgement, for
which Thula was thankful.

Gal-Athiel remained silent throughout the journey,
drawing in Her energy in case any of the other travellers
were sensitive enough to detect Her presence. From her
seat in the corner, Thula observed them. They all appeared
to be ordinary people going about their ordinary lives.
Except maybe… There was an older couple, who proudly
told her they were on their way to visit their first
grandchild, a merchant who continually boasted to anyone
who would listen that he was about to make the deal of his

life, a young man and woman – brother and sister – returning home. And him…

*   *   *   *   *   *   *

His name was Armil and he unsettled her. Made her feel uncomfortable. She felt he was reading her thoughts, picking up everything about her, and yet she sensed no mind intrusion. It was more subtle than that, a connection and understanding of her energy and frequencies. The way he looked at her with a knowing far beyond his years in his eyes made her feel he was unlocking her secrets in a way she did not know how to resist. She made every effort to avoid his conversation and that penetrating gaze.

Yet, flustered though she was, she could sense no threat, no darkness about this man. On the contrary, he glowed with an inner light and carried himself with an air of peace and comforting strength. And he was good-looking. By Sirius, he was good-looking. Wavy hair the colour of ripe wheat worn long to his collar as was the latest fashion, framing a sun-tanned face from which his vivid blue eyes twinkled most of the time with gentle mischief and good humour, teamed with a wide, generous mouth that was ever ready to break into a smile. He was much taller than she – a good head taller – and muscular, the product of an active lifestyle. This was no softened city dweller, but a man of the land, used to physical labour and the open air.

Thula had never paid much attention to the opposite sex. Of course she mixed with men – the priests and priestesses of the skulls trained and worked alongside each other – but the demanding lifestyle of her profession left little time for socialising. Moreover, serious relationships were not permitted until the priests had reached a certain seniority. Now though, outside of that rarefied environment, aware of this stranger's glances…

*   *   *   *   *   *   *

She was beautiful, he thought, corn-gold hair pulled back from her face and caught with a ribbon, eyes as green and unfathomable as his were blue, framed by long, unexpectedly dark lashes. But there was also anxiety in those eyes, and a sadness that pulled at his heart. Although she was slight of build, he sensed in her a strength of both body and mind that belied her delicate appearance. He found himself constantly assailed by an overwhelming urge to take her in his arms and protect her. Shield her from whatever she was running from, for he was in no doubt that she was running from something... or someone.

She was avoiding him. Trying hard not to make it appear too obvious, still he could feel her pulling her energy away whenever he got too close. What was she hiding?, he wondered. He had barely spoken a word to her, but something deep inside told him she would soon become an important part of his life. The connection was there and was strong, even if she was not yet ready to acknowledge it. Their destinies were intertwined in some future that he had not yet been shown.

And then, in that passing moment, he did know. Saw the story playing through his mind. Saw them entwined in a passionate embrace, wandering through strange and exotic landscapes, living their lives together. Knew that was why she was keeping her distance. She recognised it as well. Oh, maybe not consciously, not yet, but some secret part of her understood and was resisting. Let time and destiny run their course and soon she would awaken to it too. For now, he would simply watch over her and do everything in his power to keep her safe. As his eyes rested on her from across the carriage, an unexpected wave of overwhelming love welled up inside him for this captivating young woman who was a stranger to him. It was a deep and everlasting love that sprang from his soul.

221

He smiled as she looked at him, unsettled, a bewildered question in her eyes, and drew away a little more. Yes, she felt it too.

* * * * * * *

As they neared the outskirts of Carn'gà the shuttle slowed. The older man put his head out of the window and peered down the road. 'What's the hold up?' he called to a couple passing by in the opposite direction.

'Dark Ones!' The words almost spat from the woman's mouth in disgust. 'They are checking the papers of everyone who enters and leaves Carn'gà. Searching their baggage.'

Shadow Chasers! Thula did not utter a sound but Armil saw her hands grip the edge of the seat so tightly that her knuckles turned white. She was pale, all colour drained from her face; luckily none of the other passengers noticed her discomfort. She sensed Armil's stare and for the first time met his eyes fully, fear and desperation fluttering in her own. Wordlessly asking him for help. Instinctively knowing that she could trust this man who so unnerved her.

What was she hiding? Whatever it was, the Dark Ones were evidently a part of it. It really didn't matter anyway. He had vowed to help her, would do everything in his power, lay down his own life if necessary to protect this mysterious enchanting young woman and the secret she was carrying.

Armil thrust his head out of the window and scanned the road ahead. The checkpoint was still a good way away and for the moment progress was almost at a standstill. A little way in front of them a drainage ditch led off at right angles to the road. There had to be a bridge, or pipe, running under the road to carry away the water. An idea seeded itself. He looked at Thula with what he hoped was a reassuring smile. She seemed to relax a little.

Could his plan work? That would depend on everyone else in the shuttle. He quickly scanned their energies. From all except one he picked up a feeling of deep antipathy towards the Shadow Chasers. He was sure they could be trusted. The exception was the merchant, but by a stroke of good fortune he had fallen asleep and was snoring loudly in the corner, his head lolling against the window. As long as he remained asleep, he would be ignorant of what was going on and unable to tell the Shadow Chasers anything of help.

Armil leaned across to where Thula sat and spoke in a low, urgent voice. 'Gather your belongings. We are getting off now.' Her face flashed surprise, then fear, then hope. She did not hesitate. He threw a cautious glance at the sleeping merchant then spoke quietly to the other occupants of the shuttle. 'We have to get off here. We cannot take our chances with the Dark Ones. I am taking a risk in speaking to you like this, but I believe you all bear no more love for them than we do. Please, don't give us away unless your own lives and freedom depend on it. If they should ask, tell them we got out several hours ago and that you don't know where we are heading.'

Momentary confusion and incomprehension gave way to understanding, and to a person the other passengers all nodded their silent agreement. Carefully, without making a sound, Armil opened the door and surveyed the area. The shuttle was still moving at a slow walking pace, the ditch now only a few yards ahead. He lowered himself to the ground and reached up to help Thula. She handed him her precious pack and let herself drop into his arms. A whispered 'good luck' followed them as an unseen hand quietly pulled the door closed behind them.

The ditch was directly in front of them now and they dropped into it, Armil's strong arm steadying Thula as she stumbled and almost fell headlong to its base. She flashed him a shaky smile of thanks as they scrambled under the road and out of sight of anyone who might glance down from a following shuttle or passing by on foot.

* * * * * * *

Thula rested against the wall, reaction at last overtaking her now that the immediate danger had passed. She had been more terrified than she had allowed herself to feel, and as the adrenalin drained from her system she sank to the ground, her mind unable to think clearly. After a few moments Armil's hand lightly touched her arm, pulling her back to their situation. She opened her eyes and gave him a weak smile.

'Thank you,' she said. 'But why do you risk your own safety to help me? You don't know me.'

'Because you needed help.' And because I do know you, he held himself back from saying. I don't know how, but I do know you. And you know me. He couldn't say it, not yet. This was not the right time. She would not understand and the words would only disturb her further. Soon though she would see, of that he was certain. 'Are you alright to go on?'

She nodded, pulling her shattered energy back together and focussing on their situation. 'But where do we go?'

Armil's next words brought further reassurance. 'I know this land well. Just beyond the city is a valley and it's riddled with caves. No-one will find us there. As soon as you are safely hidden there, I'll return to the city to find us food and hopefully discover what is going on with the Shadow Chasers.' No questions, no curiosity, just total acceptance of her and her secret. 'Come on.'

Thula let him lead her away along the ditch, leaving the road, the shuttle and the Shadow Chasers behind. It was a narrow cut in the land, bordered with a dense line of reeds that hid them from view. Once they were no longer visible from the road, they clambered up its banks and, keeping under cover of the vegetation as much as possible, set off across the countryside.

Chapter 40

The valley was exactly how Armil had described it, a narrow rocky cleft in the land through which a sparkling stream tumbled. It was a beautiful and tranquil place, and Thula felt the tension in her body begin to melt away. It felt safe here, like nothing bad could ever happen within its sheltering folds. The grassy slopes were pockmarked with caves and Armil led the way assuredly, as if heading for a specific destination. Sure enough, before long he stopped in front of a large thorn bush. 'Here.' He pushed the branches aside to reveal the entrance to a small dry cave with a smooth rock floor. 'You'll be safe here. No-one will find this place. Wait here for me, I'll be back soon.' With those words and a casual wave of his hand, he was gone again.

She spread her cloak on the floor and laid back on it. Now that she was alone again, doubt and apprehension flooded back into her mind. What was she doing here? How did she know she could trust him? What if, even now, he was on his way to the Shadow Chasers? But even as these thoughts jostled in her head she knew that she did trust him. Trusted him completely. He still made her uncomfortable, those sky blue eyes so knowing as they looked at her with something else, something more, something unfathomable, untouchable, in their depths. For all that, she was certain he would not betray her.

He had helped her. Had risked his own freedom to safeguard hers. Why? What did he know that she was still reaching for? All these questions and more whirled around in her head until her eyes closed and she slept.

*　*　*　*　*　*　*

226

She woke to someone softly calling her name. It was a voice that echoed inside her mind. Insistent. Whispering. Gal-Athiel! In the events of the last few hours she had completely forgotten the skull's presence.

'I hear you, Gal-Athiel,' she replied, digging through her pack for the bundle that held the blue skull.

In the dim light of the cave Gal-Athiel was as dark as midnight. Thula moved closer the entrance so that she could see Her more clearly. The skull's energy pulsed as strongly as ever and a fire was glowing deep within. Thula allowed her eyes to be drawn into those golden depths, softening their focus. Letting go of the outside world as the skull absorbed her.

Images began to play through Thula's mind: this cave; a boat on an ocean; thick damp forests; small stone houses, squat and square; people unlike any she had ever seen before – some dark and sturdy, some tall, so tall. There were those with fair skin and light hair; others had a strange bronze-coloured complexion. All were glowing with an inner light. Other images drifted in now: herself and Armil, in each other's arms, their bodies entwined and moving in…

She pulled back, startled by these last visions, her consciousness returning immediately to the cave, her breath panting rapidly. What did it all mean? What were they showing her? A glimpse of the future? Or a warning… And if so…? Her mind was struggling to take it all in. This had never happened before. The pictures… The feelings… Her eyes were still on the skull in her hands though Her inner fire had now softened, but they gazed unseeing as her thoughts raced, trying to make sense of what she had just experienced. It was several minutes before she realised she was being watched. She looked up quickly, fear clouding her face. Had she been betrayed after all?

*   *   *   *   *   *   *

Armil was standing in the cave entrance, watching her, comprehension slowly dawning in his eyes. The pieces of the puzzle were fitting together. He did not seem in the least surprised or in awe of Gal-Athiel, and his easy and immediate acceptance of Her presence deeply disconcerted Thula. Why wasn't he staggered by the unexpected appearance of one of the sacred skulls, as anyone else would have been? Armil simply smiled.

'She showed you.' It was a statement, not a question.

Thula nodded, still unsure of what to make of his improbably relaxed behaviour. 'I'm not sure what She was telling me though.' It seemed bizarre that the conversation was so natural, so ordinary. In fact, Armil was taking about Gal-Athiel as if he had known Her all his life.

'She was showing you the future.'

Thula shook her head vehemently. The future was malleable, created through thoughts and intention, and it could be changed at any time in the same way. 'The future is not set,' she stated firmly. 'Any action or thought or decision can change it. Any intention can change it.'

'That is true.' His voice was gentle but firm. 'But when you agreed to the task you embarked upon, your destiny was settled. Some things are too important to be left to whim. The safekeeping of the skulls is one such thing. When we take on a mission of such importance we have to bow to the direction of a higher power and allow it to lead us where it will.'

'But free will. We always have that.' Thula argued.

'We do. And you had the choice as to whether to accept your destiny or not. You accepted it, and in doing so surrendered to it.'

'How do you know all this?' Thula's confusion was deepening by the second and she drew back from him, once more uncertain and suspicious of his motives.

228

'Let me show you.' He sat down opposite her and reached his hands out to Gal-Athiel. Instinctively she drew the skull away from him, holding Her close to her heart, wanting to protect Her, to keep Her from his touch. 'Please, Thula.' Something in his voice, a reverberation that reached far beyond her conscious mind, reassured her. Tentatively she held out Gal-Athiel once more. As Armil's hands covered hers, the fire within the blue skull immediately re-ignited in a golden blaze. 'Let yourself see,' he commanded. Thula felt herself falling into it once more, only this time she was not alone. He was with her, his presence firm and strong by her side.

*   *   *   *   *   *   *

More images, this time clearer, more vibrant than before. Of a strange silver craft moving through the stars, landing on Earth, though it was not an Earth that she recognised. Of people emerging. Tall, fair-haired people. Armil bore a striking resemblance to them; the thought entered her consciousness as a distant melody. Of these strangers, living amongst the people of the Earth, raising families with them, before returning to the skies once more.

Herself and Armil, only it wasn't them… And yet it was. Over and over again. Always together. Always as lovers. In that instant she knew why he was so familiar. She had spent so many lifetimes with him. How had she not recognised him? The cave returned around her and as she looked up, their eyes met. The connection, renewed and reinvigorated, swept over them both in a surging tidal wave. Yes, now she knew. As one, their eyes never leaving one another, they lowered Gal-Athiel to the floor and moved together.

*   *   *   *   *   *   *

Love overwhelmed her, a love carried and strengthened through countless lifetimes. As Armil's arms closed around her, a passion and desire unlike anything she had ever experienced before flowed through her body. She had never known a man – as a novice priestess it was forbidden – and he instinctively felt it. Despite the urgency of his own desire he was gentle and slow, whispering tender words of encouragement and reassurance.

His touch set her skin aflame, every nerve ending now sensitised and receptive. Stroking gently, softly, igniting a white-hot pleasure that coursed through her. His hand reached up to cup her breast, barely brushing its firm peak so that she gasped at its whisper. And then his mouth, his lips, his tongue, seeking, enticing, tantalising until she did not think she could stand any more. A fire was ablaze in her belly, her whole body was trembling, and still he did not stop.

She reached out and unfastened his shirt, slipping it off his shoulders, running her hands over the hard muscles of his chest. His nakedness pressed against hers. Her hands reached down, eager to explore further. Hungry to uncover the secrets of this man who was arousing such powerful sensations within her. Running her hands over his buttocks, feeling them tighten in desire at her touch.

Gently he laid her back and removed the last of her clothing so that she lay open and vulnerable below him, quivering and unsure. He moved above her, lost in her eyes and in her touch, caressing her tenderly as he slowly and gently pressed into her, mindful of her innocence. She was so hungry for him, so desiring, that she barely felt him break through her tender veil. And now he was part of her, and she part of him, lost in the overwhelming sensations of their love-making.

The fire within her blazed more and more fiercely, the uncontrollable waves of feeling almost unbearable in their intensity. She cried out in pleasure at every movement. She was consuming him, and in turn being consumed. Nothing existed but the sensation of him moving within her and the pulsating, agonisingly delicious tension that she didn't know how much longer she could stand but never wanted to end. And her world dissolved into an explosion of sensations and ecstasy that seemed to go on forever; as he felt her release, his own burst forth and his cry joined with hers.

Chapter 41

Much later, as he cradled her in the womblike darkness of the cave, she asked the questions that she had been holding back since the moment she had raised her head to see him standing at the cave entrance, watching her communing with the blue skull. 'How did you know? You weren't surprised at all. How did you know about Gal-Athiel?'

Armil pressed his lips against her hair and, quietly, began to speak. 'Long ago, lost way back in the time before time, visitors from the stars came to my people. It was those visitors that Gal-Athiel showed you. They lived with our people, our women bore their children, and through those children their essence and their genes merged with those of the human race. I am a direct descendant of those star-beings. Their home is the planet Theta and it was they who created this skull. Their connection to Her, their knowledge of Her, has been carried down through the generations, in some more strongly than in others. In me, it is strong. I have spoken with Her many times from a distance, but recently She has been hiding Herself from me. Now I know why. I had to trust my own intuition when I helped you. It had to happen without Her input and without me knowing that She was involved. Once that happened, She returned to me. The time had come for Gal-Athiel and I to meet. I feel incredibly blessed to have connected with Her physically at last.'

Thula thought hard. 'In those first images I saw many unusual looking people. Some I recognised; others like them have visited the temple at Yo'tlàn. Are they the travellers from the stars?'

Armil nodded. 'Yes, although they would not identify themselves as such. Once upon a time they walked the

232

lands of Atlantis much more openly than they do today. Now the fear has grown too strong. Now they would not be safe if their true origins were revealed.'

'Have other star people... you know, mated with humans?' It sounded clumsy, even to her ears, but Armil did not hesitate.

'Yes, many times. It has helped us to evolve. But it has not happened for many lifetimes now.'

'What about the other images I saw? The boat, the forests?'

'Gal-Athiel is guiding you. Showing you the next steps. Tell me, what exactly did you see?'

Thula related in as much detail as she could the information she had received from the blue skull. Armil looked thoughtful. 'We must follow Her guidance – reach the coast, find a boat and cross the ocean.'

'We?' Thula scarcely dared hope he meant what she thought.

'Yes, we.' He bent his head and kissed her deeply. 'It is clear that I am to follow this path with you. Do you really think it was chance that brought us together? You, the guardian of the blue skull and me, a descendant of the race that brought Her here? You know as well as I do that nothing in this life is mere coincidence. This is our journey and we will take it together. Besides,' he said, kissing her again, 'I love you. I could never let you simply walk away from me.' His hand tenderly pushed a stray strand of hair from her eyes. 'Now sleep, my beautiful lady. We must leave at first light and it will be a long road ahead.'

*   *   *   *   *   *   *

Their journey to the sea, though long and taking many months to complete, was straightforward and uneventful. They avoided the roads as they travelled and, when supplies grew short, Armil simply purchased more in the towns that they skirted. His papers were genuine and in order, the Shadow Chasers were not looking for him. He was just a young wanderer passing through; no-one gave him a second glance.

Despite the uncertainties and inevitable hardships of a life on the road, Thula was happier than she could ever remember. Armil was caring, funny and supportive and they were deeply in love. The days passed in laughter and companionship, sharing stories and dreams, the nights in lovemaking and untroubled sleep, curled in each other's embrace. With Gal-Athiel as their constant companion and guide, an unshakeable knowing gradually rooted itself firmly in Thula. A knowing that their successful escape and future survival was inevitable. A knowing that surrounded and dissolved in its warm certainty any lingering fears that rose within her. By the time they reached the coast, neither she nor Armil doubted that they would find the help and transport they sought, nor that Gal-Athiel would lead them to a place of sanctuary where they could live out their lives with Her in peace and safety.

GAL-ATHIEL: The Blue Skull

Part 3

THE VOICE OF THE MOTHER

Chapter 42

The quake came suddenly and unexpectedly, knocking people to the floor and tumbling the delicate structures of their light huts to the ground. Such an event was not unusual – tremors often shook the valley and no-one paid much attention to them – but this was one of the most powerful they had ever experienced.

When the shaking stopped, an unnatural stillness descended as the people gathered their wits and the wildlife was shocked into silence. Gradually normality resumed. The villagers checked for casualties – thankfully only a few minor injuries had been suffered – and surveyed their destroyed homes with only a little dismay, for the huts were simply constructed from branches and leaves and would be easy to repair or rebuild. The ancient, squat, square stone buildings that had stood since before memory had again escaped unscathed, standing as solid and rooted as ever. Nothing seemed particularly out of the ordinary.

Another violent tremor rocked the land, and then another. Aftershocks of a major earth slip close to the Earth's surface. This time, the silence held until a distant muffled crack echoed across the valley. Ominous. Terrifying. Unearthly.

The sound thundered down towards them from the head of the valley where massive near-vertical cliffs soared high into the sky. The rock appeared to shimmer and, as the village watched, the whole cliff face shuddered and hung motionless in mid-air for an eternity before dropping with a crashing roar, carrying the soil and vegetation that covered it, plummeting downwards in an avalanche of rock, earth and trees. Hundreds of thousands of tons shaken from its foundations as the earthquake shattered its grip. A dense cloud of dust plumed upwards, blocking the sunlight for several hours, bringing an early twilight to the land below.

*   *   *   *   *   *   *

Jamui stared up at the jumbled mass that drowned the foot of the cliff, his mind unable to grasp the immensity of the devastation the quake had caused. Loose debris littered the ground for a vast distance all around, stretching far out from the former base, the main bulk piling up on itself against it in an unstable mountain of earth, rock and uprooted vegetation. High above, the newly exposed rock face gleamed unnaturally in the morning sunlight, virgin stone exposed for the first time and as yet unmarked by the ravages of time and nature.

He picked his way gingerly across the outermost edges of the fall, mindful of the danger that towered above him. Jamui was anxious not to be seen for he had been forbidden to come here. Inquisitive by nature, an inquisitiveness that frequently got him into trouble but which he could not quell, his mother was fearful for his safety, knowing that he would be drawn here like a magnet. As indeed he had been, despite her stern words. It was this irrepressible curiosity that now caused him, little by little, to forget caution and, ignoring the risks, clamber higher and higher up the pile of shattered rock. He moved cautiously, in the full knowledge that one clumsy step could bring the whole slope cascading down on top of him, swallowing him up unnoticed in its fury. Gingerly, he tested every rock and boulder before putting his weight on it. Edged up and across the jumbled mass.

Suddenly he was slipping, the earth giving way under him, sliding downwards. Instinctively he grabbed at something to save himself, throwing his arms around the nearest big object – a large chunk of rock twice as tall as a

237

man that had fallen to wedge firmly against the cliff face. Jamui held his breath as he grasped his anchor, feeling the soil continue to shift beneath his feet. If the trickle of dislodged earth and stones became a torrent he would be swept away like a twig on the river. Slowly, slowly, however, as the cold sweat of fear trickled down his back, the movement stopped. Jamui opened his eyes, retaining his grip on the rock, and let out a long, slow, shaky breath. That had been close. Nor was he safe yet; his perch was still highly unstable and any further movement by him risked re-triggering the slide. But he had to move. He couldn't remain where he was.

Taking as much weight as he could on his arms, step by tentative step Jamui edged his way sideways, using the rock to support and steady himself, moving off the perilous loose ground to where a section of small boulders were wedged together to form what seemed to be a more solid footing. He was not yet safe but the immediate danger had passed.

Without making any sudden moves that might vibrate through the ground and cause further slips, he turned to gaze at the cliff face behind him, whose original surface now lay shattered and buried deep beneath his feet. As his eyes travelled across it, Jamui spotted a dark crack rising up above the large rock that had saved his life. With the resilience of youth, all thought of his recent brush with death was instantly forgotten as his unquenchable curiosity got the better of him once more and he picked his way carefully back through the debris.

The rock had fallen to lean at an angle and, sure enough, behind it he could just make out a narrow cleft that he had not noticed before. Would he be able to squeeze through? It was probably just about big enough, although the leaning rock created an awkward obstacle. Jamui had to twist and contort his body around it in order to wriggle through the tiny entrance, mindful that he could not risk dislodging anything. The chance of causing further falls was too great.

*　*　*　*　*　*　*

The crack opened out almost immediately into a small chamber, dimly lit by a narrow shaft of light filtering through from outside. There was also, Jamui noticed with some surprise, a faint glow emanating from the rear of the chamber. He ran his hands over the walls, which seemed unnaturally smooth. Those were tool marks beneath his fingers. This room had been carved out of the solid rock! 'What was this place?' he wondered. 'Who could have built it, and why?'

His eyes fell back onto the faint glimmer at the back of the room. Unsure, and not a little fearful of what he might find, he edged towards it,. Was it some form of magic? Could he be disturbing some malevolent spirit that would bring a curse down upon him? He could not see the floor under his feet in the gloom and he was wary of unseen perils that may have lain invisible in the darkness.

The light was within arm's reach now and he stretched out his hand to it. Pulled it back in sharp alarm as he touched heat and a powerful tingling sensation that shot to his shoulder. It had come from the object, whatever it was. What was it?

Gathering his courage, Jamui reached out again, this time prepared for the unexpected sensation, forcing himself to keep contact with it even as fear called on him to pull away. After a few moments the fear subsided. He was still alive. He was unhurt. Nothing horrific had happened. The sensation, the tingling was, he discovered, not unpleasant. In fact, it was strangely warm and comforting. He allowed his fingers to explore the object, which he still could not see, for despite the light it gave out its outline remained blurred and undefined. His touch

239

revealed that it was roughly spherical, the front ridged and indented. Oddly, in spite of the heat emanating from it, the material beneath his hands was cold against his skin.

Suddenly the room began to shake. Small stones, loosened from the roof by the vibration, clattered onto the floor by Jamui's feet. He froze, his heart in his throat. An aftershock. He was immediately reminded of his precarious situation. This was not a good place to linger. At any moment another rock fall could crush him or, infinitely worse, bury him here alive, never to be discovered.

He grabbed the object, surprised by its weight, needing both hands to lift it, and wriggled back out through the crevice to the outside world. As he emerged into the daylight he almost dropped his find. Stared at it in wonder and disbelief, and not a little reawakened fear. In his hands was a perfectly formed skull, not of bone but carved from some sort of transparent rock-like material. Solid. Heavy. Beautiful. It was flawless, of a clear and a delicate greenish-blue as if the water in the deep river pools had set solid. From within its core came the glow that had illuminated the rear of the chamber.

His mind captivated by the object in his hands, his attention held riveted to it, Jamui clambered back down the treacherous slope, this time paying no heed to where his feet were stepping, negotiating unconsciously the piles of fallen rocks and splintered uprooted trees. Somehow reaching the safety of solid ground without mishap.

His mind was reeling, his thoughts racing, tumbling over one another in their headlong rush. Was this...? Could it be...? No. The stories were just that – stories, made up for entertainment around the hearth. But maybe... Was it possible? Could they be true after all? He had never believed them but now, here, holding this treasure in his hands... Had he really found The Voice of the Mother?

240

*   *   *   *   *   *   *

The legends told of a talking head that had been brought to the valley a thousand generations before by the Children of the Sun.

This was a hidden, secret valley, a vast bowl cut off from the outside world, protected all around by insurmountable cliffs and churning rivers. It was a lush, fertile place in the heart of the rainforest, and provided in abundance for all the needs of those who lived there. The inhabitants were a gentle, peaceful people who lived in harmony with their surroundings and worshipped the spirits of the natural world around them as their gods and protectors. Isolated, untouched by the outside world, they remained ignorant of the existence of other tribes and races beyond the protective bastion of the peaks that surrounded their territory. It was a possibility that did not even enter their minds. Any stranger stumbling upon this place would do so only through a miracle.

And yet there they were, the golden-haired god and goddess, the Children of the Sun, walking into its heart and into the lives of the valley people, bringing with them the blue skull, Gal-Athiel, who had soon been re-named The Voice of the Mother by these people for her gentleness, love and compassion.

The newcomers and the skull had been warmly welcomed into this society, held in reverence and treated as gods. But they did not act as such, seeking friendship and equality rather than worship and obedience. They shared with the people the secrets and knowledge of the skull, holding no desire to use her to increase their own power, and for this they were loved and respected. The people prospered and grew, their primitive society slowly becoming more advanced as they embraced the technologies the Voice had taught them. The Children of

241

the Sun grew old and died but the Voice lived on, guiding the people wisely.

They created a home for her, carving a chamber deep within the mountainside, chiselling it from the solid bedrock. Here was a place where all could go and seek her wisdom, for she was freely available to all. Many would be found there simply sitting, bathing in her warm, loving energy.

Until the day she was lost to them forever. Weeks of torrential rain, unusual even in the wet climate of the rainforest, had proved to be too much for the land, filtering through and undermining the already unstable sub-soil levels. A massive mud slide had engulfed the cliff face, burying the entrance under thousands of tons of wet, sticky soil and the life it had sustained. The people had risked their lives trying to dig through it but their attempts only brought about further falls and they had had to give up their impossible task.

Their only consolation – the village had been unscathed, the people unharmed. But the Voice was gone.

Since that time, so many lifetimes previously, and as so often happens, the memories had passed into legend, recounted at the fireside by generation after generation, embellished and enlivened at each telling. The truth lost in the shadowy mists of time. Some told of how she had been a gift from the sky gods, or the river gods. Of how she was a tool of vengeance and retribution. Or cursed. Or conversely how those who touched her were blessed with riches and long life. Or that she could raise the dead… These though were just stories, for the entertainment of those who listened. No-one really believed them any longer.

Nonetheless, some vestige of this past still lived on, pointing to a truth long forgotten. The sons and daughters, grandsons and granddaughters of the Children on the Sun married into the people, became part of them. Over time, their foreign genes were overwhelmed by those of the people and their characteristics lost. But every once in a while, a golden-haired, light-skinned child was born, who kept alive the ghosts of his ancestors. The valley people accepted these children as a natural part of life and they were not considered in any way unusual or special, for, as the people would say, 'it has always been so'. Yet still they were given the nickname 'child of the sun', a gentle teasing born of ancient memories. Jamui was one of these children.

Chapter 43

Without noticing where he was heading, Jamui's feet led him to his favourite spot, a flat rock high above the river that meandered through the wide valley that was his home. Up here he could be alone and quiet, unseen and undisturbed. Up here, he could become one with the world around him, take time to hear his thoughts and feelings. Today, however, he had come to be with his treasured find.

He sat on the smooth, sun-warmed rock and took the skull in both hands. The tingling pulse he had felt in the chamber was still strong, moving up his arms, flowing through his body and down into the ground beneath him. He stared at the object he held and she drew him in. He would have been unable to take his eyes off her had he wanted to. Deeper and deeper, until he began to lose sense of the forest around him. Growing dizzy. Then falling. Falling. Down and down into nothingness, swirling colours drifting past his vision.

Several hours passed as he remained unconscious, caught up in the vortex of the blue skull's energy. Where he went, what he saw, he could not later remember. It was the sound of his name being called that roused him.

*   *   *   *   *   *   *

'Jamui! Jamui! Where are you? Your mother wants you.' Way below him, standing in the open ground that bordered the river, was one of the older men of the village, come to find him.

Jamui stood and waved. 'I'm here. I'm coming...' The words froze in his throat mid-sentence as before his eyes the man appeared to judder and then, impossibly slowly, toppled forward to the ground. Jamui recoiled in horror., Protruding from the centre of the man's back was a brightly painted wooden shaft, decorated with feathers and claws.

Blind instinct caused him to drop down and flatten himself against the rock so that he could no longer be seen. His heart was racing, his breath shallow, fear taking hold. Trembling, he peered over the lip of the outcrop. Apart from the incongruity of a lifeless body, there was nothing unusual about the scene he was looking down upon. Everything was still. Slowly, however, through his stunned senses, terrified shouts and screams penetrated his numbed brain. They were coming from the village. It was under attack! But that was impossible. Who would be attacking them? Even if other people did exist outside of the valley, as some of the villagers claimed, no outsider could know a way through the towering ridges that guarded it. It had never happened before. No-one had ever entered this hidden place. How could they have done so now? Why had they come? It didn't matter. He had to get back. Had to help.

Jamui grabbed the skull and scrambled down from his rocky perch as quickly as he could. Raced now towards the sounds without knowing what he would do when he got there, stumbling blindly, not seeing the path in front of him, his world reduced to the screams and cries that filled his ears. Tripping over something solid that lay in his path, almost falling. Steadying himself with a violent curse born of the turmoil of emotion within him. He turned to see what he had tripped over and sank to his knees, tears filling his eyes and blurring his vision. The vacant eyes of his closest friend looked back at him, seeing nothing, the ground around him stained crimson with his blood. Jamui swallowed as he stared disbelievingly, his stomach threatening to empty its contents as he took in the gaping wound that ran almost from ear to ear across his friend's neck. His throat had been cut, brutally and ferociously. He had been Jamui's age, still only a boy.

The noises were getting closer. Jamui could not afford to stay and mourn him. That would have to wait. He scrambled to his feet, wanting to run, but his legs refused to move as helplessness and futility washed over him. What was happening? What should he do? What could he do? The violence he had just witnessed in the two cold-blooded deaths was beginning to sink in and return him to his senses. Their attackers were merciless, hard and experienced, that much was clear. He was just a boy – on the verge of manhood yes, but still just a boy. He was certainly no warrior. None of his people were. They did not know how to fight, had never needed to, protected as they were by the surrounding impenetrable terrain. He had neither the skills nor the physical strength to take on those who were violating his village and his people.

As he stood, undecided, deadlocked by his confusion and uncertainty, he heard footsteps crashing towards him through the undergrowth. Ahead of him a figure burst onto the path, eyes wild and panic-stricken, skin torn and bleeding from the branches and thorns that had snagged at him in his flight. It was one of the men from his village. He caught sight of Jamui, recognising him as he hesitated, small, scared and alone on the path.

'Run Jamui!' he screamed. 'Run! They have taken the village. If they catch you, they will kill you.' The man plunged into the dense jungle once more, and Jamui heard more feet pounding as his pursuers drew closer. At last his legs obeyed him. He turned on his heels and fled.

Chapter 44

Clutching his precious treasure to his chest, Jamui lay motionless under the fallen log, barely daring to breathe. His heart was thumping so loudly in his chest that it surely had to betray his hiding place. By sheer force of will, he attempted to bury himself further into the soft soil under his body. The smell of the damp earth and leaf mould filled his nostrils as he gritted his teeth, forcing himself to ignore the creeping, slithering, wriggling creatures that continuously dropped onto his bare back from the rotting trunk that shielded him. His eyes were screwed tightly shut in a futile effort to block out the horrors of the morning, recognising that he had to stay strong and clear-minded if he was to survive.

He shrank back further, flinching, as feet pounded past him, so close that if he had reached out his hand he would have touched them. Feet that were in pursuit of those like himself who had escaped the initial attack.

The forest was eerily quiet, its usual chorus of birds, insects and animals unusually silent, its sinister stillness punctuated only by the occasional piercing shout or scream. It should have been a welcome silence, but it wasn't. This was the silence of death. And then, near at hand – too near – a shout, a scream… an ominous thud, followed by a heart-rending wail of grief. He burrowed down even further under the log as the footsteps returned, more slowly now. This time, they were roughly dragging a young woman along with them. He caught a momentary glimpse of her as she passed. She appeared unharmed but her face was a mask of terror and pain. It was one of the young women of the village, newly married only a few days before. Had that first cry been her husband, killed as he tried to protect her? Jamui was in no doubt that his own fate would be the same if he let himself be captured.

* * * * * * *

Jamui lost track of time as he lay there, not daring to move until he was sure that the attackers had called off their hunt. He didn't know who they were, or where they had come from, only that they had been vicious and merciless in their onslaught. Night had long fallen when at last he crept out of his hiding place. His back was raw and itching from the bites and stings of insects but he pushed the discomfort from his mind and set off into the forest. This was his territory and it held no secrets from him. He knew this land intimately for several days walk around and could find his way through it in darkness as easily as in the brightest daylight.

As he reached the top of a low rise he found himself looking down on the village. Torches had been lit and placed around its perimeter, illuminating clearly the devastation created during the attack. Many of the huts had been burned to the ground, although the more ancient stone buildings had withstood the flames. Tears filled his eyes as he saw bodies, so many bodies, lying where they had fallen, their blood darkening the ground around them. Huddled terrified in one of the animal compounds were those who had survived, guarded by their attackers, who appeared for all the world like macabre living demons in their war paint and masks. It was clear that the captives' fate would not be a gentle one.

There was nothing he could do. He did not know how to fight and even if he had, he was still one against many. One young inexperienced boy against a hardened raiding party numbering several dozen. He was powerless to help them. Any attempt to do so would inevitably result in his own capture – or more likely, given the bodies strewn

248

grotesquely around the huts – his death. His heart was heavy, his eyes wet with tears, as he turned his back on the scene below him and forced himself to walk away.

* * * * * * *

Jamui wore nothing but the strip of cloth around his loins that all the male members of the valley people wore. Had nothing with him except the hunting knife he always carried and the skull he had retrieved from the cliff and which he still held clasped tightly in his hands. It did not concern him. He had grown up in this forest, knew its secrets and gifts. He would be able to live off its bounty for as long as necessary, and live well. However, he was going to have to find a better way of carrying the skull, in order to have both hands free to climb and to forage. That would have to wait until he had put more distance between himself and the village though. He was still too close, and still in mortal danger.

At long last, after hurrying on at a rapid pace – a half walk, half run – for the remainder of the night and all the following day, he felt it was safe to stop. He needed the rest, needed to sleep and replenish his energy reserves. And he needed to think. He had fled without caring where he was going, simply wanting to get away as far as he could. Now that he was out of immediate danger and his flight had slowed, he realised that he had no idea of where he was heading. The truth was that he had nowhere to go. He was running but without a destination.

Jamui laid the skull on a clear patch of soft, rich earth, closed his eyes and leant back against a tree. Sleep came, but fitfully, punctuated by painfully vivid images of the previous day's nightmare that woke him time and time again with a start and a shout before he drifted off once more. Slowly however, as the night passed, the images faded and a sense of peace touched him.

The next morning he set about creating a pouch in which he could place his treasure, stripping narrow lengths of soft bark from the trunks of young trees and weaving them together to form a bag. It was time-consuming, and he was impatient to be on his way, but he knew it would save him time and difficulty in the longer term. The thought of leaving the skull behind did not enter his mind. Indeed, had anyone been there to suggest it, he would have surprised himself at his vehement refusal to do so. For as long as he was able to defend her, she would not fall into the clutches of those who had come to kill and to plunder.

As he worked, he let his eyes linger on the object that lay in front of him: Gal-Athiel, although he did not know her by that name. To him she was the Voice of the Mother, the sacred oracle and teacher spoken about in hushed and reverent whispers by the tribal elders. A ghostly presence that had disappeared so long ago in the shadows of the past. She sparkled that day in the morning sunshine, silvery highlights flashing over her surface as she revelled in the fresh air and freedom after her thousands of years of imprisonment. She was a truly beautiful object, had been part of his people's stories forever – and now she was here, returned once more. Returned once more to what? Jamui's tears flowed unchecked. The people were no more; he was the only survivor. All the others had either been slaughtered or dragged off as slaves and sacrifices.

*   *   *   *   *   *   *

Picking up the Voice to stow her safely in the newly-made bag, Jamui hesitated. Something, he didn't really know what, was compelling him to lift her up until she was level with his face and he was looking directly into those empty eye sockets that nonetheless seemed to pulse with vibrant life. 'Help me, Mother. Guide me. Show me the way.' His words sounded distant, like they came from someone else.

Immediately the answer filled his head. 'Go north.' In his surprise he nearly dropped her. He had asked in desperation, as a drowning atheist calls out to God, not knowing why he was doing it, not expecting a reply – and she had answered him. Or had she? Maybe he had just imagined it. She did seem to be glowing more brightly, somehow. It frightened him and he quickly shoved her into the bag and fastened it around his waist. Go north. Well, why not? He didn't have any better ideas. He began to walk.

Chapter 45

Jamui hadn't gone very far before the realisation struck him that he was going to have to find a way out of the valley. He had been so caught up in his misery that he hadn't even considered the problem until now. The valley formed a vast basin in the landscape, several days walk from wall to wall and considerably more in length. At the head, the towering cliffs that had shattered in the recent quake formed an impenetrable wall, to left and right sheer ridges and impassable ravines blocked any escape. North was the only possible way, the direction the blue skull had told him to take.

That distant part of the land was unfamiliar to Jamui. The village was located to the south, nearer to its head where the river flowed benignly from deep within the earth. He had never travelled to the north before, had never had cause to come this way. He prayed that The Voice was not mistaken. Could there really be a way out of the valley there? The people had never given thought to the existence of a world beyond; it was the entire world in their eyes. The events that had just taken place had proven otherwise. Those who had attacked and slaughtered had come from somewhere, and that somewhere had to be outside the valley. If they could get in, Jamui reasoned, he could get out, though what awaited him beyond the confines of the valley he could not begin to guess.

The invaders would be returning this way soon, eager to return to their own village with their spoils. There was no way of knowing how far behind him they might be. As he had looked down sorrow-stricken on his village on that last evening they had seemed in no hurry, leisurely ransacking the store houses and taking their brutal pleasure with the women and girls. Jamui's tears flowed and his heart quickened in fury at the memory. However, it was certain that they would soon grow bored of their sport and break camp, although hampered by their prisoners they would be unable to travel as quickly as he could alone. Jamui had a breathing space; nevertheless he could not afford to delay. He did not know where the path was, did not know how long it would take him to find it or even if he would.

He had to. This tragic place was no longer somewhere he could bear to be. Once so peaceful and tranquil, his much loved home was now poisoned and desecrated. Maybe The Voice would help him again, guide him to the path he was seeking. It was not to be. She remained mute, even as he reached the limits of the valley and found himself staring up at yet another barricade of rock. This one was only a fraction of the height of that at the southern end but it made no difference. It was enough to block completely any further progress.

*   *   *   *   *   *   *

Refusing to lose heart, Jamui made his way slowly along its base, keeping watch for any sign of a way through. Eventually he found himself on the bank of the river that flowed from the cliffs at the far end and bisected the valley. But whereas there its current was gentle and placid, here it was churned into a fury by the rocky, uneven bed beneath, roiling and tumbling in a seething torrent that disappeared once more into the earth through a giant, gaping black maw in the rock wall. Unless he retraced his steps for many hours there was no way he could cross. For a fleeting moment Jamui wondered if the river would be his way out, a notion that vanished as soon as it was born. He would be battered to a bloody pulp within seconds in the grip of that merciless current.

Now Jamui did sink to the floor and allow despair to flood over him, bringing with it to the surface all the trauma and heartache of the past days. He curled up and allowed it to consume him, his pain issuing forth with the howl of a wounded panther, his whole body shaking uncontrollably as powerful sobs racked through him. He stayed that way for a long time, until his pent-up emotions were finally spent and he shakily surfaced, coming out of it still grieving but lighter, cleansed. His spirit had returned to him. There was a way out of the valley here somewhere and he would find it, no matter what.

Slowly he retraced his steps along the cliff to the point where he had first approached it. Nothing. What had he missed? He walked a few hundred paces back from the rock and stared up at it so that he could see it in its entirety. Still nothing. Not even a shadow that might indicate a possible opening or path. As he took another step backwards, a faint chink sounded by his feet. He glanced down. Lying next to his left foot was a small, shiny round object – a bead maybe? He picked it up and turned it over in his hand. Yes, it was a bead, made from some kind of metal, but it was not of his peoples' making. Where had it come from? His curiosity and his hopes raised, Jamui looked more closely at the ground. No more unexpected finds caught his attention; instead something infinitely more valuable became clear. The ground was disturbed here, as if many feet had passed across it, and at the edge of the patch, the shape of a single foot, clearly imprinted in the soft humus rich soil. It was pointing out of the undergrowth into the heart of the valley. Could it really be...?

Scarcely daring to believe his good fortune, Jamui peered through the thick vegetation. Just to the right of a small stagnant pool the ground was even more churned up. It could have been caused by the animals that roamed the area but Jamui felt a strong conviction that he had found what he was looking for. As he approached his instinct was confirmed. More human footprints were visible around a jumbled pile of rocks that stood not much higher than he was. He skirted it examining every possible nook and cranny until finally he spotted a narrow gap between two enormous boulders. The owners of the footprints had come from inside there.

It would be dark; he would need light of some kind. Working quickly he cut down a vine, peeled off its outer layer and wrapped the dry pithy core around an ironwood branch. He cut down and stripped several more, which he wrapped around his waist then, striking a spark from two dry stones, lit his makeshift torch. It would burn slowly and would not give a great amount of light but it should be just enough to see by. He would have to watch it carefully though; the last thing he wanted was for it to burn out and leave him blind as he was negotiating whatever lay ahead in that narrow cleft.

He squeezed through the gap and found himself in a cramped irregular space created when the boulders around him had been piled up one on top of another by some long-ago flood. It didn't seem that this could possibly be the way. He must have been mistaken. He was just about to back out when a colourful flash caught his attention, illuminated in the faint glimmer of the torchlight. Worming his away with difficulty across the uneven boulders he reached out for it. It was a bird's claw, painted a garish yellow. He had seen one before, only a few days previously, adorning the spear that had been plunged into…

He shook the unwanted memory away as an excitement rose in him. This had to be it. They had to have come this way. How else would this have got here? The claw must have snagged on the rocks as its owner negotiated his way through the tight, awkward gaps. All thought of turning back forgotten, Jamui half crawled, half

255

wriggled forwards and downwards. To his relief, after only a short distance he left the boulder fall behind and the space opened out into a low, steeply sloping passageway, a channel eroded by an ancient long dry water course. The walls and floor were smooth and he found his feet sliding on its slippery surface. He could not risk losing his balance and plummeting downwards out of control, but by pressing his back against one wall and his outstretched hands against the other, he found he could steady himself so that he was able to stay on his feet and control the speed of his descent. To the relief of his aching shoulder muscles, the meandering passage gradually flattened out and the descent became easier. After what seemed a very long time, a pinprick of light appeared in the darkness ahead of him. He had made it. He had found the route out of the valley. What would he find there?

Chapter 46

The world Jamui found outside the shelter of the valley was much the same as the one he had so recently left behind. Another forest world. He walked for a very long time, an endless cycle of days that turned into months. He did not know where he was heading or why he went on. But he did go on because he had not found a reason to stop. There was no reason to stop. His village was far behind him, destroyed and by now reclaimed by the jungle. His people no longer existed, and in all the long months he had been walking he had not come across another human being. If he stopped he would simply give up. There would be no reason to live. As long as he walked he had a purpose.

The rainforest seemed to go on forever. If the terrain changed underfoot, the thick damp undergrowth and heavy canopy that shielded the ground from the sunlight did not. He scaled steep overgrown mountainsides, his feet slipping constantly in the thick humus-rich earth, and descended into deep, creeper-tangled valleys. From time to time he came to a deep, slow moving river which he would swim across, braving the carnivorous creatures that lurked in its depths, and the powerful undercurrents that threatened to pull him under at any moment. Since that first day, the Voice had remained silent throughout. He had begun to believe he had imagined it all.

Finally, after he had been walking for what seemed like an eternity – he did not know how long it had actually been, for he had stopped counting the moon's cycles long before – there came a time when the forest began to thin and wide tracts of blue sky showed through the sparser canopy. The air was clearer here, less moisture laden. Open, treeless spaces appeared more frequently with their patches of rough grass and wild flowers, many containing pools where the local wildlife came to drink. Jamui had been steadily climbing for many days and, unbeknown to him, was reaching the upper limits of the forest where the tree line would disappear.

The forest ended abruptly at the edge of a vast plain, which stretched out as far as the eye could see, gradually rising up ahead to meet the lower slopes of a far off mountain range. Jamui stopped, astounded by the rolling grasslands and never-ending skies. His world had always been the forest, and he had never dreamed that there could be anything else. The breeze rippled the long plains grass into the waves of an endless green sea and the snow-capped peaks of the distant mountains towered majestically up into a clear deep blue sky. He stood unmoving for a very long time, the vastness of the world around him overwhelming him, taking his breath away. He had spent his life in the forest, where he had been constantly surrounded by thick vegetation and where the limit of his view was a minute or two's walk in any direction. Here it went on forever.

Jamui hesitated, surveying the vista that faced him. He was out of his territory here, ignorant of the skills he would need to survive this place. But he was healthy and fit, and over the months of his journey he had turned from a boy into a man. He had grown taller and stronger and his face carried the traces of a first beard. His confidence, knowledge and skills had grown too, as he had faced and conquered the perils of his lonely journey, and he stood undaunted at this new challenge. He had long ago abandoned even his loin cloth as it rotted in the damp heat of the jungle, and now stood naked and proud, a young god setting out on a quest, his long golden hair like ripe corn in the sunlight, his softly bronzed sweat-glistening skin smooth and firm.

*　*　*　*　*　*　*

He was higher now, and his route north was carrying him higher still. Before many days had passed the air began to carry a distinct chill. There was no shelter here away from the heat and shelter of the forest, and in his nakedness he was completely unprotected from this unaccustomed weather. A northerly wind had sprung up, blowing down the slopes of the mountain range, bringing with it the cold bite of snowy peaks. He would need to find warm clothing and food if he was to survive much longer. Where, though, would he find that in this barren wilderness? He was existing on only berries and roots as it was, already weakening through lack of food. His meagre diet would not sustain him for long.

He had no choice but to continue, and so he trudged on, the chill seeping slowly into his marrow, stumbling ever more frequently as the cold robbed his muscles of their strength and co-ordination. He had to keep moving, could not allow himself to rest or sleep. If he stopped and lay down, which every part of his body was pleading with him to do, he would never get up again.

'Stay strong, Jamui.' The Voice of the Mother, silent since that first day, echoed once more in his mind. 'Stay strong. Help is near. Look for it.' Was he hallucinating again? Help? Here? Where? He had not seen another living soul since that horrific day when his village had been destroyed. Why would he come across anyone now in this cold, barren wilderness? Nevertheless, he would not give up his life without a fight. He peered into the falling dusk, shivering so hard now that he could hardly focus his eyes. Nothing.

'It is there. Trust,' the soft sing-song voice repeated. Jamui staggered on, scanning the growing darkness for any sign of salvation. There. As his knees again gave way under him, he imagined he glimpsed a flicker of light, far off to his right. Were his eyes playing tricks on him, some last cruel joke born in the desperation of his final moments? No, there it was again. Forcing himself to his feet with his last reserves of energy, Jamui turned and stumbled towards it. The faint sound of voices carried to him on the wind. People! Too soon his strength finally gave out, his knees buckled and he collapsed. But before he hit the ground a strong arm came out of the darkness and circled his waist, holding him up, supporting him as he half stumbled, was half carried towards the light. A voice shouting out, raising the alarm. Eager, concerned hands pulling him inside out of the wind, wrapping him in a thick blanket, pushing him down close to the fire. A bowl of hot steaming liquid was put in his hands but he was shaking so much he could not drink, the contents spilling with each violent spasm. He was barely holding on to consciousness and became aware that someone was cradling his head, lifting the bowl to his mouth so that he could drink, his chattering teeth rattling against its rim.

Slowly the tremors subsided, Jamui's head cleared and he could make sense of his surroundings. His saviours were watching him in amused but kindly curiosity, wondering who this naked young man was who had fallen into their midst, where on earth he had come from, and what he was doing wandering alone and unclothed in this bleak land. He was like no-one they had ever seen before with his yellow hair, pale soft skin and delicate features.

*   *   *   *   *   *   *

Jamui had been found by a family of mountain herders bringing their animals down to graze on the lower lands for the winter months. They were strong, sturdy people, short and dark both of skin and hair, who dressed warmly in thick woollen clothing woven from the fleeces of their livestock, and spoke in a language Jamui did not understand. Generous and kind-hearted, they welcomed Jamui without reservation. The father of this family, the man who had stumbled upon him, soon disappeared back outside to check on his animals, a task which had been interrupted by Jamui's appearance. The others chattered and laughed as they went about their chores and Jamui, comforted by this cosy mundanity, wrapped the blanket more tightly around himself, curled up and slept.

He woke early, roused by the sounds of a busy household preparing for the day ahead. After so long in solitude, it felt strange to be surrounded once more by the activities of normal family life. Noticing he was awake, one of the older woman – a grandmother perhaps, he wondered – held out a bundle to him with a smile. It was a pile of warm clothing. Gratefully he pulled on the thickly woven trousers and jerkin and a pair of sturdy leather boots. The unaccustomed garments felt strange against his skin, so used to its nakedness. The older woman nodded, her eyes twinkling and her toothless mouth grinning her approval.

Jamui pulled aside the flap of the tent and stepped outside. The morning air was icy and there was a hint of frost on the ground, but he was snug and warm in his new clothes. The father was there, taking a moment before his day started to cherish the beauty of the landscape around him and drink in the cold champagne air. He greeted Jamui with a wave and gestured for the young man to join him. Jamui stood beside him also in silence, not yet tired of the openness of this land and the vastness of its skies. At last the man spoke. Jamui did not understand his words but understood their meaning. Where was he heading?

Jamui pointed directly at the mountain range. North. Just as the Voice had told him so long ago. His companion shook his head forcibly. It would not be wise. Winter would soon be upon this land and already now, in early autumn, the mountains would be treacherous. Even the experienced mountain people were heading to lower ground, fearful of the unforgiving cold and the unpredictability of the weather. Someone as unfamiliar with that snow and ice-locked world as Jamui would inevitably soon perish in its vice-like grip. But even as he surveyed the grey, looming bulk of the mountain range, fear clutching at his stomach in an unrelenting warning, Jamui knew that he would follow the path that had been laid out for him back in the rainforest. There was within him an inexplicable compulsion to keep going, as if some force was drawing him irresistibly onwards. Was it the skull he carried that would not let him rest? Did she have a purpose in mind that he was not party to? Whatever the reason, he was unable to refuse its call.

A tug on his sleeve drew him back to the moment. It was one of the children, come to tell him the morning meal was ready.

*   *   *   *   *   *   *

Jamui left later that day, refusing to change his mind despite the vigorous attempts of those who had helped him to persuade him to do so. When they saw his determination, and ignoring his protests, they pressed on him food, warm blankets and a thick coat as he said his goodbyes. Guilt touched his heart at taking such hard-earned items from these generous people, understanding how much they would have laboured to create them. He had little choice, they would not take no for an answer. He was deeply grateful, knowing their generosity would likely spell the difference between survival and death for him. With the Voice safely fastened around his waist he accepted their gifts and, waving his thanks, struck out for the mountains. He did not know what to expect, was heavy with apprehension, but not once did it cross his mind to

262

turn back. Yet again he was heading into the unknown, with only Gal-Athiel to guide him.

GEMMA

Chapter 47

'It's next Saturday evening. Oh come on Gemma, what do you say? It's about time you got out and about more. You're becoming a real hermit tucked away out there in that cottage of yours.'

Cathy was right, of course. I was becoming a bit of a recluse. It wasn't that I didn't like meeting people or going out into the big, wide world, more that I loved my home so much. Enjoyed the peace and solitude that gave me the space to appreciate the beauty and feel of the countryside that surrounded me. Was so wrapped up in my writing and enjoying every creative moment of the process.

It was true though that my circle of friends had dwindled as a result of my self-imposed exile. I was becoming uncomfortably aware that when I finished this book, which would be very soon now, I would find myself with a huge empty gap in my life that I would need to fill. So, although at that moment I wanted more than anything to say no and to stay at home curled up in front of my cosy, crackling, flickering fire, instead, I said yes.

The event was a barn dance that Lou, a friend of Cathy's, was organising in aid of charity. Lou's husband Mike was a farmer and the dance was to take place in one of his barns. Now I know a barn dance isn't everyone's idea of an exciting evening out, but I love them. They are invariably good-humoured, friendly affairs where the beer and conversation flows freely in equal measure, and the air is filled with laughter as everyone falls over everyone else while attempting to negotiate complicated weaves and chains. Confusion and laughter that inevitably increases as the evening progresses, beer consumption rises and brains become even more befuddled. As soon as I'd agreed to go my recluse-self stepped aside and I started really looking forward to it.

'Brilliant.' Cathy was delighted that I had at last agreed to emerge from my cave. 'One more thing - what are you doing during the day on Saturday?'

'Why?' I was wary. Knowing Cathy as well as I did, I wasn't going to leave myself open to anything until she told me what it was.

'Lou has asked for some volunteers to help clear out the barn ready for the evening. Mike was going to do it last weekend but he's really busy on the farm at the moment. It's just shifting some junk, sweeping it out, setting up tables and what have you. I think it'll be fun – and she said she'll feed us. There will be cake.'

Well, why not? It would be something different and a chance to get my muscles working. One thing I'd noticed about writing is that it doesn't involve a lot of physical activity, and recently I had been starting to feel the effects of that. Besides which, Lou's baking was legendary.

*   *   *   *   *   *   *

At ten o'clock on Saturday morning Cathy and I were at the barn, each of us armed with wellington boots and a large broom. There were six of us there, all willing volunteers and ready for some serious work. We were not disappointed; the barn needed a bit more work than we were expecting. It was filled with junk, old logs and farming debris, much of which hadn't been moved in a very long time, and we set to with a will. Lou worked hard raising money for charity and deserved as much support as we could give her.

'Hello Gemma.' Joe appeared at my shoulder. Where had he suddenly popped up from? 'I've just dropped something off with Mike. Can't stop, I'm off out with a mate of mine, Callum, but wanted to say Hi. I'll be along later this evening though.' He indicated the doorway where a tall, thin figure stood silhouetted against the bright sunlight. I couldn't make out anything about him, he was just a black shape against the sunshine outside, but he waved at me cheerfully. I waved back. 'It would be good for you to meet him sometime, Gemma. I think you might be able to help each other out.' Then with a shouted 'cheerio' he was gone.

Mike appeared in the doorway. 'Lunchtime folks, if you're hungry.'

We didn't need telling twice and hurried up to the farmhouse. I caught sight of myself in the kitchen mirror. What a sight! I turned to Cathy and she wasn't any better. Both of us were covered in dust, our faces streaked in dirt, hair festooned in old cobwebs as neither of us had thought to bring a scarf. We looked at each other, then at the others who were gathered around the table, and both burst out laughing. We were all the same – grubby, tired and happy.

* * * * * * *

The dance was as good as it had promised to be. I laughed so much I couldn't breathe and my stomach ached; I couldn't remember the last time that had happened. Yes, much though I loved my isolated little world, it was good to be out with people and having fun again.

The only minor fly in the ointment was that I had caught Joe looking at me oddly once or twice during the evening. A couple of times I felt he was about to say something, only for him to fall silent. I wondered if anything was wrong but, knowing he would tell me in his own time if he wanted to unburden on me, I dismissed it. Nevertheless, something I couldn't put my finger on continued to niggle at the back of my mind, long after I got home.

GAL-ATHIEL: The Blue Skull

Part 4

THE FINAL JOURNEY

Chapter 48

'Father. Here. Come quickly!' The girl knelt by the side of the figure that lay motionless on the rough stones of the desert floor. He was young, scarcely older than her own fifteen summers, and barely alive. Indeed, until she noticed a faint pulse tremble in his neck she had believed him dead. He was unlike anyone she had ever seen before with pale skin, now burned fiery red by the sun, and wavy golden hair that reached to below his shoulders.

Her father, Grey Wolf, was at her side in an instant. 'Run back to the camp, Wailaila, and tell Koshe she will be needed, although I fear even her skills will not be enough. I will follow on with the boy.' Wailaila did not need to be told twice, her lithe sun-tanned limbs flying as she raced back to the encampment. Gently, easily, her father lifted the boy into his arms as though he weighed no more than a child, cradling his broken form like a baby. He moved steadily, as rapidly as he could, mindful of the urgency and the precarious knife-edge between life and death his charge was treading.

At the camp, Grey Wolf headed straight for Koshe's tepee and laid the boy on the bed she had hastily prepared for him. For the first time, he stood back and took a good look at this young stranger who had appeared in the heart of this unforgiving desert land. The boy was ill, desperately so, and seriously injured. His skin was burnt and blistered by the scorching unrelenting sun, and he was suffering from a potentially fatal level of heatstroke and dehydration. A filthy rag of animal skin wrapped around his hips was his only clothing, displaying a painfully thin body. As well as heat and thirst, this child – Grey Wolf could not help but think of him as a child, for the young man looked so young and vulnerable lying unconscious on the bed – had clearly been tormented by near starvation.

But it was his hands and feet that drew the most pity from those tending him. Several fingers and toes, as well as a good part of his left hand, were blackened and dead, the surrounding skin angry and swollen. The man recognised the signs immediately: frostbite. It was a constant fear amongst his people during the icy winter months as they trekked through the mountains hunting game. Where though could the boy have succumbed to these wounds at this time? The last snows had melted over two moons ago, unless… Could he have come down from the highest mountains? Surely that wasn't possible. They were too far away, many days' walk for even a fit, healthy man. For a boy in his condition? Surely it was impossible. But what other explanation could there be? And then the womenfolk were shooing him from the tepee as they attended to their patient and the wise woman, Koshe, mixed healing herbs into soothing salves and lotions, offering prayers to the spirits for their help and guidance.

As he left the tent, Wailaila ran up to him, her face anxious. 'How is he father? Will he live?'

'I don't know, Wailaila.' He would not lie to his daughter. 'He is gravely ill and his injuries are severe. But if anyone can make him well again, it is Koshe.' He smiled reassuringly. 'At least he has a chance now, thanks to you. You found him. If you had not…' He turned at the sound of someone approaching from the tepee. One of the women was walking towards him carrying a woven bag that held something heavy and roughly spherical, which she held out to him.

'He had this around his waist, Grey Wolf. As the Great Chief has not yet returned, would you hold it in safekeeping until he does?'

He took it from her and nodded. The bag would be kept safely – unopened and untampered with – until the

271

boy's recovery. A man's property was sacred in their eyes; not one of their people would have thought to touch another's without clear permission. This bag would be held by the Great Chief for as long as was necessary. If the boy died, it would be left with his body for him to take with him to the next world.

*　*　*　*　*　*　*

For four days and four nights Jamui hovered in that no-place that is neither life nor death. Time after time he cried out, battling imaginary demons and fleeing unknown terrors as the fever wracked him. Koshe summoned every ounce of her skill and knowledge to keep him walking on the Earth, and the shaman was called to travel deep into the dangers of the lower world in order to retrieve the splinters of the boy's fractured soul. Towards noon of the fifth day, in answer to everyone's prayers, he woke and the fever had left him, although he was still desperately ill. Even breathing exhausted him. He was immediately aware that his precious bundle was no longer with him and he fought to get up, his eyes darting everywhere in a panic-driven search. He was so weak, however, that he could not lift his head from the pillow, and the slightest movement sent excruciating darts of pain through his scorched skin and damaged limbs. Spent, he fell back into a restless but natural sleep.

When he awoke, Wailaila was sitting on the ground beside him and with her she had the bag that contained the Voice of the Mother. She smiled at this blond stranger whose colouring was so different from her own dark skin and straight jet black hair. 'Hello. I've brought your belongings back to you now that you are awake.'

Once again the words were a meaningless jumble to his ears, so alien to his own tongue, but he heard the kindness held in them and smiled back at Wailaila as she

272

set the bag by his shoulder. His blue eyes – which she had not seen until this moment, and which were as vivid as the sky that soared above her land – bewitched and thrilled her, and her heart began to beat a little bit faster. He was beautiful, even now, lying there so frail and pallid. A wave of sadness touched her own eyes as she took in his ravaged body. It was a sadness that would not leave her. He would not be with them for long.

*   *   *   *   *   *   *

From that moment Wailaila was constantly by Jamui's side, helping him to eat and drink, teaching him her language and learning some words of his, walking by his litter as they moved their camp across the desert, following the herds of bison and antelope. His wounds were slowly healing, and yet he was growing weaker by the day. There was no obvious reason, and Koshe too was at a loss as to why he was not recovering. It was as if he had given up the will to live. There was a simple explanation, although they were in ignorance of it; his internal organs had been so damaged that they were unable to recover. Little by little they were shutting down. The boy knew he was dying and did not resist. His journey from the rainforest had been long and arduous and he was too tired. He had brought The Voice to safety – these people would protect and honour her now – and he could let go. He did not fight it.

*   *   *   *   *   *   *

In the early hours of the morning, less than three moons after he arrived in their midst, Jamui whispered Wailaila's name. Koshe hurried to wake the girl; his time had come. Wailaila was joined at his bedside by many who had grown to love this good natured golden-haired youth who had been with them so short a time. Amongst them was White Raven, Great Chief of the tribe.

Tears tricked down Wailaila's face as she knelt beside the boy. He raised his hand with difficulty, for it cost him a huge effort, and lightly brushed them away. Then, in halting uncertain words, offered in the language of Wailaila's people, his weakened voice barely above a whisper, he spoke.

'Thank you Wailaila. Thank you for finding me and bringing me here. Thank you for helping me to find what I was searching for.' He touched the bag that lay beside him. 'This is a treasure beyond price. A treasure that must be used wisely and with integrity. Your people will do so. You are beautiful, Wailaila. Beautiful and kind and good. I ask you to become its guardian and, when your time finally comes, to hand it on to your successor. Take it, please.'

Wailaila hesitated, but she saw the pleading look in his eyes and reached across to take the bag.

'Open it, Wailaila.' She unwrapped the binding and peered inside, an involuntary gasp escaping her lips as she saw what it held. Slowly she withdrew its contents and the blue skull emerged into the firelight. A murmur of amazement and wonder ran through those present. 'This is the Voice of the Mother,' the boy continued, each word fainter than the last, the effort they were costing him written in his face. 'Speak with her, listen to her and let her guide you. She has much power. Use it wisely.'

Wailaila stared at the boy in fear and confusion. 'I-I-I can't. I don't know how. There must be someone else…'

She looked at White Raven for help but he merely nodded. 'He has chosen you, Wailaila. He has his reasons. You must honour his request.' She looked down at the blue skull resting in her lap. It seemed to be surrounded in a glowing golden light, and something else as well – a warmth, a strength, emanating from the skull, flowing into her body bringing an understanding and familiarity that came from she didn't know where. Her resistance lifted as she saw clearly that this was the path she had always been destined to take.

Gal-Athiel's sweet voice spoke to Jamui for the last time. 'You have chosen well, little one. Sleep now.' He slipped softly and gratefully into death's gentle embrace.

Chapter 49

Wailaila allowed the sorrow and loss welling up within her to break free. Tears flowed down her lined, still down-soft cheeks and dripped onto her tunic. She did not wipe them away. This had to be. She had to allow herself to grieve. It was a healing, a closure and a farewell.

It had been over sixty years since she had found the golden boy lying in the desert. Over sixty years since he had placed Gal-Athiel, whom she had always known only as The Voice of the Mother, in her care. From that day, she had watched over and protected the blue skull, learned her secrets and wisdom, shared her guidance with the people who had prospered and thrived under her love. And now she had to let her go. It was so hard, but Wailaila knew there was no choice.

Over the past four moons she had begun to dream more vividly than ever. Powerful dreams. Disturbing dreams. Dreams that quickly turned into nightmares. Dreams that carried a message for her and for those whom she loved. Of men who had travelled across vast expanses of water, setting foot on this land – men with pale skin like the golden boy – coming at first in friendship, friendship that would later turn to anger and violence. Of exploding sticks that killed from a distance. Of the destruction of her land and the people who had lived on it since before memory. Of war and bloodshed. Of her people lying dead and bleeding on the red sand of the desert, or driven from their ancient homelands, starving and dispossessed.

Although Wailaila knew these dreams held a warning, she did not know what she was to do about them, so one morning she had taken The Voice and made her way slowly to a small clear pool at the base of a low, sparkling waterfall – a rare oasis in the heart of this scorched desert. There she had bathed, the clean, pure water caressing and healing her frail, aged body, cleansing and purifying her spirit. Bringing the blue skull into its waters with her to be cleansed likewise. Afterwards, seated on a flat rock in the warm sunshine, she had taken The Voice in her lap and allowed the skull's energy to merge with her own. 'What does it mean Mother? What must I do?'

'It is coming and it cannot be stopped.' The sweet tones of The Voice had filled her mind. 'They are already on their way. These newcomers do not understand the ways of Spirit as your people do. They do not understand the connection, the One-ness of all. So they will come, in good faith and genuine friendship at first, but as more come, so this will change. Greed and power will grow and overthrow the peace and co-operation between you. Life will be hard. The people of this land will suffer much in times to come.

'I was brought to this world to help the evolution and understanding of the human race, but I cannot speak to those who will not hear – and those who are coming will not wish to hear. If they find me then it is not just I who will be in danger; the future of all humankind will be in peril. Many of those who come will not understand my purpose, and because they do not understand, they will fear me and seek to destroy me. Those who do understand will fight to possess me in order to use my power to fulfil their desire for greed and control.

'Wailaila, my beloved guardian, I ask you now, please take me to a place where none will find me. Keep me safely hidden there until the day comes when all of humanity is ready to hear what we have to teach you.'

Wailaila had listened, and she had heard the truth in the blue skull's words. The moment she returned to the camp she asked to speak with the great Chief and elder of the tribe, Bright Eagle.

*   *   *   *   *   *   *

Wailaila stood in front of Bright Eagle and waited.

'You speak wisely Wailaila,' he said at last. 'We must give up The Voice, sacrifice our beautiful Mother, as she asks of us. Who though do we entrust with this most important of tasks?' It was almost unheard of for a chief to ask the advice of a woman on such matters, but Wailaila was far from being an ordinary woman. In the years that she had been the skull's guardian she had gained a wisdom, insight and knowledge that far exceeded that of even the old Chief himself. Bright Eagle trusted her judgement completely.

'Takuanaka.' The reply was unhesitating. 'He is strong, loyal and courageous. And he will welcome the opportunity.'

Takuanaka. Bright Eagle's heart saddened at the choice, even as he knew it to be the right one. He had always held a deep affection and respect for the younger man, watching as the rebellious, hot-headed child grew into a strong and generous man, a brave, honourable hunter and warrior with an infectious passion and hunger for life. Until… The old man's eyes clouded with sorrow even now at the memory. Takuanaka and his beloved Dancing Star, twin souls destined, so they believed, for a long and blissful life together. Only for her to have been stolen from him so cruelly within a few short months of their wedding day.

Takuanaka had believed himself doubly blessed when he heard about the child, a gift that the Great Spirit had unexpectedly granted to them so soon after their union. Although it was the way of their people to keep their feelings to themselves, no-one could fail to notice the extra spring in his step and shine in his eyes. His joyful spirit was contagious.

278

When her time came, Dancing Star had slipped away quietly from the camp to bring this new soul into the world in the stillness and purity of the desert, surrounded by the spirits of the earth and the ancestors. But it did not go well, and her screams woke the camp. A desperate search had found her just after daybreak, sightless eyes watching the new sun rising over the horizon, her contorted body lying in a pool of her own blood. Between her legs, by some miracle alive, lay the child.

After that morning, Takuanaka was a changed man who recklessly – and unsuccessfully – pursued his own death at every opportunity. Whereas he had once been a thoughtful and calculating warrior and hunter, now he rushed in with no forethought or heed for his own safety and survival, or for that of those who fought alongside him.

The child, a boy, was raised by Takuanaka's sister. Despite the tragedy and difficulties of his birth, he was a strong lusty child who thrived and grew rapidly and who was blessed with the same rebellious streak and stubbornness as his father. But Takuanaka ignored the boy, unable to face such a clear reminder of his cherished wife's death. So the boy never knew that Takuanaka was his father, was never told, was taken in to his aunt's family as one of her own as Takuanaka remained locked in the dark prison of his grief. Takuanaka had never shed the tears of his grieving and pain, never shown them to those around him, but inwardly they consumed him relentlessly, ravaging his spirit, robbing him of reason. All he desired was to be reunited with his Dancing Star.

Though he would never admit it, it had saddened Bright Eagle beyond endurance to see this once alive and passionate man build a wall around himself to shut out the world. He knew that hidden there still was the good and honourable man he had once known. Yes, Wailaila was right. It must be Takuanaka. This way he would find, without stain or dishonour, the resolution he had been chasing for so long. This way, he would be given the opportunity to end his torment. Bright Eagle knew he would seize it gratefully.

Chapter 50

The drum began to sound its slow steady heartbeat. Unchanging. Hypnotic. Little by little drawing all those present into its rhythmic spell. One by one, other drums joined in. Drum upon drum. Rhythm upon rhythm. Heartbeat upon heartbeat. Its intensity building and then falling, only to rise again stronger than before, echoing through each body, seeping into every cell. The air reverberating with the deep primal pulse.

A sense of anticipation rippled through the assembled group as the drumbeat reached a crescendo and then, as suddenly as it had begun, fell still. An expectant silence settled on the camp. The children, clustered together on one side of the circle, stood in wary excitement, hardly daring to breathe as they waited in awe and wonder for what would happen next. There. They grabbed at each other wordlessly, pointing.

From a large tepee at the rear of the camp, a procession of women was making its way slowly towards the circle. They came in twos, young women and old – mothers, daughters, grandmothers – singing a low melodic chant as they walked. In their midst, one woman walked alone. She was Wailaila, elder of this group, the wise woman who had seen more than seventy summers, a venerable age that few in these tribes accomplished. Her hair was grey, and the hardships of her years were etched in the lines on her face and the slowness of her steps, but her eyes were still those of a girl. Soft, clear, laughing, and filled with love for her people.

She carried with her a pillow made of soft antelope hide on which rested a life-sized skull, skilfully and delicately carved from pale sea blue obsidian, every detail accurate from the finely chiselled sutures of the skull

281

plates to the complex delicacy of the jaw joints. This was the Voice of the Mother, the precious treasure that had been passed to this people so many years ago.

The procession had reached the perimeter of the circle. Here the pairs of women parted, moving to stand around its outer edge until Wailaila stood alone. Slowly, she came forward, the women's soft song accompanying her as she approached Bright Eagle. With some difficulty she knelt before him and carefully laid the pillow at his feet. Then, at his nod of acceptance, she rose stiffly to her feet once more and returned to where her sisters were waiting.

*   *   *   *   *   *   *

Bright Eagle stood before the blue skull that glittered at his feet in the torrid sunshine of the desert afternoon. He too was old, older even than Wailaila, but he still held himself tall and erect, a proud man who wore his undisputed power and authority in a shimmering cloak around him. It was clear to those who had gathered here that this occasion was of huge importance. Never before had the Voice been paraded with such ceremony and solemnity.

The chief raised his arms, commanding attention, his eyes surveying those gathered before him. In a clear, still powerful, resonant voice he began to speak.

'My people, for over sixty summers we have held in our lives and in our hearts a gift from the Great Spirit, brought to us by the Golden Child. That gift is our cherished Voice of the Mother. She has taught us and guided us well, but the time has come for her to leave us. She has spoken to us for the final time, and in those final words was a request. A request that we allow her to leave us that she may be safely hidden from those who would wish her harm.'

Although no-one spoke Bright Eagle sensed the consternation rippling through the crowd at his words. He gestured for calm.

'It must be so, although it saddens all our hearts to say farewell. The Voice has foretold that one day soon our people will face much hardship and troubled times. These times cannot be avoided, simply endured. She has told that strangers will come. Strangers whose hearts are not open to the unseen worlds as ours are. Who cannot see or feel the magic and mystery of the Great Spirit.

'Our wisdom, our understanding of the world we live in, of the Great Spirit, will fade, but we must hold strong to the belief that it will not be lost forever. For one day it will be needed, will be recognised and accepted. One day, many generations in the future, the descendants of those who come to crush us now will call us friend and brother, and will in their turn understand the truth of what we know. We must wait patiently for that day to come.

'For in the times that face us, they will not honour or respect our beloved Voice. They will not do so because they do not and will not understand. Because they do not understand, they will fear her and try to destroy her. This cannot be, so we must let her go.'

The crowd listened to Bright Eagle's words with sadness and a not a little apprehension. The Voice's wisdom had served them well. None knew how they would fare without her presence, which for most of them had been a constant comfort in their sometimes difficult lives. Through Wailaila, she had taught them to deepen their already strong connection to the world around them, to see things invisible to their physical eyes and gather information from the unseen energy of a person or place, shown them the power of the mind to heal and to create. From today she would no longer be there for them.

Bright Eagle was still speaking. 'Her destination will be known to only one man, the one in whose care she will be placed, and he will reveal it to no-one. None will follow him and the council has decreed that anyone doing so will forfeit his life as punishment. He who has been chosen to safeguard the future of the Voice is Takuanaka.'

The crowd stirred and parted as Takuanaka stepped forward, crossing the empty circle to stand before his Chief. He was a commanding figure. Tall, even by his people's standards, strongly built, and still heart-meltingly handsome, even with the hard lines of loss etched into his face. But he carried with him a heaviness of spirit and an aloof, almost arrogant air, that kept people at a distance.

The crowd exchanged wordless glances. Where once Takuanaka had been the most popular of men, his later recklessness and volatility, though their cause was understood, had lost him the friendship and respect of many of those gathered there. None however would dare question Bright Eagle's decision.

'I call upon you, my people, to sit now with our Mother for one last time, to say your farewells and spend these last hours sharing her company and her love.' The Chief knelt then in front of the Voice of the Mother, bowing his head in respect and honour. Takuanaka did the same. One by one, all those present followed suit, opening their hearts and spirits to the love and peace that emanated without end from the beautiful ocean blue skull. One by one, from the oldest grandfather to the youngest child, they approached her, laying before her gifts of feathers, flowers and crystals in gratitude and blessing. Whispering their prayers and thanks.

*   *   *   *   *   *   *

As the first rays of dawn lightened the eastern skies, Bright Eagle took the Voice in both hands and raised her high above his head, feeling her powerful energy surging through his body as he did so.

284

'Father Sky. Mother Earth. Great Spirit. We call on you now to watch over and protect our beloved Voice of the Mother. Hold her in your arms until such time as she returns to the people of the Earth.' He turned to Takuanaka. 'Takuanaka. You have been chosen as the new guardian of the Voice of the Mother. Her safety – and the future – is in your hands. Take her and go now with our blessings.'

Takuanaka bowed his head in acknowledgement as he received the Voice from Bright Eagle's hands, then wordlessly turned and retraced his steps through the circle as the hushed crowd watched him leave.

Chapter 51

In that early morning light Takuanaka walked out of the camp. He took neither food nor water, only his hunting knife tucked into his belt, a rough woven blanket and an antelope skin bag, both of which were slung over his shoulder. In the bag, carefully wrapped in soft furs, lay the blue skull, The Voice of the Mother.

Takuanaka did not yet know his destination. It would be revealed to him during his coming vision quest. For this night and for as long as it took, he would sit alone, silent and unmoving, on the high rocky outcrop that stood sentinel at the end of this vast valley, waiting for the sign from the spirits that would lead him forward. Only then would he know the final resting place of the Voice. A place the spirits had chosen and would protect from discovery for as long as necessary. He did not concern himself with fears that he could be followed for he would leave no tracks. He was a skilled and experienced warrior who had learned to walk silently upon the earth.

This land was dry and barren, a rocky desert where little grew. His tribe were nomads, following the herds of game – mostly bison and antelope – that sustained them and provided for almost all of their needs. It was a parched land, baked hard by a fierce pitiless sun that could kill the careless or the inexperienced within a day or two. But Takuanaka knew this country, had been raised in its stark savage beauty. He knew how and where to find water and food where none could be found, to navigate by the sun and the stars, and to listen to the guidance and signs of his ancestors. He was strong, not yet old, and the gruelling trek through the dusty oven-hot desert did not touch him.

For several hours he walked at a swift but steady pace until at last he reached the foot of the bluff. It towered above him, its dark silhouette imposing and intimidating against the clear, deep blue of the afternoon sky. Steep boulder blanketed slopes gave way here and there to crumbling vertical cliffs and stomach lurching overhangs.

There was no obvious – and certainly no easy – route to the top. Takuanaka's feet slipped constantly on the loose, precariously balanced scree, threatening at every step to send him plummeting back down to the valley floor, a fall which at best would result in several broken bones. It was early evening when he finally reached his chosen site, his leg muscles cracking with exhaustion, his breath coming in rapid gasps from his exertions. It was right on the edge of a narrow spur that pushed out from the main bulk of the bluff, which at this point fell away in an almost sheer drop of several hundred feet. Nothing impeded the view to the front and sides, so that Takuanaka looked out at an uninterrupted panorama. The crag faced west, direction of the setting sun, of endings, of moving into darkness. He had deliberately chosen it for those very reasons.

Takuanaka sat crossed legged on the ground and pulled the blanket closely around his shoulders. The light was fading, and with the dusk came a biting cold which, already noticeable, would intensify as the night progressed. In front of him the setting sun was turning the sky to flame. Rich gold and vibrant orange danced with deep pink and soft lilac, constantly yet imperceptibly melting and merging through each other, flowing around the fiery red sphere that was slowly sinking below the distant horizon. As the last of its rays abruptly disappeared, extinguishing the dazzling kaleidoscope display in the sky, a sudden and total blackness fell. Slowly his eyes adjusted to the transition, and the night was suddenly lit by millions of tiny pinpricks of light, its radiance rivalling that of the recent sunset. But where that had been vibrant and alive, the incandescent swansong of a dying day, this was a quiet, cool, serene beauty. Diamond flakes glittering on a backcloth of deep indigo velvet.

Takuanaka had already taken the bag from his shoulders and laid it by his side on the rough ground. He would not be using the skull's wisdom this time. His guidance would come from another source – from the spirits of this place, of nature and the elements, and from his ancestors. He closed his eyes and began to sing a low rhythmic chant, invoking their help and guidance in the way his people had done for generations. When the prayer finished, he slowed his breath and opened his senses fully, so that he would be ready receive their answer when it came. And then he waited.

For a short while, silence settled over the world. Gradually, hesitantly, the sounds of the night awoke. He was aware of the small animals that scuffled around him as he sat motionless. Insects chirruped and buzzed. He heard the cry of owls and other night birds, the roar of a distant mountain lion.

Slowly the night passed. Takuanaka did not know how long it would be before the spirits came to him, only that it would not be until his own spirit was ready to receive them. So, unmoving, he waited patiently. As he did all the following day and night. Not moving, not eating, not drinking. Just waiting, silently absorbed in his vigil, maintaining his awareness. Feeling, listening, searching, with all of his inner senses.

*　*　*　*　*　*　*

By the evening of the second day he was much weakened physically. Two full days in the searing heat with no food or liquid had dehydrated his body, and the night spent in sub-zero temperatures with just a blanket for protection had also taken its toll. His limbs were cramping from their immobility, his joints and muscles screaming their protest.

288

Still he sat and waited, unwavering and impassive. Still no sign appeared.

*   *   *   *   *   *   *

On the third night she came to him. Walking towards him through the starlit sky, taking him in her arms. He could taste her spicy sweetness. Breathe her delicate scent. Feel her gentle hands on his face, caressing and soothing him. His Dancing Star. She was as real as she had ever been in life and as she kissed him tenderly he felt the love and desire rise in him.

He scarcely dared to breathe in case she melted away into the moonlight once more. Then he was holding her, touching her. With hands that shook, he unfastened her tunic so that it slipped from her shoulders and she stood naked before him, smiling at him in that half-shy, half-teasing way that had always melted his heart and fuelled his passion. She moved to him, loosening his own garments so that they too fell to the floor. Kissing him, hungry for his lips and the taste of him, pressed hard against him, flesh on flesh, setting his skin on fire. Reaching for him, her cool fingers enfolding him, their firm softness arousing him more.

Neither of them had spoken and no words were necessary. Their eyes whispered their love and need. It was as if they had never been separated and he could hold back no longer. Gently he lifted her and laid her on his blanket. His hands, his eyes, his tongue explored every inch of her, lightly tracing every line and curve of her adored and so familiar body. He felt her tremble as waves of pleasure pulsed through her, her breath coming in ragged gasps as his tongue traced her hot swollen depths. Sensing her eager hunger and desire as she opened to him, his own need for her growing beyond bearable.

Then her mouth was on him, teasing, licking, stroking until he grew so hard and full that he felt he would explode. He did not want this to end, never wanted it to end, but he could hold on no longer. With a gentle roughness he pushed her to the ground, his mouth demanding, hungry on hers, seeking to lose himself in her once again. And she responded, taking him in her hand, guiding him into her with an urgency to match his own. He lost all sense of the world around him as she opened to take him into herself, and he felt her hot pulsing need to engulf and absorb him, heard her gasping shuddering ecstasy as he thrust deeply into her, sinking into her hot moist depths, all sense of himself dissolving.

Entwined in each other they became as one, rising and falling together, moving in harmony, oblivious to everything outside of their lovemaking. To everything beyond their desperate all-consuming need for each other. Time stood still and the world around them stopped. As the flame exploded within them, engulfing and overwhelming all other sensation, they reached their climax and the night sky echoed to the sounds of their release.

*   *   *   *   *   *   *

His senses reeling, his body trembling, Takuanaka became aware of his surroundings once more. He had not moved. He was still sitting motionless in the darkness of the outcrop... and she was gone.

But she had come to him. It had been real, he knew that. For the first time since her death he allowed the grief to consume him, allowed himself to endure it and fully give himself up to it. Allowed the tears to come and flow unchecked down his face, and his heart to break. When it was over, he recognised that he had experienced a cleansing. A release. And in doing so he had awakened a deeper understanding of what lay ahead of him. In that moment he knew that his wait was almost over.

Chapter 52

As dawn rose, Eagle came, soaring high above him on the
early morning thermal currents, at first only a speck
against the pale watery blue of the new sky, drawing closer
until he hovered right above where Takuanaka sat. Eagle
would lead him, had come to show him the way.
Takuanaka still did not know where he was going, but
Eagle would take him there. He simply had to follow.
'Thank you, Brother Eagle,' he whispered. 'I will follow
where you lead.'

It was time to leave, to set out on the next stage of his
journey. He knew now. Knew that he would be guided
each step of the way. Knew that he would find the place
that he was looking for. Knew too that at the end, she
would be waiting for him. He felt alive and strong, at
peace for the first time since she had been taken from him.

He got stiffly to his feet, his muscles rebelling
painfully at the movement, for he had been sitting in the
same position for two full days and three long nights. But
he was steady on his feet, all traces of hunger and
dehydration gone. Dancing Star's spirit had revived him,
given him the strength he needed to go on. He would have
to find water soon, but for now he could continue his
journey.

He looked up as a shadow tracked across his vision.
Eagle was there, waiting for him, impatient to start. 'I'm
coming, Brother Eagle. Lead on.' With that thought, as
restless to start the journey as Eagle, Takuanaka threw the
blanket over his shoulder, picked up his precious bundle
once more and set off out into the desert.

For four days he walked; all the time Eagle flew just
ahead of him, guiding his footsteps. Ever deeper into the
stony, arid landscape he pushed, finding water and food

where he could, resting briefly from the ceaseless assault of the midday sun only when his body insisted. They were heading towards a range of low hills that lay strung out like beads across the far horizon. They had to be his destination, but would he find in them the sanctuary he sought? It had to be so, or Eagle would not be leading him here.

It was a further day's walk before Takuanaka reached the lowest slopes. The hills were not large but they had a forbidding air: desolate slabs of crumbling brown sandstone stacked one above the other, ravaged by the wind and the extremes of temperature that had assaulted them for millennia. Here and there a dark shadow marked the entrance to an underground chamber. There were caves here, that was a good sign. He felt it was a cave he was looking for... but which one? He had to trust he would be guided. The spirits had drawn him to this place. The spirits would show him the way forwards from here.

A high-pitched whistling cry drew his attention. Eagle was calling him, but where was he? Takuanaka's eyes searched the landscape. There, on a small outcrop far off to his right. He followed the cry, slipping and sliding on the loose surface. As he drew nearer he could see a low opening in the hillside, right beneath where Eagle rested. Takuanaka closed his eyes and opened his inner senses. Was this the place he sought? An unmistakeable 'Yes' flooded through his body. He drew a deep breath. He had found it.

Takuanaka dropped the bundle of scrub he had gathered over the past days as he journeyed through the desert and surveyed his haul. It was meagre; wood and brush were scarce in this parched landscape. In the fading daylight he scoured the hillsides for more but there was little to be found. Once he had bundled up his supply into rough torches he saw that it was barely enough for six. But he had taken all there was. To find more he would have to spend many extra hours searching deeper into the surrounding high ground with no guarantee of success. In addition, night was already falling and any further scavenging would have to wait for the following day. It was time he was not prepared to waste. Now that he was here and the reality of his task was before him, he simply wanted to get on with it.

Six torches. Would that be enough? He didn't know. Didn't know for how long they would burn. Didn't know how far beneath the ground he would have to travel until he found a safe hiding place for the skull. Well, six torches were all he had. Six torches would have to suffice.

*　　*　　*　　*　　*　　*　　*

With night settling around him, Takuanaka clambered up to the dark opening in the hillside. This was it. His heart was pounding. Standing there before the cave mouth, he was standing before his own death. There was a dryness in his mouth and a clammy dampness on his palms. He was not afraid of dying. Indeed, over the last five years since Dancing Star had travelled to be with the ancestors he had actively – and unsuccessfully – hunted it. Nevertheless, faced now with its certainty, preparing to walk towards it with cold deliberation, he could not prevent the apprehension rising within him. This would be no warrior's death in the heat and passion of battle, but a slow, lingering, and solitary end.

Dancing Star. Her lovely face filled his mind as if in response to his summons. She would be waiting for him, of that he had no doubt. She had come to him during his vigil to bring him the strength to do this. To remind him that she was there, her arms open, impatient to hold him. Calling him to her once more.

With no further hesitation he struck a spark and the bone dry scrub torch blazed immediately into life. Ducking under the entrance, he stepped inside the cave. It was wide and deep but low, its roof scarcely higher than Takuanaka's head. He could stand upright, but only just.

Cautiously he moved further into the cave, mindful that this would be the perfect lair for a wolf or mountain lion. Thankfully, no warning growl greeted his intrusion. He began to circle the cave's perimeter, searching for some passageway that would allow him to push on deeper under the ground. As he neared the back wall, a sudden draught of cold air flared the torch flame. Thrusting the torch ahead of him, Takuanaka peered through its flickering light. The opening he was seeking was here somewhere. There, a black shadow in the wall, running from the roof almost to the floor. It was a narrow cleft, which Takuanaka struggled to squeeze through even sideways. To his relief, after a few feet it widened into another small chamber. It was a relief that was short-lived as his torch revealed a further two openings facing him. Which way now?

'Left.' A musical whisper sang in his head. He stopped, startled. 'Take the left passageway, Takuanaka,' it repeated.

'Who are you?' Even as he uttered the question, he knew the answer. His back had grown unnaturally warm where the bag rested against it, and he could feel waves of powerful energy pulsing through his body.

'Yes,' the whisper confirmed. 'I am Gal-Athiel, she who you call the Voice of the Mother. I will guide you now, if you will listen.'

'I am listening.' Takuanaka was too taken aback to say more. The Voice had only ever communicated through Wailaila, the chosen guardian. In their history, no-one else had ever connected with her.

'Just because I did not, does not mean I cannot.' It was as if she had read his mind and he could sense the amusement in her words. 'There were reasons. Now it is important that I communicate with you, to lead you to our destination.'

Chapter 53

The cave system was a labyrinth of inter-tangled passageways, dead ends and steep inclines. Tunnels branched off tunnels that branched off tunnels. Takuanaka made no effort to record his route. He would not be leaving this place. He was certain that it would have been an impossible task even if he had tried. Deeper and deeper they went, ever downwards, until they had to be far beneath the desert floor. He lit the final torch. He would not have light for much longer and when it went out he would be completely blind, yet still they went on, the Voice guiding him whenever they reached a fork in the path.

The torch sputtered ominously as at last the passage opened out into a small, almost circular chamber. They had arrived. This was to be their destination. As Takuanaka walked to the centre of the space the last flames flickered and died. He was left in total darkness. But a few seconds later, as his eyes adjusted, he realised he could see. The immediate blindness that had struck him as the torch went out had passed and he could now clearly make out the contours of the cave. Lifting his hand, its silhouette was just visible against the floor. The light was dim, certainly, but it was enough to see by. Where was it coming from? He was far underground. No daylight could penetrate here.

As his eyes grew more accustomed to the gloom, Takuanaka realised that the light was coming from within the cave itself. The walls and roof were emitting a faint greenish glow. He did not know how, could not know that it was coming from a form of phosphorescent mineral embedded within the bedrock itself. Although ignorant of its source, Takuanaka offered his heartfelt thanks to

Mother Earth for providing him with this blessing. Brave and stoical though he was, the prospect of sitting in Stygian blackness for he knew not how many days as he waited for death to claim him had unnerved him more than he had realised. Only now, when its spectre had passed, did he allow himself to feel this fear. Even this pale, eerie luminescence would make it more tolerable.

It took Takuanaka only a few moments to explore the small room. The tunnel through which he had entered was its only opening; the remaining walls and roof were smooth, solid bedrock. The floor was sandy, a memory of its long distant past as the underground reservoir whose long gone waters had carved out the rounded contours of the chamber. To his left, at chest height, ran a narrow natural ledge – an obvious resting place for the blue skull.

He took a deep breath. It was time. Delay would not serve him. Kneeling on the hard floor, he closed his eyes and called in the spirits of his ancestors to bless and guide him. Then, with the handle of the spent torch, he traced a circle on the floor and divided it into quarters. He was creating a simple medicine wheel, allowing himself to be led by the spirits who surrounded him, feeling for the directions with his senses and marking them with small stones collected from the cave's perimeter. The centre he left bare. This is where he would keep vigil and await his death.

Takuanaka's voice rang rich and deep, the sing-song chant of his prayers echoing through the underground labyrinth as he invoked once more the ancestors and spirits of the earth, calling on them to protect and watch over the Voice as she sheltered here. Then he reached into the antelope skin bag and drew her from it, unwrapping the protective furs that had cushioned her throughout this final journey.

This time, as he laid his hands on her, he staggered. As his skin came into contact with her, impossible amounts of energy unexpectedly surged through his hands and up his arms, then flowed back down through his body to the ground. He hadn't experienced this when he had carried her from the camp. Steadying himself against this pulsating tide of power, Takuanaka gazed into the heart of the skull lying in his hands. The greenish glow of the cave had deepened her colour to a rich ocean blue. Within her depths, flashing light danced through the solid crystal of the brain cavity, forming into flickering patterns and symbols that came and went again before his mind could grasp them. As he stared into her empty eye sockets he was shocked to feel a deep compassion flowing to him, enveloping him, and he felt himself falling... falling... By a huge effort of will, Takuanaka wrenched his consciousness back to himself and his surroundings, tearing his eyes from her compelling, hollow gaze. Unsettled, he quickly set the skull onto the ledge and took his place in the centre of his drawn circle. He would not move again from this spot.

He had neither food nor water with him and he knew death would not come quickly or gently. He was no longer afraid. He would endure, as he had endured the last five painful, endless years. Whatever he faced now could not test him more than that had done.

*　*　*　*　*　*　*

'Takuanaka, look at me.' The soft lilting voice filled his head. No. He would not. She would not cast her spell on him again. 'Takuanaka.' It was gentle and compassionate but commanding, enfolding him as a mother's love enfolds her child. 'Takuanaka.' Persuasive, encouraging. A compulsion he was unable to resist drew his eyes to the skull once more, locking them onto hers, empty of flesh, yet somehow so vital and alive.

299

'I am Gal-Athiel, skull of Theta. I am compassion and I am creation. But know this. That which holds to power to create also holds the power to destroy. For creation is always a beginning, and a beginning must always be born of an ending.

'I bring you now that gift. The gift of an ending from which the new may arise. The gift you have been seeking for so long. And in your ending and your beginning, you will know my truth.'

As her words faded into the unearthly glimmer of the cave, a crushing pressure surrounded Takuanaka's head. His forehead blazed, a white hot shaft of light penetrating his brow at that sacred point where the unseen becomes visible. Dazzling brilliance exploded inside his head. As it faded, there in front of him stood a breathtakingly beautiful woman, shimmering and ethereal. He felt that if he reached out his hand to touch her, she would simply dissolve into the air.

She was tall, taller than him, and slender, with long, silken hair the colour of ripening corn. Her eyes were a pale sea blue, the same colour as... She smiled wordlessly, a slight nod her only acknowledgement that he had indeed understood. She was the essence of Gal-Athiel, the living consciousness that was embodied within the blue skull.

She reached out to him and her slim, delicate fingers brushed his temples like a cooling breeze, resting there so lightly that he could barely feel them. 'Go now Takuanaka. Your work here is finished. Leave here and move forward into your new beginning.'

The strength began to seep from him, draining from every pore, every cell, soaking into the sandy floor beneath him. He swayed, no longer able to hold himself upright, and slumped heavily to the ground. This was the end. Death was coming to claim him, bringing with it the relief he had been pursuing for so long. As his vision faded and he slipped further into unconsciousness, comforting arms surrounded him, holding him tightly, softly whispered words telling him he was not alone. Dancing Star had kept her promise. She had come to meet him. Without a backwards glance, he let go of all that he had known and walked with her into a brand new world.

Chapter 54

The two skulls, Gileada and Gal-Athiel, still lie where they were hidden so long ago. Deep in the heart of the Earth, far from the light and warmth of the sun, they wait patiently, knowing the when the time is right they will be revealed to the world once more.

Eleven others too lie scattered across the surface of this planet, biding their time. Some, like Gileada and Gal-Athiel, have been lost and forgotten, their whereabouts unknown. Others, though very few, are held in the care of ancient bloodlines and societies, who have sworn to keep their existence a secret until the time of awakening comes.

That time is nearly upon us. The ancient skulls are once more making contact with those who are willing to listen, as our blossoming consciousness allows us to hear their call once more. Soon, those who have been chosen will notice the clues that are filtering into the world, clues that will lead to these skulls. Then is the moment they will be brought back into the light.

GEMMA

Chapter 55

I had finished it! I was doing a full-on happy dance around the kitchen to celebrate, jigging around in delight at my achievement. The final word had been transcribed onto my laptop and the book (well, the first draft at least) was complete. I had revised it and reviewed it, re-revised it and re-reviewed it, and as far as I was concerned it was ready to go. I was bathed in a feeling of satisfaction and accomplishment unlike anything I had ever experienced before.

The next step was to find myself a publisher. The big question was, would anyone actually want to read it? Was it really any good? I thought so, although I was hardly coming at it from an unbiased position. Before I even thought about submitting it to anyone, though, it would be sensible to conscript some people to read it and give me honest feedback. Cathy was eager to contribute her views and I was thrilled and immensely grateful for her unwavering belief in me. But she had been bubbling over with enthusiasm and support for it from the beginning, so while her praise was exactly what my lack of self-belief needed to shore itself up, and I very much appreciated it, to be honest I also recognised that she was totally prejudiced in my favour and could never be completely objective. I needed someone who wouldn't be afraid to tell me openly (but gently, please) if it was complete rubbish.

So I asked Joe, and to my delight he agreed. He had been a pillar of support too, but I knew he wouldn't hold back from giving me an honest opinion and constructive criticism. If something didn't work, he would tell me so. I had only ever shown him one small section before, and he leapt at the opportunity to read it in its entirety before anyone else set eyes on it. I jumped straight in the car and drove over to his flat where I proudly presented him with the bulging manuscript. He looked impressed.

'Come on.' He laid the folder on the coffee table. 'I've got all of tomorrow free so I'll be able to spend all day on it and give it the time it deserves. Tonight I'm taking you out to dinner to mark this memorable occasion.' I glanced down at myself. I was wearing a pair of old jeans and a tatty sweatshirt I'd thrown on that morning so I was hardly dressed for it but what the hell. I didn't get invited to dinner every day (well, let's face it, at all!) so I wasn't going to turn this opportunity down. And after all, it was something to celebrate.

Joe treated me to a first class dinner and a thoroughly enjoyable evening. We drank a toast to the book's future success (and to finding a publisher willing to take it on), and had fun speculating where that success might lead. We laughed and joked, and mulled over what was happening in our lives. As usual, Joe was easy, relaxed company, and yet... I couldn't shake the feeling that, despite his smiles and teasing, he had something on his mind.

*   *   *   *   *   *   *

It was late when we left the restaurant, and Joe walked me back to my car. Once again I was certain that he was going to say something. Instead, as I opened the driver's door he took hold of my hand to stop me getting in, and leant in towards me with an odd look on his face. Was he going to kiss me? In that moment, I wasn't sure whether I wanted him to or not.

The shrill call of his mobile phone broke the spell. I drove home with my mind whirling. Joe was really a good friend, that was all. Someone I trusted implicitly, with whom I could relax, laugh, talk about anything and simply be myself. Even though I wasn't blind to his obvious recently surfaced charms, I had never thought of him any other way and, despite what had just occurred, my mind was still refusing to allow me to entertain any other possibility.

* * * * * * *

The next time we spoke, Joe was his usual self and I decided I had imagined it all, read into the situation something that hadn't been there. I felt a bit foolish, questioned for a brief instant why I'd even had the thought and then let it go. He had called to say he'd read the manuscript from cover to cover, several times.

'I love it, Gemma, it's great. There are a few things that I think might need tweaking – a couple of inconsistencies, continuity stuff, you know – but nothing much. Let me know when you've got some time and I'll come over and go through it with you.' I was thrilled. Joe's opinion meant a lot to me. 'That's not the only reason I called though, Gemma. I showed it to Callum, a friend of mine who, uh, dabbles in this field, and he's really taken with it. Thinks there's a lot of good information in it and wants to meet you. Can I bring him over to see you?'

I felt a bit put out that Joe had shown the manuscript to anyone without asking me first, particularly someone I didn't know, but then told myself I was being silly and a bit petty. I couldn't think of a good reason why I shouldn't meet this Callum if he was interested in what I'd written, although I wasn't sure what Joe meant about good information.

Chapter 56

'Hello-o-o? Gemma?' I'd heard the kitchen door open. It was Joe. 'Come in Joe, I'll be down in a tick. Grab yourself a seat.'

I bounced into the living room a minute or two later and stopped dead in my tracks. Joe wasn't alone. Of course he wasn't. I'd totally forgotten that he was bringing this friend with him. 'Gemma, this is Callum, the friend I told you about.'

I thrust out my hand and beamed at Callum like an idiot, completely unable to speak for a few seconds. I had been poleaxed! I had never believed in love at first sight but if this wasn't it, it was sure as hell lust at first sight. My legs were trembling, my pulse racing, my mouth dry... This was ridiculous. I knew nothing about this guy, had never even seen him before and here I was acting like a twelve year old with a crush. With a considerable effort I pulled myself together and tried hard to act normally. Joe was looking at me as if I'd gone mad.

'Pleased to meet you, Callum. Coffee?' The words came out in a high pitched squeak and I dashed into the kitchen, bustling around to give myself time to gather my wits. Callum. Something about this man had got to me even before he'd opened his mouth to say hello.

As soon as I felt a bit more normal I took the drinks through to the living room. Joe was chatting away but I hardly heard a word he said. I was too busy studying Callum over the rim of my coffee mug. He was close to six feet tall, suntanned, with long, straight mid-brown hair streaked with grey pulled back into a ponytail, and a devastating smile that he flashed at me as I handed him his coffee. What was it about him that was having such an effect on me?

307

He wasn't especially good looking, not in a traditional Brad Pitt or Keanu Reeves type way. His nose was a bit crooked where it had evidently been broken at one time, and that greying brown hair was beginning to thin on top. But his slate grey eyes flirted with me at every glance, twinkling with mischief and a healthy disregard for rules and regulations. This man was a maverick; perhaps that was why I was so attracted to him.

'Callum has read the manuscript.' With some difficulty I concentrated on what Joe was saying.

'Wd you think?' Somehow I kept my voice steady and light, longing to hear Callum say that he'd loved it.

'Interesting.' Oh, not quite the response I'd hoped for. Irrational as it was, I felt a bit deflated. 'I'm an archaeologist and I've been researching the ancient crystal skulls for over twenty years. That's how I met Joe, at a seminar I was giving in London last summer.'

'Skulls like Duncan's?' I wasn't sure where he was going with this. How could I possibly have any information that would help him?

'No. Older, much older. Skulls that came from civilisations like Atlantis. Most people consider them as simply myth and legend, are convinced that they don't exist and never have. Certainly the scientific and academic communities dismiss it all as stuff and nonsense.'

'But you don't,' I said slowly.

'No. I suppose I'm a bit of a renegade.' (I'd already worked that one out. He had it written all over him). 'They refuse to take my theories and research seriously. They fall into two camps. Those who see me as dangerous and claim that I risk bringing their serious research into disrepute, which is most of them, and the others, who at best think I'm a bit of a nutcase. Which is fine by me, because it means they leave me alone to get on with my work.'

'You really think these skulls actually exist?' I couldn't believe what I was hearing.

'I'm convinced of it. Or at least that they did exist. Whether they still do is the question my latest research is aiming to answer.'

'He's a skull hunter,' Joe broke in. 'He's been all over the world countless times following leads in an attempt to pick up their trail.'

'I've spent all my working life researching this, trying to fit the pieces of the puzzle together, to gather as much evidence as I can. I know they exist but I haven't been able to prove it. Up until now. Your book could very well change all that.'

I was flummoxed. How could my stories, taken out of dreams and thin air, help him?

'I believe that the information in your stories is accurate. Has been given to you so that the skulls can be found and brought into the world once more.'

Was he serious? I looked at him closely – he was. OK, sexy and irresistible he might be, and there was no denying the overwhelming attraction I felt towards him, but he was also stark, staring bonkers. I had made it all up. Hadn't I? Joe's words echoed faintly in the far recesses of my mind. 'The skulls have work for you, Gemma'. Oh, don't be so ridiculous.

As the battle raged within me, Callum leaned forward and grasped my hands in his. Immediately all thought became impossible. It was with immense difficulty that I forced my attention away from that warm, firm grip and the sensations it was arousing in me to concentrate on what he was saying.

'Gemma, I know you think I'm crazy. So does everyone else. Humour me. Just for a moment consider the possibility that I'm right. That these skulls do exist and that you are being given the information that leads to where they are hidden.'

'Even if it was true, so what? What do you want me to do?'

'Give me a head start. A chance to begin searching before the book goes public. Once it hits the shelves there could be hundreds if not thousands of people with the same idea.' I doubted that very much!

'Please Gemma?' His eyes met mine and a flame coursed through my veins. He had charm in bucket loads did Callum, and he knew exactly how to use it. The warning bells should have sounded at that moment but I was oblivious to the danger. I had a real life Indiana Jones in my living room and I had fallen for him hook, line and sinker. I gave in without a fight.

'Look, I haven't even begun to approach publishers with it yet. I only finished it last week, for heaven's sake. I'll print you off the sections you want and you can go off on your quest. But if you do find anything, I want to be the first to know.' My mind was swept back to the vision I'd seen so recently through the black skull, of the red desert and the man on horseback. In a flash I believed I knew exactly who he was.

'I promise, Gemma... But maybe you could come along on our expedition to look for them? See for yourself?' A deeper, unspoken invitation was explicit in his eyes.

Chapter 57

Now that the stories had been told, the dreams stopped as suddenly as they had started all those months ago. Was that it then? Was it the end? I had always believed there was much more to come but at the moment it certainly didn't seem that way.

I felt flat. I had been on a roller-coaster of an adventure and now it was all over. Furthermore, Joe had disappeared off again on his travels and we hadn't parted on the best of terms. I still wasn't really sure what had triggered it but we'd had a huge row and he'd stormed off. That was it. The next thing I knew, Duncan informed me he'd flown out to Bulgaria. Apparently there was some recently discovered pyramid in the Balkans that was creating a great deal of excitement.

I can't recall having said anything in particular out of turn that could have started the argument. All I'd done was ask him about Callum. I'd been thinking about Callum a lot. No, that's an understatement. Since that evening I'd met him he was never out of my thoughts, and it was driving me nuts. Especially as I'd not heard a word from him since. Not to tell me whether anything in the books was helpful and had given him any additional clues. Not to let me know how his search was going. Certainly not to repeat his invitation. Obsessed, besotted, infatuated Cathy called it. And she was right.

Not that I'd told Joe any of this. My instinct had told me loud and clear that it wouldn't be a good idea. But I had tried to get some information out of him – subtly, I thought. Obviously not subtly enough. He'd turned on me angrily.

'What the hell has got into you, Gemma? Why do you want to know all this stuff about Callum? Leave the poor guy alone.'

I was rocked back on my heels. Where was all this coming from? Anyway, the argument had escalated to that sorry point where neither person means what they are saying, knows it is unfair and untrue, regrets saying it as soon as it come out of their mouth but won't admit it. Joe had accused me of throwing myself at the first man to pay attention to me (Ouch! Unfair!), and I had responded by telling him that what I did with my life was none of his business and to stop interfering in it. (Ouch! Also unfair). The point of no return had been reached. He had stormed out of the door and gone abroad. I had to admit it, I really missed his company.

Not that I had much time to mope. Now that I had finished the writing, the hard work was just beginning. If I wanted to find a publisher I would have to write a top class submission. I hated every moment of it. It was a painful combination of CV and school exam paper but doing it right mattered, so I put my head down and got on with it. Within a month I had sent it out to a dozen or so different publishers and agents. Now all I had to do was sit down and wait.

I took some time out. With the book finally finished I had some serious decisions to make about where I was going next, and my money wasn't going to last indefinitely. I found it really hard to concentrate. Cathy, as always, was there to help.

'You should know by now, Gemma, don't try to find the answer. Let it come to you. The next step always becomes clear when the time is right.' I couldn't argue with her. It had happened every step of the way up until now. She was to be proven right again.

I'm sure people would have heard my shrieks of delight from miles away the morning the letter dropped onto my doormat. After several disappointing and discouraging rejections, this one looked different. It was. This publisher wanted to take on the book and was even prepared to pay me a tasty advance. Not huge, but enough to allay my money anxieties for a while. Enough to give me a breathing space for who could say what new opportunities to open up for me.

The email popped into my Inbox a few days later: 'Making good progress. Back in the UK next week & will call you. Callum.'

*   *   *   *   *   *   *

Whoa! Yet again, I found myself sitting bolt upright in bed, my heart nearly jumping out of my chest. Breathing hard. Groping for reality. The skulls were back....

TO BE CONTINUED...

OTHER BOOKS IN THE SKULL CHRONICLES SERIES

THE RED SKULL OF ALDEBARAN
(Book II)

The adventure continues...

Gor-Kual: the red skull whose origins lie on the distant star worlds of Aldebaran...

Gemma Mason: an ordinary Englishwoman, chosen by these ancient sacred skulls to be their mouthpiece, sharing their stories through her writing...

In this fast-paced sequel to Lost Legacy, the story of Gor-Kual unfolds, from the barren plateau of an ancient land to the fabled continent of Atlantis and, ultimately, the empty deserts of North Africa: a story of loss, heartbreak, courage, sacrifice and love, all to protect this most powerful and sacred of objects.

Meanwhile, in 2013, Gemma is undertaking a quest of her own, travelling to the deserts of the south west USA with a group of maverick archaeologists in search of the blue skull Gal-Athiel, whose story was told in Lost Legacy. As her own journey of self-discovery unfolds further, Gemma is forced once more to step beyond the boundaries of her fears. What will she find there?

~ Even better than the first one.
~ I couldn't put it down
~ Excellent read.'

DAUGHTER OF THE GODS
(Book III)

The game turns deadly

Maat-su, daughter of the gods. Object of beauty & power brought to Earth to watch over the human race. Lusted after for tens of thousands of years by those who sought to use her for their own dark purposes.

Maat-su, the lapis lazuli skull, created on a world far from our own. Present at the birth of the first great civilisation of Atlantis, rescued at its fall and carried half way across the world to guide the emergence of a second. One whose legacy strikes wonder into *hearts* even today.

Far in the future, in 2013, Gemma Mason returns home to England after an abortive expedition through the deserts of Arizona in search of the blue obsidian skull, Gal-Athiel.

Wanting only to return to her quiet life, Gemma soon realises this is not to be. After a series of murders, break-ins, and a disturbing encounter with a sinister stranger it becomes clear that someone else is looking for the skulls. Someone who is prepared to stop at nothing.

Will Gemma be their next target?

> *~ Detailed and wonderfully told. Couldn't put this one down till I finished.'*
> *~ 'This series keeps improving with each book'*
> *~ Absolutely enthralling*
> *~ Expertly written (..) A must read...'*

OTHER BOOKS BY THIS AUTHOR

FORGOTTEN WINGS
(Dawn Henderson)

Is your life filled with Life? Or do you feel that somehow you're missing the point but don't quite know why?

We are all born with glorious powerful wings that will carry us through life joyfully and effortlessly if we let them. But all too often we forget their existence and they lie dormant and unused.

In Forgotten Wings, Dawn Henderson offers us 10 simple keys to remembering our wings and opening up to the magical and limitless potential of life. Knowledge that seems new but is as old as existence.

Through the insights, wisdom and reawakened knowing she has received on her own on-going voyage of spiritual discovery, Dawn reminds us of who we truly are and why we have chosen to play this game of life. Guiding us gently by the hand, Dawn shows us how, by changing the way we perceive these 10 key areas, we can reawaken our wings and open them once again to the light.

'Uplifting & inspirational'…'An amazingly beautiful book'…'Wonderful self-help book'

'Keep a copy by your bed and take nightly doses to keep you sane' *Kindred Spirit review (5 stars)*

ABOUT D.K. HENDERSON

D.K. Henderson lives in the beautiful county of Wiltshire, surrounded by its mysterious ancient landscape and stone monuments, which are an important source of inspiration for her writing.

She writes several occasional blogs and is passionate about spiritual development and the metaphysical side of life.

WEBSITE:
www.dkhenderson.com

BLOGS:
www.soulwhispering.wordpress.com
www.thenakedheartblog.wordpress.com
www.thebigadventureblog.wordpress.com

FACEBOOK:
www.facebook.com/DKHendersonAuthor

72361526R00192

Made in the USA
Columbia, SC
20 June 2017